E-JIHAD

INTERNET
WARFARE

TRACING THE ORIGIN OF COMBAT
ON THE WORLD WIDE WEB

Shahid Khan

Some facts can never be stated.
Some events are destined never to be disclosed.

Tales can however be told.
Stories can be written.

On lines
And
 Between them.

A part of this book is fiction.
The rest is stranger than fiction

Prologue

Harry switched on the computer in the basement of his New York home. Working to a strictly defined set of instructions, the machine started an extremely comprehensive procedure, testing various parameters, collecting information, checking hardware, processing data and executing commands. And, when it was required, it sought the system clock to establish the date and time.

The clock circuit responded. It provided the required reference to the operating system. The operating system updated itself and the time-date information was then used by numerous other subroutines, programs and processes. As always, a tiny subroutine buried deep within the computer also sought this information. The time-date stamp matched the one that it had been programmed to seek. The subroutine could now execute itself. It could modify the startup procedure to include a new set of instructions. The computer cancelled the normal boot process and forced itself to execute a shutdown cycle followed by an immediate reboot. Harry did not even notice the screen flicker, go off, and then come back on. Harry saw his familiar desktop appear on his screen and commenced his computing tasks. For all intents and purposes, Harry's machine was behaving completely normally. However, unbeknown to Harry, it had started executing new commands and was invoking additional processes in the background. Harry could not have known that his computer was now running additional programs, doing additional tasks—that his machine was now working for someone else.

It first checked whether Harry was connected to the Internet or not. It was. Using a random seed generator, Harry's computer created a list of IP addresses and then connected to these addresses using the TCP port 80, hoping that at least one of these addresses would be that of a Web server. A Web server was found. In fact, a total of five Web servers were among the addresses generated by the code. Each server was then addressed directly by Harry's computer, and it sent a HTTP GET request to each machine, trying to force a buffer overflow in the Indexing Service. Each server was then instructed to go through the same process as that of Harry's machine, generate IP addresses using a random seed generator and then send similar HTTP GET requests to each of the randomly chosen IP addresses. Within a very short span of time almost half a million machines worldwide were flooded with the requests. Half a million buffers overflowed. This done, the tiny piece of code sent out the message it had been programmed to send.

Harry was startled to see the screen go blank and then come up with the cryptic message:

"Oh Puck, What have you done?"

Like Harry, millions of computer users were to see this message on their screens in the coming days. A powerful and sophisticated computer virus had arrived.

The computer community, not surprisingly, gave it the name "Puck." They soon realized that the virus was very smart. Not only had it been triggered on a particular date, it was also capable of mutating and behaving differently on different dates. Some days it would spend propagating itself, using the random seed generator. On other dates it would start attacking a particular fixed IP address to flood it and force a denial of service for that particular site. On yet other days, it would hibernate, doing nothing; it would remain dormant, waiting, monitoring, assessing and then arise, wreaking havoc on specific devices that were connected to the Web; devices such as routers, switches, DSL modems, printers. It would force them to either crash or reboot.

The world's first electronic warrior had been born.

Internet Jihad had begun.

1

"Nobody, but nobody can breach the computers of the Pentagon. We have the ultimate in encryption, the last word in firewalls. We have security of a level that you cannot imagine. You cannot even begin to comprehend what we have."

Robert Forrester was adamant in his statement. He was irritated by his childhood friend's assertion that a determined hacker could take apart any computer system; it only required tenacity and time. Forrester was absolutely sure that no one could negotiate the extensive barriers that had been put in place within the information management systems of the Pentagon.

"No way. Not anybody. Not even you Pakistanis. So what if you guys did create the very first computer virus. Big deal. That was then. This is now. This is way, way beyond your capability. Whatever expertise you can boast of, it is useless when it comes to our systems. There is absolutely no way anyone can get into the computers of the government of the United States. Not you, not anybody."

Pervez Khan was equally firm and remained committed to his stance. "Don't you be too sure about it, R.F.", he said reverting to their old habit of calling each other by their initials. "It has been done, it is being done. It can always be done. And there is nothing you can do about it. Trust me."

"Pervez, what makes you so sure? Surely the Pentagon knows what can be done, and those guys would definitely have protected themselves. It is, after all, the United States we are talking about. I am sorry, but I have to go with Robert. He has to be right. How could anyone breach the computers of a place as secure as the Pentagon?" This from a now-famous doctor involved in the esoteric concepts of nuclear medicine but not too knowledgeable about computers.

"Listen up Doc. It's all about ports. Not the kind of port the admiral has a wife in. Or the port you sip after dinner. In this case ports are the doors, the electronic holes through which the information highway connects systems together. The channels used by the Internet, cable, cellular, telephone, and satellites to communicate; the electronic gates that everybody uses—has to use. The Pentagon is no different; it uses them also, just like everyone else. These are the gates that allow movement of information. These are the channels through which you can move an e-mail message or a bank can move trillions of virtual money. Whatever happens on the Net has to happen through these ports. They enable flow of information between computers, and whenever you have a path for legitimate information to pass, you also have a path for an unauthorized person to enter. Such visitors can be harmless or they can be deadly. They can be computer geeks who enter just to prove that they can do so or they can be malicious assaults designed to wreak havoc in the systems."

Robert bristled at the suggestion. "Don't you think we know that? Do you really believe that we would not be able to prevent anyone from entering our systems?" he retorted. The conversation was now getting animated. Others had started listening in. Soon it would be the two of them talking, while others, drinks in hand, stood around in silent attentiveness.

"Robert, for Christ's sake, you damn well know that any computer network is one big highway for information exchange. It has to be accessible; you have to allow legal users to access the computers. And when you have legal users, the illegals can come in too. You know very well that everyone uses the same codes; everybody speaks the same language. The language of TCP/IP. Everyone uses the same 'handles,' and you also know that every computer has many, many ports that can all be compromised."

"What's a port then?" the wife of a multinational's CEO chimed in. She had obviously missed the earlier part of the conversation.

"It's a door. Put simply, a port is like a door. Let me give you an example. When your computer wants data from any other computer, it sends a message to that machine indicating that it wants to talk to it. For this, it uses port 80, the TCP port. The server, seeing that you've asked for port 80, allows a connection to your computer so that it can handle your request. A link is established. Both computers start talking. Services spring into action, Daemons start working." Pervez saw the brow furrowing and preempted the female by continuing, "Daemons are the programs that enable the dialogue. It is these daemons that allow conversation between the machines. Now, the conversation may be brief or may continue indefinitely. It all depends on what you are planning to do. The simple truth is that now a door is open. In fact, at any given time, there are quite a few doors open on any computer. Any computer that has an open port is vulnerable. Any program that listens on a particular port represents a potential liability. This is when the hacker comes in. This is when harm can happen.

It does not have to be anything very complex. It can be the simplest form of invasion; a denial-of-service, or DoS, attack. In a DoS attack, the attacker does not attempt to actually complete a connection with the victim, but instead it just sends a stream of message packets to the host in an attempt to disrupt the host's capability to function. If the program isn't equipped to recognize when too many requests come in at once, and if it is not designed to reject at least some of them, it will tie up the entire machine as it attempts to service all these requests. If the program has a weakness that allows an intruder to overwrite memory, to cause a buffer overflow, there is a good chance the system can be taken over completely. Once this is done, you can then insert a program into a computer, any computer . . ." This was said with a meaningful stare at Robert, ". . . and tell it to open a particular door, to start listening on specific ports! And there are millions of them out there, millions of machines spread across the world that have this weakness. Machines that are screaming across the Internet 'Probe My ports, Please probe my ports!'"

"You mean to say that every time I log on to the Internet, a hacker can enter my computer, even with my firewall?" someone asked but before PK could answer, Robert interrupted his friend.

"Come off it, Pervez, this is not what we are talking about. We are not talking about common cyber attacks using port 80. We are not talking about cross-site scripting, buffer overflows, cookie poisoning. Nor are we talking about spoofing, changing header addresses of packets, embedding host addresses within mail files. This is child's play. This is stuff that kids do on a daily basis when they are not jacking off. We are talking of the computers of the Pentagon, managed and controlled by the most capable computer professionals in the world. This is what we are discussing. That is the security I am talking about. And that is what cannot be breached," an obviously annoyed Robert interjected.

"I know, I know. This is, as you said, child's play. I too am not talking of this. I am talking of real evil. I am talking of steganography and beyond. Highly complex, killer programs hidden so cleverly within legitimate data that no one can recognize them. I am talking about inserting instructions within harmless files, within genuine data. I am talking of worms that can enter a computer hidden inside a legitimate document, change themselves, hide their tracks, open back doors and take over the host. I am talking about programs that reprogram antivirus software, coding that instructs the machine to ignore its presence. I'm talking of polymorphic software containing its own antiforensic tools. Programs that are able to evolve rapidly, even as they are attacking systems. I'm talking of software so powerful that once inside a machine; the machine needs no further penetration. The machine itself goes out in search of additional viruses."

By now, there was a tense silence in the room. The music had stopped. The bartender had stopped dispensing. He too was listening attentively as the host waxed eloquent on the subject of computer viruses.

"Viruses, worms, probes, infections, firewalls, antivirus software. This is chicken shit. This is not what I am talking about. I am talking about the drugs of the cyberworld. We are all familiar with people doing drugs. We all know about addicts hooked on shit, desperate for the next fix. That's people on drugs." He paused, surveyed the listening faces and then continued, this time in a somber tone. "I am talking about computers on drugs. I am talking about the crack, the cocaine, the heroin of the computer world." Computers hooked on shit so bad they cannot work without their daily or monthly or annual fix. I am talking about machines that can be made addicted to malicious software. Servers that go screaming forth at the appointed time, searching the Net for their next high. I am talking of machines that are programmed to seek out other machines, to seek programs that are designed to destroy them, just as the junkie seeks out the pusher. And just like a junkie can be made to do anything for the next fix, the computer can also be ordered by the drug provider to do his bidding. And I am saying that it can be done. There is no such thing as absolutely safe.

"And, now, Robert, let me tell you something else. Let me tell you that I can do it. Pentagon or no Pentafrigginggon. You know damn well that there is nothing that a fighter pilot cannot do. And I am telling you as clearly as I can; I can do it. So, General, don't you go betting anything on it. I'd hate to collect."

"Five hundred dollars says that you're full of shit," said Robert, testily.

"Don't do it, R. F. You'll lose," Niles interjected. "Trust me, you'll lose."

Niles Barrington had listened with amusement as his two buddies argued. This was, after all, a hallmark of their relationship. Open, no-holds-barred discussions. For the forty-odd years that the three had been together, there had been many such exchanges. The "Falcons Three" as they were known among friends and foes alike had been close associates since adolescence - since the time they had trained together at the Air Force College in England. Each had then gone on to become fighter pilots within their national air force. Each had excelled in his chosen profession; each had climbed the ladder of success within his national military hierarchy. Thanks to a shrinking world, with nations interacting militarily through pacts, training programs, and personnel exchanges, they had been able to maintain and indeed strengthen the bond they had forged as cadets.

When Niles cautioned Robert not to make the bet, he spoke with knowledge and conviction. He remembered the cold wintry London morning when he had accompanied P. K. to the Tottenham Court Road store to buy the newly launched Apple computer. He remembered P. K. drooling over his new toy; he remembered the long hours P. K. spent learning to program the machine. He knew how good

11

P. K. had become at machine code. More pertinently he remembered the very first virus ever placed on the Internet and propagated across the world. Analysts had tracked its origin to the Pakistani city of Lahore and had further determined that the program had been created using an Apple computer. Niles knew that P. K. had been living in the city of Lahore when the virus had appeared on the scene. Niles remembered asking P. K. about it at the time. Niles also remembered P. K.'s mysterious smile and the fact that he had failed to respond. This is why Niles warned R. F. that he would lose.

But Robert was adamant. He was not backing off. P. K. would lose the bet. The challenge would be made.

P. K. had taken the dare. He would do it. He had absolutely no doubt about his ability.

Everything had its counter. Everything came in pairs. Right and wrong, black and white, day and night, keys and locks, firewalls and backdoors. Guards and intruders.

2

It had been just one week earlier that Robert had caught up with Niles at Heathrow airport to travel together to Karachi for the reunion. Thus far the three had always met in North America or Europe, but Pervez had insisted that this time the annual event be held in his country. The two Westerners had been apprehensive, yet, once the plans were finalized, they looked forward to the visit with keen anticipation. Though both had very detailed knowledge of Pakistan, they both had multiple, conflicting perceptions of the distant land and were excited at the prospect of gaining firsthand experience of P. K.'s complex country.

Their flight arrived at night. As the aircraft circled overhead, waiting for its turn to land, they could see a vast sea of lights spread out below. Karachi, a huge city of twelve, maybe fifteen, maybe eighteen million people living together in splendor and squalor, shimmered in the tropical night. Nobody really cared about the number, no one was counting. As the aircraft continued circling and as they watched from up above, a whole area of light suddenly vanished while simultaneously another area of inky blackness lit up. Karachi, touted as a city of lights was actually a city of rolling blackouts, of shifting darkness, elusive electricity; resigned residents.

The aircraft slid to a gentle stop and docked. The passengers tunneled into an impressive airport; polished marble walls, gleaming floors, moving walkways, brightly lit corridors, billboards, advertisements, display panels carrying ubiquitous messages from global companies and, in the distance, a smiling recognizable face. P. K. strode forward and embraced them both together in one big bear hug, welcoming them warmly to his land. While the other passengers were left to contend with baggage carousels, cascading suitcases, boldly emblazoned stickers on packages, "this side up," "fragile," "handle with care," tossed aside with gay abandon, the three friends were escorted into a VIP lounge, where they were served tea and biscuits while the staff completed the formalities of arrival. Paperwork completed, they moved onward, through smoked-glass doors that slid open silently.

They stepped into Pakistan, a step forward into uncertainty, a step back in time. A step sideways into a parallel dimension; into a world that moved of its own accord, at its own pace, gyrating weirdly on multiple axes.

The two Westerners experienced a simultaneous attack on all senses. Their eyes were stunned to see the seething mass of humanity. A sea of people of all colors, shapes, and sizes. Men, women, girls, boys all straining, surging, pushing, searching for the faces of those they had come to receive. Panicked olfactory nerves were assailed by a curiously fascinating potpourri of smells, aromas, odors; pungent, sweet, sour, tangy, fruity. Flowers, farts, heady oriental oils, sweat, exotic Western perfumes, curried halitosis—a veritable bouquet of confusion. Their ears were attacked by an incessant chatter; strident males, raucous females. The clamor, the rattle, the cacophony of an unruly nation. Whistle-blowing cops, screeching brakes, nerve-jarring horns, deafening music emanating from gaudy taxis, exhorting hawkers, loudspeakers wailing from minarets, calling the faithful to prayer. And finally, as the escorting staff carved a passage through the crowd, there was the touching. Hands. Helpful hands, tugging, guiding, protecting. Outstretched hands, wanting, begging. Uncouth hands, ill-mannered bodies, pushing, shoving, pulling.

Two foreigners had entered the Land of the Pure.

Pakistan, a Stan of the Pak, a Land of the Pure. A nation striding forward purposefully to its destiny, the only problem being that no one was sure of where or what the destination was. A nation saddled with pathetic leaders who had forced themselves onto the hapless masses—leaders who were, in reality, devious opportunists adept at convincing the simple folk that they had been tasked by Allah Himself to lead the nation. They knew well that Pakistanis, Muslims all, submitted to His divine will readily. One only had to invoke the Almighty and the masses would follow willingly, even as the self-appointed leaders pushed them further into misery and despair. Pakistani leaders fought tooth and nail among themselves for the right to rape their fellow countrymen, while an amused military watched from the wings, stepping in whenever it so desired. Pakistan was blessed with an army always ready to conquer its own nation - a nation already defeated by poverty, illiteracy, ignorance, and disease.

"I don't think I shall ever understand the Pakistani psyche. It's amazing how mixed up you people really are. One has to wonder what makes you guys' tick."

P. K. smiled and told Robert that there was nothing too complex or devious about him or his people. They were children all; both emotionally and mentally. By some strange, cruel joke of nature, their bodies had matured but their brains remained locked in a juvenile form. Behind twirled mustaches, beefy exteriors, ample paunches, swaggering gaits, and guttural voices—behind their mature physiques, Pakistanis were actually trapped firmly in a child's world. They were children both in thoughts and actions. Their thought processes and reasoning were a curious mixture of impishness, naïveté, simplicity, and tantrum-throwing typical of a juvenile. Captains of

16

industry or roadside vendors, generals of the battlefield or alms-seeking beggars, Pakistanis were children at heart and childish in their actions. Every adult, irrespective of his status and demeanor, was, in fact, an irresponsible adolescent.

"We are not supposed to be responsible for our actions; we are free to do as we please. If we are caught, we express surprise and resentment. If things are not going the way we want them to, we promptly throw a tantrum. Our perception of right and wrong is simply based on our needs and the prevailing environment. Our respect for the law is very similar to the attitude of a juvenile toward rules and regulations. Laws are meant to be broken. If we can get away with it, well and good, if caught, then we must resort to anger, pleading, begging; whatever it takes to get us of the hook. We are exempted from all concern about right or wrong, truth or falsehood, legal or illegal.

"We are a free people. Free from slavery, free from occupation, free from subjugation. Sadly, however, we are also free of responsibility, unhampered by any disciplining constraints. We are free to do as we please, whenever we please, and in whatever manner it pleases us. We do not care about self-discipline, we do not have any personal code of ethics, nor do we have any worry about peer pressure. Everything is all right as long as we are not caught in the act, and when caught, it is perfectly acceptable to behave brazenly, lie glibly, deny everything.

"And just as a juvenile is extremely self-conscious and desirous of public adulation, we too are obsessed with 'Honor.' We are willing to go to any lengths and act in the most unethical manner just to ensure that our 'honor' is not compromised. We are quite comfortable demeaning ourselves in private in the chambers of our superiors while ensuring that our public image does not suffer. We emerge from our bosses' offices having compromised our dignity and principles in every which way, twirling our mustaches, giving the impression that it was we who really chewed the boss out."

Pervez then told them of the fascinating tale of a friend of his, a son of a landlord or "Chaudhry," the lord and master of his domain. As son of the village chief, this friend had grown up in a huge country house with dozens of servants and attendants at his beck and call. Soon after achieving puberty, he was introduced to the wonders of sex by one of the more mature maidservants. She very easily convinced the horny teenager that time could be better spent in sweaty copulation rather than studying or pursuing other agrarian interests. Every afternoon the two would sneak away to a secret rendezvous where P.K.'s friend would indulge in his newfound, delightful pastime. It took him a long while for the realization to sink in that every time they engaged in their cavorting, the maidservant, having disrobed completely, would however keep her face completely covered throughout the sweaty event. Intrigued, he

18

eventually asked the naked female why she did so and was stunned by her answer.

"Saadie bhi Izzat hai. Assie besharam te nahin."

"I am an honorable person, not a shameless hussy". Stark naked, gyrating expertly, bucking fiercely, whimpering ecstatically in carnal lust, she had to hide her face because she could not be seen enjoying herself in an illegitimate and socially reprehensible act.

In a semi darkened room of an insignificant village in the rural backwater of Pakistan, an illiterate village woman of indeterminate age had paraphrased, in an extremely succinct manner, the true psyche of the Pakistani people. In one simple sentence, she had encapsulated the mind-set of an entire nation. In one breathtakingly simple observation, she had paraphrased it all.

"Saadie bhi Izzat hai. Assie besharam te nahin."

The denizens of the Land of the Pure could engage in the most immoral of acts but had to put up an honorable face; they had to project an image of dignity.

Niles and Robert could not help wondering at this nation of amazing paradoxes. A complex mixture of races, Pakistanis came in all shapes, sizes, and colors. From the tall, blue-eyed, blond-haired, fair-skinned tribes of the north, to the Negroid, thick-lipped, curly-haired, black-skinned villagers of the Makran coast. Dissimilar in looks; equally diverse in habits, cultures, customs, and languages, they ranged from the greasy, rotund, potbellied, foul-smelling, foulmouthed residents pursuing carnal pleasures, to highly cultured, literate, art-loving, creative geniuses. Dissimilar in dress; ranging from the braless, tit-swinging females of the village to the cantilevered breasts of the boutique-frequenting city dwellers. Diverse in thought; from the lofty ideals of philosopher poets to the crass financial greediness of unethical businessmen. Pakistan contained a wide-ranging assortment of the human race, bound together by religion.

Islam.

Pakistan was a nation created in the name of a religion, created by the Muslims of India wanting freedom to practice their religion and to live their lives according to the tenets of their faith. Unhampered and unhindered.

"And you, Niles, you, the Brits, orchestrated the creation of this unique state."

It had been decreed that British India, the Jewel in the Crown was to be divided. A separate state for the Muslims of the subcontinent was to be created. The faithful had flocked from all corners of the subcontinent toward the new nation. Princes and princesses journeyed to the new land, foregoing their estates, leaving behind their wealth and their fortunes as they sought freedom to practice their religion unhindered. The poor, the impoverished, the downtrodden, the denied; they surged toward the new country, hoping to be free, yearning to be unchained. The greedy, the opportunists, the carpetbaggers; they flocked to the nascent country, wanting more, grabbing more, seizing more. The intellectuals, the idiots, the able bodied, the handicapped, the young, the withered old men and women; all flocked to their new home. They came on foot, by animal-drawn carts, by trains, by buses, by cars, by airplanes, by boats and ships, clutching their belongings to their chests and, within their chests, their most treasured belonging. Hope.

As the Muslims moved toward their newly created country, the Hindus moved eastward. They were forced to leave their ancestral homes and find for themselves a new home in Hindu India. They too were similarly unsure, similarly uncertain, similarly stripped of their lives, their homes, their hearths, and, sadly, they carried an additional burden: despair. Because, while the Muslims surged forward toward hope, the Hindus had no such morally uplifting sentiment to console them. For them it was a forced eviction. It was a simple question of survival, a retreat to safety. And as this mass of humanity moved in both directions, it created a migration that was to be the largest mass displacement of human beings the world had ever seen.

A nation was being born; humanity was in labor, the pain was horrendous. There was unbearable agony, intolerable suffering. Human vultures, rapists, looters, plunderers had a field day stealing, robbing, raiding, marauding, pillaging. The powerful preyed on the helpless, slitting throats, slashing pregnant bellies, severing heads, chopping limbs. Gold rings were ripped out leaving behind torn ears and bleeding noses. Bangles, difficult to slide off the wrist, were impatiently removed from the quivering stump of a hacked limb. Muslims, Sikhs, and Hindus; all were abused; thousands were slaughtered, hundreds of thousands maimed, millions traumatized. Families were broken, children were separated from parents, wives from husbands, the old from the young. The beast within had been let loose. It was on the rampage; innocence was being devoured. Man was desecrating mankind.

A land was being partitioned; India would now become India and Pakistan. The division would enable a nation for the Muslims of the subcontinent. It would also enable a divisiveness of minds, a creation of an unbridgeable chasm of mistrust and hostility that would result in periodic conflict, both armed and otherwise. Indians and Pakistanis would spare no effort at trying to upstage each other whenever the two interacted. They would fight in the air, on the ground, on cricket fields, in academic environments of international universities. They would delightfully seek out a chance, any chance to pass a jibe at each other. In the movies they made, the books they wrote, the songs they sang. To the casual observer this would appear to be a result of hatred for one another. It was in reality a perverse expression of love denied, hope shattered; a juvenile reaction of an industrious and creative group of people forced apart.

3

They made a strange sight. A tall, gaunt, balding man, striding ahead, erect in his posture, self-assured in his step. Following him deferentially, a few steps behind, a young girl still in her teens. His, an expression of purpose, of determination, hers of bewilderment, of confusion, of innocence. A child lost in the open wilderness of the huge expanse of sun-drenched concrete, trapped in a surging mass of humanity, pushing, shoving, straining. A juvenile who would normally have been roaming comfortably in the huge, airy verandahs of an ancestral home, now forced into the unfamiliar environment of an airfield. One hand lugging an oversized suitcase, almost too big for her to carry, the other in the firm, bony grip of the blind woman trailing behind. Another female, old, bewildered, desperately clutching onto the hand, her only hope, her singular contact with a black world.

A child bride was sandwiched between a husband and a blind mother-in-law. Lost, confused, alone, helpless.

The unlikely group scurried across the blistering tarmac, herded together by bossy officials intent on keeping the group intact. Their goal was the giant silver bird that shimmered in the distance. She had seen these graceful metallic objects in the sky from the courtyard of her home, but this was the first time she would see one up so close. Not only that, she would sit in it and be transported aloft! She was going to fly. That thought terrified her more than the fact that they had just had a narrow escape from death. They had barely managed to escape the marauding mob that had rampaged through their neighborhood, a mob that had raided and put to fire the stately mansion that had been their home for generations. She had no idea why their calm and peaceful lives had been so rudely shattered, why their idyllic, private and intensely personal lives had been destroyed.

The day had started just as any other. A normal day, a regular routine. Slipping out from the silk and velvet warmth of the huge four-poster bed, she had completed her toilette with the assistance of the ever-present maidservants flitting around her. She had dressed and then gone across to her mother-in-law's room to help the blind lady dress for breakfast. They had sat down at the well-stocked table while the fleet of servants served their needs, easily sensing their demands, delivering before being asked. Little did she realize that this was the last breakfast she would enjoy in such luxury. In the next few hours, swiftly, brutally and completely without warning, her safe, secure and contented world would shatter irreparably. A wealthy homemaker would turn into a wandering destitute.

Her husband had rushed into the female quarters of the rambling mansion. He had ordered her to pack her jewelry and the ornaments of her mother-in-law in one suitcase. "One," he had emphasized, "just one, pack it and be ready. We are going on a trip." She had obeyed unquestioningly, deciding that she would also include her most prized possession, more valuable than all the gold, all the diamonds or the precious stones she possessed. She laid out her wedding dress in the leather suitcase, smoothing the creases, ensuring that the folds were even. It was her most cherished possession, a reminder of the most thrilling day of her tender life. Upon donning that dress she had entered a house where she would reign and, upon removing it, she had entered womanhood. In that dress she had found her being and her kingdom, she had become a woman, a wife, a housekeeper.

She could hear the cries in the distance—angry voices, aggressive sounds. They had left their home hurriedly through the backdoor, the breakfast unfinished, running along the winding alley, through the maze of the old city lanes, eventually reaching the street where a servant was waiting with the horse carriage. They clambered aboard and the horses took off. She had recoiled at the fury of her husband as he struck the animals repeatedly, urging them to go faster. The carriage careened across the roadway; people tried to grab hold of the horses but then jumped out of the

26

way as they failed. They had broken through the human barrier and raced on toward the airport.

As they labored up the few steps of the tail-wheeled DC-3 aircraft, the man checking them through grabbed hold of the large suitcase and, in a gruff voice, ordered her to let go. She could not take it with her, it was not allowed. She resisted, clinging desperately to her wedding dress, looking toward her husband, her silent eyes beseeching intervention. He looked directly at her with eyes instructing her to let go. She obeyed the eyes, understanding the language they spoke. She entered the aircraft, a hot, stuffy, smelly tube. It was nothing like she had imagined the inside of an airplane would be. They found a vacant space and squatted on the warm metal floor. Someone instructed them to hang on firmly to the ropes that criss-crossed the circular chamber. As the plane filled rapidly with others like them, she squeezed herself toward a window, a round globe of light. She tried to open it but could not. They huddled together, clinging desperately to the ropes as the aircraft started moving. From the window she caught a glimpse of her suitcase; now open, the wedding dress tossed aside on the tarmac, the man going through the contents gleefully.

The machine picked up speed, bumping, rattling, engines roaring, propellers beating the hot Indian air. Airborne, they settled down as best as they could. Someone vomited. Many more would be airsick. August afternoons could be very turbulent in the skies above Delhi. By the time the aircraft landed in a strange and distant land, in a country just born, the plane's interior had new smells intermingled with those of oil, fuel, hydraulic fluids, and engine exhaust gases.

Vomit and Fear.

As they were guided into the crowded refugee camp, his eyes fixed protectively on the two women. He looked at them with tenderness, a sentiment that was strange for him. A young bride and a blind old mother. A flushed, radiant, confused face. A beautiful face. Another, a wizened, wrinkled face, yet equally beautiful. It was a body shriveled by age. The breast that had fed him had long been dry; the hands that had cared for him, fed him, sustained him, slapped him, and caressed him were now frail and helpless, clutching desperately to her daughter-in-law, sensing bewilderment through touch.

He had absolutely no idea what the future held for them, no knowledge of what lay ahead. Yet, he remained undaunted. He knew that they would be taken care of. Allah, the All Powerful, the All Mighty would protect and sustain. He would provide. He herded the two women into a corner and spread out the sheet they had been given to sleep on. They prayed. Facing Mecca, they praised Him.
They thanked Him for His bounty. They thanked Him for the harsh sunlight of a new land, for the stark emptiness of the refugee camp. They expressed their

humble gratitude for the tiny room, for the bare floor, for the coarse blankets, for the semi cooked gruel, for the solitary earthen bowl in which they would eat together. They had been taught never to complain. It could never occur to them to question why they had been so suddenly and so violently stripped of the comforts they had enjoyed ever since they could remember. There had to be a reason. God always had a reason. The Lord giveth and the Lord taketh away. He had given. He had taken away. He would give again. God is Great. Allah O'Akbar.

She had not been sick on the plane. While others around her had thrown up, she had not felt the need. Now, safely on ground, in the severe environment of the refugee camp, lying on the hard floor, her insides heaved. She scrambled for the open doorway, pushed apart the canvas curtain that served as a door, and ran outside. She bent down, gripping her stomach with unsteady hands and retched violently. Nothing came forth. Her body had nothing to disgorge. She stayed bent, straining, retching.

The blind mother-in-law heard it all. The scramble, the heaving, the gagging. These were sounds she had heard many times in the past. These were delightful sounds; they were the sounds of a pregnant female. Fatima was with child. Her son was soon be a father, she a grandmother. It would be a male child; she knew it, she simply did. It would be a handsome boy and she, the grandmother, would name him after her dead husband. Pervez.

Pervez was born. He survived, as did Pakistan. The country consolidated and secured its place in the comity of nations. Pakistanis moved outward, beyond the borders sallying forth to better their lot, venturing into the world seeking their fortunes. Most headed for Great Britain, drawn to their rulers, the home of their erstwhile masters. Leaving behind a bright, sunny, tropical environment, these brown-skinned, black-haired oriental Dick Whittingtons traveled thousands of miles in search of the gold that paved the streets of London. And they found the yellow metal exactly as promised; on the streets of London and, indeed, below it. They found it behind the wheel of the red double-decker buses; they found the yellow metal in the ticket dispensers hanging round their necks. Many found gold down below, in the London Underground, driving the tubes, cleaning lavatories, sweeping platforms. They found wealth operating machinery, stoking furnaces, shoveling coal, laboring, toiling, enduring, dreaming, hoping. Starting from the tenements of Paddington, the squalid surroundings of Slough, the stark houses of Southall, these newcomers fanned out into the heartland of the mighty industrial nation, making their homes in the cold, uniformly dreary council houses of Sheffield, Bradford, and Birmingham. Living cheaply, sharing beds, working long shifts, toiling, scrimping, saving, denying themselves, dreaming, hoping.

And Britain had welcomed them. These brown foreigners had stoked the British economy, outperforming the indolent, beer-guzzling locals.

They were disciplined, quiet, industrious, remaining to themselves, working long shifts in the factories, living in crowded basements, sleeping on the floor, one worker arising for his shift, vacating a warm bed for another to slip into as he returned from his labor.

They had few needs, fewer wants, minimal desires. Something to fill their stomachs, simple, basic fare, minimum sleep. Their waking lives were spent working and praying. Muslims by faith, they prayed to Allah whenever they could. Most were married, forced by economic considerations to live alone, away from families, their wives and children subsisting in mud houses of their ancestral villages in Pakistan. They led a life of denial and celibacy, but when natural urges could not be kept restrained, they sought out the prettiest and the most attractive of white females. Gorgeous, beautifully proportioned, stunning women from London, Paris, New York, San Francisco, and other Western cities. Models, supermodels, actresses, the cream of the crop. Those among them with different tastes, the homosexuals, sought out the best of the Western males. Tall, blond, muscular, willing golden bodies. They brought them into their squalid tenements, into their smelly beds, and made wild, passionate love to them; furiously, powerfully, repeatedly.

It was easy, it was simple. It was cheap. All one needed was half a crown and a bit of imagination. For the two shillings and sixpence it cost to buy the glossy magazines, one could fuck the prettiest. Even that sum could be saved if one really wanted to do it on the cheap. It was the age of the miniskirt and the microskirt. Rising hemlines and plunging necklines had laid bare cleavage, thighs, and areas beyond. Dark-skinned conductors working the London buses had enthusiastically begun directing the scantily clad females to the upper deck. "Mind the steps, luv". Voicing concern for their safety, they ensured that every female was carefully monitored as she proceeded up the spiral staircase.

And thus, time passed. Praying, saving, scrimping, masturbating, these industrious individuals progressed up the social and financial ladder, slowly but surely, working their way through laborer, supervisor, shop assistant, shop owner, retailer, wholesaler, trader. Morphing from floor sweeper to mill hand, machine operator, shift in-charge, factory manager, factory owner, business magnate. Their progeny became doctors, lawyers, engineers, politicians. Pakistanis became lords, members of Parliament, captains of industry, men of letters.

The attachment with the motherland, however, remained strong. Britishers of Pakistani origin remained emotionally tethered to their country. They watched it stumble back and forth from democracy to dictatorship, from affluence to poverty, from enlightenment to blind ignorance. They were saddened by their country's inability to find competent governance, its helplessness to find leaders who could guide it to the glory that was their due.

Sadly, the Pakistani nation remained frustrated in its attempt to rise and find a meaningful place in the hierarchy of nations. It was a country that did not have clean drinking water for its citizens, but it had a space program. It was a country where millions lived below the poverty line, but it boasted an enviable nuclear weapons arsenal. Pakistan was a nation that could not educate its mushrooming population but nonetheless boasted of world-class scientists, academics and philosophers, settled in other countries. It was a nation without playing fields that yet managed to produce the world's finest cricketers, squash players, field hockey champions, snooker experts, yachting professionals, bridge players. Pakistanis would attain brilliance and global recognition as doctors, engineers, scientists and in a myriad of other professions. A Pakistani would create the Bank of Credit and Commerce International, a complex and unique financial structure that would threaten the entire Western banking system and would need to be destroyed. Yet another would set up an amazingly intricate smuggling ring and build nuclear weapons for a state that had decided to 'eat grass but become a nuclear power'.

Pakistan was a nation that boasted a military that had humbled a much larger and more powerful enemy more than once. A nation whose pilots would nonchalantly volunteer to participate in Arab-Israeli wars, shooting Israeli aircraft out of the skies effortlessly; repeatedly. A nation whose citizens would rise to prominence, a nation whose citizens would fall from grace. Brilliant professionals gaining accolades, devious criminals and drug runners being executed in foreign lands. A people who would travel the world in private jets, landing at airports where their fellow citizens would be cleaning the lavatories and sweeping the floors. A country where the streets would be overflowing with garbage and dirt, while inside the obscene mansions that lined those streets, liveried servants would be serving its depraved and corrupt occupants the finest of wines, the best of Parisian gourmet dishes, the choicest of imported meats. It was a country where labor and monetary reward did not go hand in hand; it was a country where labor needed little reward and money needed no labor, just guile.

Pakistan was a nation of innocents; it was a nation of the most devious. Of pious young men and debauched old Satans. Of gold-bedecked, devoutly religious, burqa-clad prostitutes. Of naked, impoverished females, their clothes in tatters, their bodies bare, cringing, ashamed, strangely dignified despite their nakedness.

A Pakistani would win the Nobel Prize for science. Another would create the first computer virus to ever infect the Internet. Pakistanis would marry into Arab royalty, into English nobility. Pakistanis would produce the world's finest aromatic rice, breed the world's finest tropical fruits, grow the finest cotton. Those who did so would themselves go hungry, remain malnourished, naked. Pakistanis would sweep the streets, the buildings, the palaces, and the shopping malls across the globe, while their own cities and villages remained dirty, foul smelling, garbage ridden, festering pockets of disease and despair. They would breed like rabbits, rich and poor alike, reproducing with careless abandon. A poor nation, getting poorer by the minute. The poor, unable to afford a condom, procreating uncontrollably. The elite, impervious, oblivious, fornicating wantonly. All ruled by a government that was always unimaginative, unintelligent, compromised, helpless. Pakistan, The Land of the Pure, a country created to provide dignity to its people, a country prevented from doing so by those very same people.

Niles and Robert were truly overwhelmed by their visit. They were thrilled by the diversity of this strange land; they were enamored by the genuine warmth of the people toward foreigners. They liked what they saw, they enjoyed what they heard, and they delighted in what they tasted; at least Niles did. And, in doing so, it was he who ended up getting the "squitters". No visit to the subcontinent could ever be complete without one having the runs.

"Serves you right, going off like that, acting a bleeding gourmet," said Robert, who had studiously avoided any adventurous meals and had ensured that he drank only bottled mineral water.

"This is what's different between us, R.F.; between the Brits and the Yanks. This is exactly why you don't get to understand the world. You travel across the globe, staying in five-star hotels, eating Western meals, visiting fabricated tourist sites especially set up for suckers, and then you go back with armloads of photos to show to the neighbors. You stand tall and boast that you have been to so and so place, done this and that. Balls. You have not been anywhere, done nothing. You might as well have stayed at home.

To have been somewhere, to have understood a country, you need to experience it. You need to mingle with the masses, you need to see what they see, hear what they hear, feel what they feel. You need to mix, to understand. This is how we ruled the world. We understood. We saw, we heard, we felt. And the natives responded. They welcomed us and they still do. The Commonwealth is still going strong. And you know why? Because we did not mind the squitters, we did not mind the bugs, the smells, the dirt, the grime. We mingled. We shared our lives. We reached out and touched the natives. And you, what did you do? In the short time you have been a nation, you buggers have managed to piss off the entire world."

"Tell you what, 'mate,' you crap your guts out, you mingle," said Robert, in an almost flawless cockney accent. "Me, I'm staying with Perrier water."

Niles recovered rapidly but not before he had lost four pounds. Ever the optimist, he found the silver lining in his cloud. "I think I've found my gold mine. I am going to be a bloody millionaire soon. I am going to make my fortune with Paki water. Bottle it and sell it as the perfect weight-reduction formula."

And as Robert started to say something, he continued blithely, "to fat Americans!"

4

Reunion over, it was time to become weary adults once again. P. K. was there to see them off at the airport and couldn't resist the parting shot.

"Keep the five hundred bucks ready, my friend," he remarked to Robert as they hugged each other good-bye. Robert chose to ignore the remark, his mind busy trying to comprehend the drama being enacted across the hall. A burqa-clad female was being fussed over by a whole gaggle of well-wishers and family members who had come to see her off. Veiled women and bearded males were gathered around the female, agitated and excited. It was quite apparent that the burqa-clad individual was about to embark on a perilous air journey alone and unescorted. A worried mother was praying loudly, beseeching Allah to protect her innocent daughter from the evil Western society. Concerned brothers were demanding that the airline staff give her the best seat on the aircraft. Yet another burly individual was pleading with the man behind the counter to overlook the excess baggage;

they were poor people; they did not have the huge amount needed to pay for it.

"She's probably a student at one of your universities, Robert. The parents are obviously wealthy despite their vocal protestations to the contrary. They may be illiterate villagers, but they have obviously made their fortune and now want the next generation to move up the social ladder. They want their children to be educated in the best manner possible; they want their children to go to the Western Universities." P. K. continued explaining to the two confused foreigners that his country was full of such families. Parents who wanted to give their offspring the most expensive education, knowing full well that this would raise the family status and help obscure their humble origins.

Pakistanis had amassed wealth both legitimately and otherwise. Honest workers had acquired it doing menial tasks, working hard and long hours as barbers, sweepers, construction workers, blue-collar laborers; denying themselves, saving and striving hard to elevate themselves to a higher economic status and thus, by implication, to a higher social status. Crooked parents had made fortunes running drugs; selling children to Arabs as camel jockeys; smuggling exotic artifacts, reptiles, and birds; selling pornography, liquor, and guns; pimping; prostituting themselves; doing whatever the market wanted, whatever made the money flow toward them. Money made, it was then necessary to purchase dignity and status. The West had provided the means. Generous admission policies of fund-seeking Western universities and colleges fitted perfectly with the needs of the nouveau riche parents. A child studying in a Western school was the ultimate status symbol, and therefore Pakistani children flocked to these centers of learning. Having completed their studies, some stayed on, but many returned. Each returning child had to bring back two things: a set of American car plates and a bunch of bumper stickers of a university, preferably Ivy League. These were then displayed proudly on the cars that plied the roads of Pakistan. They meant the world to the driver behind the wheel and indeed to the person following.

As they settled into their seats, R. F. nudged Niles and pointed to the burqa-clad female being guided to her seat across the aisle, all the way to the front of the aircraft.

"Not bad for a student, eh, first class," he remarked. Niles was equally surprised at the female's choice of travel. Once seated, she pivoted toward the window, seeking out her family. It was not difficult to see the group of excited individuals crowded up against the glass of the visitors' gallery, waving excitedly in the general direction of the aircraft.

"Silly, she could see much better if only she were to remove the restrictive veil," said Niles in a low voice. As the aircraft was pushed back, she waved a gloved hand. Niles wondered if the family could have seen her waving farewell. Most likely not, he decided.

The aircraft taxied, took off. Climbing rapidly, it headed west. As it reached the cruising altitude, the captain turned off the "Fasten Seatbelts" sign and then followed this by the inevitable announcement over the intercom system. "Ladies and Gentlemen, this is your captain speaking. It is my privilege to have you on board our nonstop flight to London and then on to New York," he continued, giving the passengers a rundown of the flight plan.

Niles watched the girl unbuckle her seatbelt and remove the burqa. A strikingly pretty female, dressed in the native attire, the "shalwar-kameez," emerged from under the weird garment. Although she was wearing no makeup and her hair was rolled up in a severe, tight bun, Niles could not help realizing that she was extremely attractive. She removed her carry-on bag from the overhead bin, unzipped it, and stuffed the burqa inside while simultaneously removing another bundle from the bag before returning it to the stowage bin. Carrying the bundle, she headed for the toilet. The door closed and the red light went on.

"Occupied."

The light remained red for fifteen minutes before it changed to green and the door opened. A stranger emerged. Painted lips, mascara eyes, shiny loose tresses falling over bare shoulders. Designer skirt, a skimpy blouse, bare midriff, unhampered, firm breasts, nipples firmly outlined against the flimsy

41

material. The tantalizing smell of expensive perfume. She headed toward her seat, her gait now voluptuously seductive. She stopped the passing stewardess and asked her if she would be kind enough to fetch her a drink. "Johnny Black, double, ice, no water."

While Niles watched with amusement, Robert could not resist winking at the girl, giving her a thumbs up, and saying aloud, "Way to go!"

She smiled invitingly. Robert picked up his drink and walked over. Pointing to the vacant seat next to her, he asked, "Is this seat taken?"

"Will be when you sit in it."

Perfect English, perfect smile, perfect teeth. Robert slid into the vacant chair. They chatted. She was returning from a vacation, from a visit to her loving parents. She had spent two delightful months with the family.

On long haul flights, airlines distribute an overnight kit to passengers in first class. It contains some pretty basic, but useful stuff. Eyeshades to help you sleep better, a cheap toothbrush, a tiny bottle of perfume, breath fresheners, a pair of tube socks, and, perhaps the most important of them all, a small container of moisturizing lotion. The air in the cabin is conditioned and the humidity is kept low. Dry air depletes the body fluids and dries the skin. Dryness on board airliners is all pervasive; it invades the very center of a person. Hence the lotion. If you fly from Karachi to New York with only one short stopover at Heathrow, your body moisture is considerably lowered. Drinking Johnny Blacks, double, ice, no water, does not help; alcohol accentuates the dryness. By the time you are midway across the Atlantic, even the moistest of vaginas has dried up. The tube of moisturizing lotion therefore comes in extremely handy as you enroll in the mile high club. You however have to follow the rules. You have to wait for dinner to be over, the lights to be dimmed, the blankets to be handed out, and until the other passengers have drifted off into their own dreamworlds. You also have to ensure that the attendants have completed their service and are now resting in the galley. It helps considerably if you are seated in the very first row in first class on board a Boeing 747.

You can then fuck your way to America.

She was good. Very good indeed, Robert admitted to himself when his mind could focus once again. He never had had such fantastic sex, so quietly, so expertly. She was young, wild, exotically oriental; she was a deprived female who had not had a man for two months. Now, laid back in her fully reclined seat, luxuriating in the satisfying experience she just had, she mulled the problem over in her mind. Technically, her vacation did not end until she was back in the United States. And she did actually like the handsome American. It did not take her long to make up her mind. This one was going to be for free. She would forego the five hundred dollars she charged per trick from customers in New York.

Money she could forego, but not the cleansing. Sex was impure, carnal, base. A Muslim could not remain tainted. A Muslim had to be pure. She headed for the toilet to perform the "Wadhoo," the Muslim procedure for washing and purifying the body.

Had she asked for the money, Robert would have been surprised, but he most probably would have paid, because he knew that he would soon be receiving $500 from P. K. It was, after all, a sucker bet that P. K. was sure to lose.

5

"Oh Puck, What have you done?"

Harry could not have known that the message on his screen was to take the world by storm. He could not have known that he was witnessing a profound moment in the development of warfare. He could never have understood that the message on his screen announced a paradigm shift in the way warfare would be conducted henceforth.

Puck was not smart, not very smart, it was, as one computer expert put it, fucking brilliant. It was alive. It could adapt, it could mutate. It would challenge itself, checking each machine to ascertain whether it was already infected or not. It could change ports, crafting its own entry to the computers it penetrated, creating its own backdoor so that it could come and go as it pleased, reaching in and withdrawing from the machine as and when it wanted to, taking what it wanted, bringing in what it desired. Puck installed processes for remote, root-level access to the machines it infected. This allowed any code to be executed on the infected machine and, using the hidden backdoors, the machines could be accessed whenever required, at any future date.

Puck was multilingual. Depending on the language of the computer, it varied the number of threads it used to probe other machines. Puck was cautious. It avoided probing multicast and loopback IP addresses. Puck was disciplined. It created a systematic hierarchy of machines, servers, concentrators, routers, switches, hubs, masters, slaves, nodes, globally distributed machines, some ordering, some relaying, others executing, yet others reporting.

Puck was unique. It was, after all, the progeny of a frivolous union between two males, one boastful, the other confident. Two fighter pilots, one a challenger, the other accepting the challenge. Two friends, one, an American, the other a Pakistani.

Robert refused to pay up. "Get real, P. K. This is child's stuff. Kids do this all the time. We are talking of invading large, secure computers, not frigging baby PC's."

Five hundred dollars needed to be won. Puck would have to be ordered into action again.

One fine morning, quite suddenly and without any warning whatsoever, a router located in the United States began executing an illegal instruction. It generated over two million http port scans within one hour. This caused massive bandwidth paralysis, and inbound Web access into most networks was totally shut down. Interestingly, the http inbound streams were not port 80 http connections but cleverly constructed http reply or response packets using all the port numbers above 1023. They were augmented by an additional million plus probes per hour by two additional worms. One attacked computers through port 80, while the other carried out its attacks on port 25. Everybody thought that the infection was originating in China because there had been earlier attacks on these two ports by worms that had already been identified as having that origin.

Computer engineers soon realized that this attack was directly aimed at the gateway doors. They worked furiously to stave off a major disaster in the computer community. Bandwidth was increased to counter the attack by using high-capacity routers, but all the increase was quickly consumed and the attack continued unabated. Once again the message started flashing across screens:

"Oh Puck. Look what have you done now?"

Traps were set. Unprotected NT4 servers were reconfigured with Internet Information Services software version 4.0 to trap the virus. Within minutes, Puck had stormed across them. An immediate upgrade to Windows 2000 servers running Internet Information Services version 5 software was undertaken. The software, advertised aggressively as being highly resistant to any buffer overflow vulnerability, proved to be otherwise. Puck continued replicating with wild abandon. Puck rampaged across the Net, seeking out servers, implanting within them a file called "root.exe." In some cases even the router access lists did not block Puck executables from entering the scripts subdirectory of Web servers. New software was developed and installed on servers by engineers working round the clock, software that could examine packets with worm signatures, software that instructed routers to intercept and trash any code Puck tried to "ftp" to its victims. Major hardware changes were also implemented. In some cases of particularly debilitating attacks, complete server farms were scrapped and replaced with new, more powerful, more capable machines.

All these measures failed to work. Puck stayed one step ahead. It had already decided to change itself. Soon a far more dangerous Puck was running through the Internet, forcing companies to shut down their servers and e-mail systems. And this time it was truly malicious, designed to infect a complete system when someone opened an infected e-mail or visited an infected Web site. Whereas Puck had earlier attacked using three different types of worms, it was now an all-in-one worm that attacked with http probes, smtp mail floods, and netbios file shares. Not only did it infect sites, but it also ensured that any visitor to the site picked up the infection. It then traveled across the network, attacking the entire corporate network of the visitor. It located the address book of the e-mail user and sent itself to all the contacts as an e-mail attachment. It then overwrote critical Microsoft Windows system files.

And then, having wreaked havoc across the World Wide Web, the virus disappeared just as rapidly and suddenly as it had appeared. Puck vanished. It seemed to have died. Puck had appeared, it had morphed, it had mutated; it had disappeared. Security specialists congratulated themselves that they had defeated another attack aimed at the Internet. No one could have guessed that it had been turned off by its creator. A point had been proven, a bet had been won. R. F. would pay, and therefore Puck could be turned off.

"Sorry, buddy, no can do. No way do I pay. The bet was for the computers of the Pentagon. Not your crappy civilian computers."

The bet had indeed been specific. It had to be an attack on the computers of the Pentagon. Not the wide-open, insecure Net. The five hundred dollars remained uncollected.

P. K. had hoped that it would not come to this even though, in his heart, he knew that this was where the bet would end up. It would turn into a war game. He had prepared for that eventuality, and as he sat down on the computer once again, he felt a both a twinge of remorse and indeed, a thrill that this combat would have to go the whole way. He busied himself with the task ahead, reminding himself that $500 is $500, and there is nothing a fighter pilot cannot do.

Pentagon computers were attacked in what was to be later characterized as the most destructive computer intrusion ever to be experienced by the American nation. The attack targeted all the Defense Department network domain name servers and was serious enough to merit its own codename; "Solar Sunrise". The Pentagon recognized that it was facing an unprecedented, widespread attack on its entire information infrastructure and it reacted immediately with full force. Expert computer programmers recruited specially by the Pentagon for exactly such eventualities worked furiously, searching, analyzing, tracking, and eventually succeeding in identifying the problem. It did not take them too long to find the virus. It was a malevolent piece of code that had entered the Pentagon network through a backdoor. The entire network was purged, hard disks wiped clean, completely fresh installations of operating systems were carried out, backups restored. The specialists were sure that this would bring the network systems back to normal.

They were wrong. The Department of Defense efforts were really good, but the virus was better. It changed itself and continued rampaging across the military networks, now attacking servers that operated on the Microsoft Structured Query Language. Within hours, more than seventy-five thousand gateway ports were blocked. Of the total of 14,774 Structured Query Language servers the Defense Department had, this attack breached all except two. The experts were incredulous at the magnitude of the attack but were unanimous in their verdict that this could not be Puck or a variant of Puck. Puck was never that good and, Puck had been neutralized. This had to be something new.

The entire computing community of the Pentagon worked round the clock, establishing traces, checking routes, scanning sources. Brilliant minds busied themselves trying to trace the origin of this infection. They could not, however, track the source down to one single location. The attack appeared to be originating from scores of different sources, spread globally.

The deputy defense secretary whose job it was to oversee all Pentagon computer security matters was the most concerned. His assessment was that these sophisticated attacks were originating from Russia, but he could not tell whether they were coming directly from Russia or whether someone was simply routing them through Russian computer addresses in an attempt to disguise their origin. An emergency meeting of the information technology staff was called. They discussed the other, high-profile hacker intrusions into U.S. military systems. They reviewed the long-running spy investigations "Storm Cloud" and "Moonlight Maze." They recalled those times when government computer operators had watched helplessly as reams of electronic documents had flowed from Defense Department computers onto the Internet. The specialists had seen millions of pages of sensitive data, including the contents of the e-mail inboxes of military personnel flow out of their repositories. Were these attacks once again attempting to collect information just as their predecessors? An aide suggested that this could once again be the work of the two young British hackers, "Kuji" and "Datastream Cowboy." These youngsters had broken into the U.S. Air Force's Rome laboratory, planted eavesdropping software, and started monitoring e-mails and other sensitive information. The two had never been found. The deputy secretary disagreed. He was adamant that this was something much better, much bigger than the two kids could come up with. If it was similar to anything at all, it had to be a variant of Puck; after all, it did have the telltale signature of that virus.

The Pentagon was only concerned that its own computers were under attack. No one even thought of checking what was happening elsewhere across the nation. Indeed, there was no centralized authority that could have seen the big picture. No one could have recognized that similar activity, albeit at a very low level, was being experienced by other military organizations, research and technology systems, air traffic control computers, power plant systems, rail and shipping traffic control systems, nuclear weapons laboratories, colleges, universities, banks, investment and brokerage firms, and even the casinos of Atlantic

City and Las Vegas. The deadly virus was spreading, mutating, burrowing deeper and deeper, and becoming more efficient, more powerful.

To be absolutely fair, there was one American agency that could have assessed the true extent and widespread nature of the infection, but unfortunately its tasking did not include this function. The U.S. National Counterintelligence Center was only assigned the duty of conducting espionage activities worldwide. Its charter was limited to tracking global computer networks beyond America's borders. In exercising this function, it was fully aware that many organizations and individuals were regularly penetrating computer networks across the globe. The networks of Russia were especially vulnerable, because that country had a very poor security system in place. It also knew that British, French, German, indeed most of the major governmental systems worldwide had major security holes. The center had noted with thinly disguised admiration that a large number of these intrusions were originating from within the United States. Some were actually originating from within the United States government! The agency was not worried about computer intrusions of the networks within the United States, because it was aware that historically such attacks invariably originated from within the U.S. government and were internal tests for the resident security systems and processes. Indeed, the National Counterintelligence Center itself regularly attempted to penetrate the Defense Department information infrastructure to eavesdrop on military personnel and their activities. It also penetrated the systems of the other branches of government and the systems of other countries, friendly, hostile or neutral. The United States government earnestly believed that it had in place a powerful capability not only to protect its own electronic data networks but to breach those of other nations with impunity.

This latest attack challenged that belief and a rudely shaken Pentagon decided to act aggressively. It did what any military worth its salt does in such situations. It conducted an exercise. The first-ever exercise conducted on a massive scale, designed to test the ability of the U.S. military to identify and respond to an information attack.

Exercise "Eligible Receiver" scared the Pentagon. It proved that the intelligence community had little capability to detect or assess cyber attacks. Firewalls could be breached, sensitive information hijacked, passwords hacked, secrets compromised. A frenzied effort was launched to make the Pentagon systems secure. Software was written, codes reinvented. Systems were cleaned, data purged, disks wiped, memories erased, operating systems reinstalled. New and emerging technologies were incorporated, and no expense was spared to guarantee the protection of its systems. The Department of Defense and its huge team of computer specialists worked tirelessly, striving to ensure that its information systems were made impervious to attack. Information operations were a core competency for the Department of Defense. They had to be; success or failure in war depended on accurate and secure information.

The Defense Information Systems Agency—DISA— was created and tasked to design and deploy proactive protections, create attack detection methods, and secure the department's enterprise systems. A Computer Emergency Response Team, CERT, was put together, a department-wide antivirus license was acquired, a Public Key Infrastructure secure code was created, accreditation and certification processes were instituted; new policies were defined and implemented.

All systems were tested repeatedly, over and over again. There was no trace of any virus, any worm, any malicious code. Systems were subjected to repeated attacks by exotic new viruses designed by young and innovative computer engineers, some of them still in their teens but working full time for the U.S. government. None were successful. Everyone heaved a sigh of relief. All systems had been cleansed, Massive firewalls and overwhelming security had been put in place. All viruses and worms, all bugs had been exterminated. Sure enough, following these extensive measures, there was no repeat penetration by any hostile code. Puck was history.

More importantly, a bet had eventually been won. It was a very sober Robert who handed over five crisp one hundred dollar bills to P. K.

"Buddy, I hate having to take your money, but you need to understand that this is the new face of combat. Warfare as we knew it has now changed. No longer do we have to go around burning holes in the sky, pulling "G"s, blacking out, killing ourselves. The game has changed and so has the playing field. This is the battlefield of the future. We shall have to fight a different kind of war from now on. Different weapons, different tactics, different theaters.

"And, different rules, I suppose" responded Robert, his voice heavy with sarcasm.

"No, Sir, no way. The rules do not change. They never change. The rules remain constant. We have to fight by the same old principles, the same old laws. Same old Sun Tzu, same old Clausewitz, the same old principles of war. Surprise, secrecy, stealth. And don't ever do what you did when you placed the bet. Never, never, underestimate the opposition. Never be vain. We need to recognize that the enemy also has balls! And that even though you may be from Texas, his balls might be bigger!"

P. K. sat staring at the screen in the otherwise sparsely lit study. His mind wandered over the events of the past few months, the almost childish bet and the not so childish actions that followed. He slid back in his chair, placed his feet on the table, and, with his head pushed back into cupped hands, he smiled wistfully in the lonely room. If only John could see this. He was perhaps the only person who could appreciate what P.

K had done. If only John were alive and present to witness this. John would have understood Puck; he would have loved the code.

It was then that he remembered John's stern advice. "Don't ever think that programming computers is a job. It is something much bigger, much greater. A program is like a child. You conceive it, you father it, you nurse it and you make sure that it functions, it works, it survives, it is successful. And you, the creator, must make sure that it can do all this in the adverse environment of the electronic jungle out there."

P.K. realized what he had to do. He could not kill his creation. Puck could not die. Puck would not only have to live but it would need to be empowered further. Puck was weaponry for warfare; information weaponry for information warfare.

He sat upright, pulled the keyboard toward him, and began hammering away. He changed the code, refined the command processes, created additional subroutines and modified existing ones. Puck was retrained, recertified. Additional backdoors were created, additional avenues of attack developed. An already battle-hardened warrior was further empowered. Puck was then tasked for a massive recruitment campaign and instructed to create a complete electronic hierarchy, a complete organizational structure similar to that of a modern military force. Soldiers were to be recruited, field commanders identified, a chain of command established, an army readied. The Top Level Domain or Root servers, responsible for all resolution activities on the Internet, were pressed into service. Puck was tasked to span the entire Internet and position itself in almost every server on the World Wide Web. A new battlefield had been identified, a ubiquitous battlefield whose frontline fighters were the workstations on the desktop of every home, office, and Internet café. Assisting them were millions of mobile soldiers carried across the globe by commuting professionals—laptops that could be called up at a moment's notice to respond to commands, to execute instructions, to obey orders. Mobile systems carrying Puck and the sons of Puck or, as P. K. would later christen them endearingly, "Little Puckers." Viruses and worms were metamorphosed into powerful capacity-building tools and programmed to provide the creator of Puck real-time feedback on the situation that existed across the entire battlefield. Having hammered out the final instruction set, P. K. logged on to the Internet and hit "Enter."

Nothing happened. No one across the entire planet noticed anything.

They weren't supposed to. A stealthy warrior had entered the battlefield of the future. Quietly, surreptitiously, without fanfare.

Oh Puck.

P.K. switched off the computer and the desk lamp but continued sitting in the darkened room. Past memories came flooding back. He remembered the first time he had met John. Almost a quarter of a century had passed since the day the two had met.

It was almost a quarter of a century ago that P.K. had experienced the Net.

6

John pushed himself away from the terminal. It had been a long and tiring day and he was ready to call it quits. The letter he had been writing to his friend in Berkeley would need to be finished later. There wasn't any real rush, because he knew that no matter when he wrote the letter, it would be delivered within seconds. Not because the United States Postal Service had suddenly become superefficient; it still took at least four days to turn around a letter. John was going to send his message using electronic mail, a computer-based message sending and reading process that used software that had recently been developed. It was computer code envisioned and created by what was earlier the Advanced Research Projects Agency, ARPA, now transformed into the Defense Advanced Research Projects Agency, DARPA. While the name could, and indeed would, seesaw back and forth between ARPA and DARPA, the constant factor would be the suffix it was about to acquire. NET.

The NET was what the agency had created. A series of computers, geographically distant but connected to each other electronically, each able to communicate with the others, using and sharing each other's resources, each other's databases. The NET was the result of the efforts of some very brilliant and dedicated minds in the computing world that had convinced their superiors, peers, and many other disbelieving minds of a new concept: networking. In 1972 these visionaries had given the first public demonstration of this new networking technology. The demonstration had been a success; they had prevailed. The University of California at Los Angeles had been selected to be the first node on the NET.

John had been intensely involved in the ARPANET project since its inception. He was there when they designed the hosts, the IMPs, the Interface Message Processors. He was there when UCLA, UC Santa Barbara, University of Utah, and the Stanford Institute were linked together. He was there when they first transmitted the letters "L, G, and O between UCLA and Stanford. And he was there when Ray Tomlinson had developed the software, the first e-mail file transfer protocol, and named the routines SNDMSG and CPYNET. He was the one to recommend that they choose the @ symbol as the separator between the username and computer name. And he was there now, studying for his doctorate in computer science at UCLA. He spent most of his waking hours in the well-equipped computer labs of the prestigious university and was specializing in computer communication protocols, both at the operating system level and the application level.

"Time for a break," he thought, glancing at the clock. It was past eight in the evening, and he was tired. A beer, a meal and then to bed. The letter was not really important; it could wait.

He entered his favorite eating place, situated in the main square of the village of Westwood. It was a large, almost cavernous, restaurant in the UCLA neighborhood. German in name and theme, it was decorated as a medieval cellar of a Teutonic castle. It was a noisy, boisterous, and busy place with pseudo Frauleins, some buxom, some not, with half-exposed bosoms, some ample, some not, darting about carrying unwieldy trays and beer steins. He jostled his way to the large bar, squeezed himself a place against the polished expanse, and ordered a beer. Served, he took a long, refreshing gulp of the amber liquid and then turned around to survey the crowd. He had already noticed the foreigner standing next to him, obviously different, possibly Asian, probably a newcomer; he had not seen him in this establishment earlier.

"Hi."

The foreigner smiled back, acknowledging his greeting silently with a nod. Must be a language thing with him, John surmised. Poor guys, flocking to the United States burning with a desire to jump across the divide between the third world and the first. Eager to learn, keen to study, hardworking, able, intelligent, blessed by God with the tools to progress but placed in countries where their talent and abilities would never be realized. Sad, he mused, how sad it must be for these simple folk to be thrust into a land where everything was so different and alien. New places, different customs, an unfamiliar language; America must be a formidable and lonely place for these people, unable to converse, unable to express themselves, driven by want, motivated by need, propelled by ambition.

The lights of the establishment flickered. The large hall went dark as power was lost and then, almost instantly, the room brightened as power returned. It happened again. And again. And again. The power company must be having major problems tonight, John thought. Trust California; always hungry for power, always sucking up the watts. He glanced at the foreigner and sensed some tension and bewilderment in the individual.

He thought that the Asian would appreciate a consoling voice in a hostile, strange land. "Fluc-tu-a-tions" he said, taking care to pause between the syllables, careful to enunciate the word properly, aiming to have the foreigner understand why the electricity was misbehaving.

The Asian appeared to have difficulty in comprehending him. His eyebrows were coming together, a furrow was forming on his forehead. John waited for the message to sink in. The alien continued looking at him in a strange manner. And then the brown foreigner shrugged and smiled.

"Hmmm. If that is the way you feel about it, Fluct-u-americans," came back the retort, equally slowly, equally minced, each syllable articulated in impeccable English without any hint of an accent!

It was now John's turn to be confused. As understanding dawned, he broke out in a loud, hearty guffaw. The foreigner joined in. Both laughed. Heads turned, people stared, some amused, others mystified.

"Touché." He stuck his ample hand out. "I'm John." A firm grip. "Pervez." Warm, open, friendly.

"Buy you a drink?

"Sure," and before John could ask, "beer's good."

The ice broken, they talked. The American talked to the Pakistani. Yes, he knew where Pakistan was. He knew a lot about the strange and fascinating land. There were quite a few Pakistanis at UCLA and the other universities that dotted Southern California. He had seen them, sat with them in the same class, attended the same lectures, but he had never chatted with any Pakistani or, for that matter, any Asian. They looked so, er, so, different.

"I'm starving. Care to eat?"

"No, thanks. Just ate."

"Come sit, watch me eat. We'll talk." John wanted to get to know the stranger better.

"Didn't your mother tell you not to speak with your mouth full?"

They moved to a table and sat down. John was delighted. This was the first Asian he was talking to in any meaningful manner. He was amazed that he could converse with the foreigner as he would do with a colleague or a peer. Here was a person from a different place, a different time, so completely different in experience and origin yet so remarkably similar in his perception of life. He found that they both shared a sense of humor, a desire to learn, a passion for living. He had to get to know him better. They parted, promising to meet again.

A beautiful friendship developed. A PhD student, a genius working on esoteric technicalities in the fascinating world of computers and another, a military pilot, practical, dynamic, searching, enjoying, living. Both explorers in their own rights. Both bold, thrusting, permissive. Both shy, withdrawn, reticent. Two persons oddly opposite, uncannily similar.

He was pleasantly surprised to find out that Pervez was studying at the University of Southern California. It was a U.S. military-funded training program designed to bring in foreign officers and train them in

65

a variety of disciplines. He was doubly surprised to find out that P. K. was interested in computers. Indeed, he had more knowledge than some of his contemporaries who were supposed to be specialists on the subject. They discussed bits and bytes, programming and debugging.

He told the Pakistani of what had happened when the Russians had launched Sputnik One. "President Eisenhower had been really pissed off. This was totally unacceptable. America would never again lag behind in technology. The proud nation had to be out there in the front". Eisenhower had created two new agencies, the National Aeronautics and Space Administration, NASA, and the Advanced Research Project Agency, ARPA. The first was designed to make America conquer outer space. The second was designed to make America conquer Earth.

He told him about the NET. This had floored Pervez. "You mean to say that you can get one computer to talk to another computer? That's impossible," he challenged the expert. "There is no way you can do that."

They had and they were doing it, right now, right here in UCLA.

This Pervez had to see.

This John would show.

He was the first foreigner, the first Asian, the first Pakistani, to experience ARPANET. He watched John log into the UCLA computer. From there he reached out to Berkeley. From Berkeley to Harvard. And then to Illinois. John was zipping across the United States at the speed of light. P. K. was fascinated. He did not sleep that night. A whole new world had opened up for him. Computing at a distance; the concept was mind boggling.

John and Pervez became close friends. Together they wandered the wonderful world of ARPANET. From the West Coast they could reach out and access computers on the eastern seaboard as easily as if those machines were right there in the very same room they were working in. They accessed files in faraway locations. They sent messages to distant computers and, presto, back came an answer. They went into distant data banks. P. K. saw those distant files show up on his screen.

P. K. could not hide his amazement. He was stunned. This was fantastic. Could he do this from his apartment on West Adams, out at USC? Sure. He could do it from anywhere. Even from Pakistan. The phone bill would be horrendous, but he could do it. He could connect to a computer and get on the NET from anywhere.

P. K. knew what he had to do. He would have to buy his own computer. No longer could he make do with working on the large systems of various institutions.

He would do this when he stopped over in London on his way back to Pakistan. He had, anyway, intended to stop to catch up with Niles, his close friend and fellow aviator. Theirs was a friendship that had formed during training at the Air Force College. It was a friendship that had grown over the years, because they were in regular contact. Now it would be a stopover to meet a friend and pick up a new love. He could hardly wait. He was not sure now whether his impatience was because of the computer he would buy or a result of his desire to meet his friend.

7

Ornate, wrought iron gates; a circular driveway
enclosing a wonderfully green, evenly mowed, orange
shaped cricket field and imposing steps leading up to
the majestic entrance. The Air Force College was an
institution with a history as rich and impressive as the
establishment itself. The main hall, its expansive floor
covered with a beautiful, air force blue carpet, its
imposing walls decked with massive portraits, the
circular balcony draped with flags, battle standards
and colors, had a perfect aura of awe and reverence. If
the walls could talk, they would tell fascinating tales
of tradition, of royalty and nobility, of marshals,
generals, admirals, kings, queens, dukes, and
duchesses. The walls could not talk, but Charles, the
hall porter could. Especially after a few pints to
lubricate the vocal chords and further define the
bright pink capillaries on his rotund, cherubic face.
Charlie had seen it all.

And therefore, he was not particularly enthused with
this new lot of entrants. They came every six months.

Raw, ill mannered, undisciplined sods, thinking that they were the cat's whiskers. "Just wait until the drill sergeants gets hold of them," he thought gleefully. "They would soon know, their supercilious smiles would rapidly disappear off their pimply faces." And the foreigners. Poor buggers. They were really up the creek. Lost and wandering in a strange land, confused and unsure. Her Majesty's government encouraged the induction of foreigners, because it helped preserve the dwindling empire. The service liked it because it gave the institution an international flavor. It built camaraderie on a global scale. The participating nations liked it because it enabled them to have high quality training for a select few. The staff at the college loved it because the foreigners lent color to the environment. The villages around the college loved it because the foreigners contributed to the economy. And the students at the nearby teacher training colleges loved it because it enabled them to learn the mating habits of the foreign males.

Charlie loved it because the foreigners always needed help and guidance. He was there to help them and guide them. He took great pride in seeing the cadets metamorphose into officers over the three years they would spend in these hallowed surroundings. They would be educated, refined, polished, trained, and turned into the finest officers that any air force would be proud of having in its echelons.

This was an interesting lot. An American, an Australian, a West Indian, a couple of Saudi Arabian princes, a Jordanian, a Sudanese, a Pakistani, an Indian. He picked up the roster and started reading the names of the new arrivals. Not unnaturally, his eyes focused on the longest name that occupied the list. Pahul Srivandarum Omparkash Laljee. The cadet from India. Jesus Christ, he murmured softly. This was not going to be easy.

They were all lined up. A new class was being called to order, the first roll call for the new entry was about to take place. The sergeant had arranged them in neat rows, as, in the distance, an officer paced up and down, arms clasped behind him, strutting imperiously, waiting for the NCO to report that all were present. Just as he was about to start, there was a commotion at the far end of the parade square, the sound of gravel being crunched by hurried footsteps resounded as a tall, lanky youngster loped across the open space. He approached the assembly and waved nonchalantly to no one in particular. "Hi, guys." And then, turning to the sergeant, who was now interestingly changing colors, he asked innocently, "Hi, General. How come you started without me?"

The sergeant was apoplectic. His handlebar mustaches twitched nervously, his face had reddened, the knuckles of his hand that clutched the drill instructor's measuring stick turned absolutely white. He strode up to the offender, stuck his face out until it was almost touching the other, and let forth an almighty roar, a long, drawn-out command.

"Siiiiillllllleeeennnce." And then in double quick time, "Justwhatthebleedinhelldoyouthinkyouredoingdraggingyourarseinnow."

Robert Forrester was stunned into immobility. He had not expected this outburst. He tried to say something, but before he could, the sergeant continued, "Fallintoline," and then, sneeringly, "Sir."

Robert's eye caught that of the tall fair Britisher standing in the front row. His piercing blue eyes conveyed alarm. They were sending a message that, strangely enough, Robert understood. It was an unspoken message that seemed to make sense. "Don't mess with the sergeant, just join in." He quietly stepped up to the line, found himself a place behind the tall lad. He assumed the posture everyone else held.

At Tension.

Sanity restored, the sergeant started rattling off the names, and as each name was called out, a person responded. The NCO was an old hand at this. He prided himself in being able to handle all names, even the weird ones of the foreigners. He already knew the trickiest one in this lot. The name of the Indian. Undaunted, he carried on because he had rehearsed it to perfection earlier. The officers supervising the roll call would definitely be impressed by the ease with which he handled these difficult foreigners.

"Pahul Srivandarum Omparkash Laljee?"

A stony silence greeted the call. Once again, the sergeant repeated his cry.

"Pahul Srivandarum Omparkash Laljee?"

And once again, there was silence.

The sergeant took a couple of steps forward and focused his attention on the petite, dark individual standing in the second row and repeated his cry for a third time, this time directly into the youngster's face.

"Pahul Srivandarum Omparkash Laljee?"

"Pleeze. Pleeze, not Pahul. Please to make it right, Sir. My name is Rahul. Rahul with an R."

The sergeant grimaced. This was not going well. Not well at all. First the offensive American. And now a cocky wog. A wispy brown guy with a name longer than his peter.

"Right, then. Rahul with an R. No P, just an R."
He made the correction on the list he carried and completed the roll call without further incident. The newcomers were assigned squadrons, Sections, dormitories, rooms. The assembly was then dismissed. Pervez turned away, uncomfortable with himself, his surroundings, the foreign, white men. He sought out the Indian, looking for kinship with someone like him.

73

Brown, lonely, lost, afraid. Or so he thought. The Indian was neither lost nor afraid. He refused the outstretched hand and surprised Pervez by responding, "Sorry, Not mention. Not please. No, no, no. I am Brahmin from India. Not to shaking hand with Mooslah."

Pervez was taken aback at the hostility. He recognized "Mooslah," the derogatory term for Muslim and guessed that it had to be a patriotic thing with the Indian cadet. The two nations had recently been through another war, and, while the overall outcome of the clash had been inconclusive with both sides claiming victory, the smaller air force of Pakistan had completely overwhelmed its larger, more potent Indian counterpart. Pervez assumed that this must be the reason for this antagonism. Chastised, friendless, he headed for his room, now more alone and lonely than before. Robert quickened his pace and caught up with him.

"Hi. I'm Robert."

"I'm Pervez," diffidently.

"And you're from?"

"Pakistan."

Robert nodded wisely, making a mental note to find out what and where Pakistan was.

They walked, they talked. The two were in the same squadron, the same group. They had been assigned adjacent rooms. "Should be interesting," thought Robert. Being an exchange cadet in the United Kingdom was most probably going to be more fun than being trained at the USAF Academy in Colorado Springs. Robert could not have realized then that this foreigner, this brown-skinned Asian, would become his lifelong friend. Their lives would remain intertwined as the years rolled on. Despite their disparate origins and their widely separated countries, they would interact frequently and would, one day, stand together, shoulder to shoulder to fight the most amazing battle of the future.

It was almost two weeks before the group got together for their first meeting. It was also an occasion for considerable acrimony. Foreign cadets objected to being addressed in a derogatory manner. Some resented the nicknames they had been given. The American suggested a solution. Why not do what they did back home in the United States? Call each other by their initials.

Huh?

Robert explained. He, Robert Forrester would be called R. F. Niles Barrington would become N. B. Pervez Khan would henceforth be P. K. And so on down the line. Until they came to Rahul Srivandarum Omparkash Laljee. There was a problem. R. L. was already taken. The awkward silence was broken by the Pakistani. P. K. jumped up, eager to suggest a solution. Why can't he have four initials? After all JFK had three. "Why can Rahul not use all his initials? R for Rahul, S for Srivandarum, O for Omprakash and L for Laljee."

Rahul was surprised that the Pakistani was not acting hostile despite having been snubbed during their first meeting. His elders were right! The upstart Pakistanis needed to be put firmly in their place. Only then would they behave, only then would they respect. He was also very pleased with the suggestion of the heathen Mooslah. Just as he had the longest name, he would have the longest initials too. It was agreed. Rahul Srivandarum Omparkash Laljee would henceforth have four initials as opposed to everyone else's two.

It was a furious Rahul Srivandarum Omparkash Laljee who confronted P. K. the next morning. In a language both understood, in Urdu, the succinct language of the subcontinent, in that graphic and extremely colorful language, he informed the Pakistani that his sister was a whore who had daily intercourse with Ali Baba and his forty thieves, that his mother had copulated with a donkey, and that his father was the product of the congress between a monkey and a rat.

P. K. looked upon the irate Indian in true astonishment.

"What exactly is the problem?" he asked feigning innocence. This seemed to infuriate Rahul further. The somewhat insubstantial and physically disadvantaged Indian now informed the much larger Pakistani that he would grab hold of his mustache and insert it in his rectum. He would castrate him; chop up his gonads into tiny pieces. He would then fry the pieces in the fat extracted from the massive posterior of his mother and feed the crispy pieces to the whores of Bombay. He would do all this unless P. K. undid what he had done.

P. K. was stunned at the ferocity of the Indian. He explained to the irate individual that he did not have a mustache. Nor indeed a sister. Nor did his mother have an extensive posterior. That this was no way to treat a friend who had helped him out in difficulty. All he had done was suggest a use of initials. The smile on P.K.'s face however belied his innocence.

"I'll try to fix things up, Rahul. I promise. I'll ask them to stop. I hope that they do," he said. Then, as a furious Rahul stomped away down the corridor, he continued, raising his voice to make sure that Rahul heard, "The problem is that it won't change anything. You are an RSOL, and no matter what you do, you shall always remain an RSOL."

The receding figure pivoted and charged in the direction of the Pakistani. P. K. took off. There was no point in hanging around with a high-speed RSOL headed directly for him.

Rahul vowed to get even. He did not know how presently, but he would find a way. He would seek divine help. The gods would show him the way. He was, after all, their favorite. Rahul was a devout Brahmin, who performed all his religious duties faithfully. His gods would not let him down.

Each morning Rahul carried out his ritualistic prayers before venturing out into the world. And, being a true Brahmin, he always started each day with a steaming glass of his own body produce. The "Water of Life" that would help him attain enlightenment and live a long and healthy life. The cure of everything from the common cold to cancer! As a child he had been made to memorize the entire chapter of the ancient spiritual text "Damar Tantra," which was devoted to drinking "shivambu," the water of the god Shiva. A divine nectar that flowed from one's own loins. A magical fluid that would unleash his "kundalini," sending it straight into the third eye, bringing instant enlightenment.

Rahul believed, as did his forefathers, that drinking urine was not only a religious duty; it was also a divine way of remaining pure and free of disease. The venerable Mahatma Gandhi and his family always drank the amber fluid. Rahul's distant relative, the chief minister of Bombay and later the deputy prime minister of India, Morarji Desai, started his day by drinking his own urine. In fact, Uncle Morarji Desai had actually devoted his life to spreading this custom among the general Indian population. Many Indian food preparations used the amber liquid liberally to give that unique "Indian taste" to their exotic curries. It was an article of faith. Drinking urine accelerated one's progress toward Samadhi, or spiritual enlightenment.

It was in pursuit of that enlightenment that Rahul would, having arisen each morning, find his way to the washbasin in the corner of his room. He would open the medicine cabinet, take out the special glass dedicated for this purpose and collect his first morning urine. He always made sure that he collected the golden liquid as his father had taught him, allowing the first squirt to go to waste, ensuring that the morning tonic was picked up midstream. Glass full, he would then prepare for the ceremony. He would squat on the floor, arranging the statues of his gods against the wall for the Morning Prayer. Depending on his particular need and the time of the year, he would position the most appropriate deity from the whole range of gods that he had available to him at the center of the arrangement. Some days he would pray to the monkey god, on other days he would prostrate himself before the elephant god, or the snake god, or the cow goddess, or any of the plurality of gods he had in his considerable divine arsenal. As he sipped the fresh, steaming fluid, he would invariably wonder at the amazing qualities of this miracle fluid. Water tasted watery; Beer, beery; wine, winey. Always. Not urine. This magical potion had a truly wide-ranging taste. One single fluid, multiple tastes; a positive indication of its divine nature. At times it tasted soapy, at other times salty. Sometimes bitter, sometimes tinged with a hint of sweetness. Sometimes strong and pungent, sometimes mild and smooth. Over the years, he had learned to enjoy the harsh tastes that followed meals that contained garlic, asparagus, beans, peanuts, dairy products, or eggs.

Rahul prayed. He beseeched his gods to show him a way to sort out the cocky Pakistani. He implored them to show him the way to humiliate the heathen Mooslah in a manner that would never be forgotten.

The gods would respond. They would show him a way.

8

The English instructor strode down the aisle, handing back the test papers. As he did so, he lectured the cadets in a voice that was a curious mixture of sadness and wonder, sarcasm blended with praise, ridicule mixed with annoyance. Fifty students, fifty of the brightest, the most talented scions of British families with impeccable backgrounds, impressive educational credentials. Boys who had studied in the finest of schools, had the best of tuition, the best of upbringing. And, amidst them, a foreigner, a citizen of an erstwhile colony, a native who he had believed would need coaching and leniency. It was this foreigner, this alien whose mother tongue was not even English, this individual had secured the highest marks in the language test. He spared no words berating the fifty whose mother tongue it was. What was the world coming to?

Like the instructor, Niles too was stunned. He thought that he would have secured a perfect score in the test. After all, English was his favorite subject. He loved the language; he adored its literature; indeed, he had grown up surrounded by it. He had spent long hours immersed in the books that filled the cupboards of his father's well-stocked library. As a child, he would often creep out of bed, sneaking down the hallway into the darkened balcony overlooking the sitting area where his parents had their regular literary get-togethers. From his vantage point, he would listen, as they read passages, debated, argued, and discussed books and authors. Enthralled by the words, he would be transported to strange places and mystical lands full of interesting people and fascinating events. And then he would play act. Sometimes he would be Oliver Twist, trembling, hungry, asking for more. Another day he would be Mark Anthony, exhorting the Romans to lend him an ear. He loved English literature—its drama, its emotion, its wondrous web, woven of magical words.

He would never forget the day he had chanced upon a book written in some strange foreign language in the home library. He had been confused because while the title was English, the content was not; the words did not seem to make any sense. Yet he had persevered until recognition dawned that it was indeed English but of a peculiar kind. As understanding sunk in, he reread the book excitedly.

Niles had discovered Chaucer. In discovering him, Niles had discovered his own pubescent sexuality.

Derk was the nyght as pich, or as the cole
And at the wyndow out she putte hir hole,
And Absolon, hym fil no bet ne wers,
But with his mouth he kiste hir naked ers
Ful savourly, er he were war of this.
Abak he stirte, and thoughte it was amys,
For wel he wiste a womman hath no berd.
He felte a thyng al rough and long yherd,
And seyde, fy! allas! what have I do?
Tehee! quod she, and clapte the wyndow to,

His quest now became focused. Seek and ye shall find.
He sought and, sure enough, he found. In the well-
stocked library of his home, he found D. H. Lawrence.
"Oh, and far down inside her the deeps parted and
rolled asunder, in long, fair-travelling billows, and
ever, at the quick of her, the depths parted and rolled
asunder, from the centre of soft plunging, as the
plunger went deeper and deeper, touching lower, and
she was deeper and deeper and deeper disclosed, the
heavier the billows of her rolled away to some shore,
uncovering her, and closer and closer plunged the
palpable unknown, and further and further rolled the
waves of herself away from herself leaving her, till
suddenly, in a soft, shuddering convulsion, the quick
of all her plasm was touched, she knew herself
touched, the consummation was upon her, and she
was gone. She was gone, she was not, and she was
born: a woman."

And just as Constance Chatterley was born a woman, so too was born Niles Barrington, a pimply teenager, an excited male.

He had not expected to lose the first position and that too to a foreigner. However, unlike the instructor, he felt no remorse. He was actually quite thrilled. He had met an equal, a competitor, a challenger. That it was a stranger from a distant land made it doubly exciting. Him he would get to know. Him he would try and understand.

Pervez was secretly pleased when Niles fell in step with him during recess. He had admired his class fellow from a distance, feeling strangely close yet very much apart in reality. The two had hardly talked to each other thus far. Thus far their earlier conversations had been very limited, very businesslike. Niles congratulated him on the test results. How did he manage to do so well? How come he spoke such good English? A cascade of questions spouted from the excited Englishman.

Over the next few years, Niles would learn a great deal about a distant country called Pakistan. He would learn of missionary schools; of fathers, brothers, mothers, and sisters; of robes, tunics, headgear, dangling chains, crosses and rosaries. He would learn of dedicated English and European men and women who had given up lives of comfort and ease and had traveled to distant shores, noble individuals who had devoted themselves to educating the world. Some had elected to spend their lives in Pakistan, the Land of the Pure. Pervez would tell him about the considerate and caring manner in which these individuals had educated the children of this distant land. Pervez would recount his experience of education and enlightenment. Niles would understand, having been educated similarly in one of the finest boarding schools of England. He knew of encouragement, of motivation, of education, of love, of affection, of rulers on the knuckles, of the sting of a cane on tender buttocks.

Before parting, Niles suggested that they walk to the academic block together the following day. P. K. said he already had a walking partner, the American, R. F. This was not a problem, Niles responded. Three could walk just as easily as two could.

And thus, the seed was planted. A friendship took root to blossom, grow, strengthen, mature, and withstand the tests of time. The three friends would henceforth be inseparable.

9

The Air Force College was a purely male domain. Females were not allowed to set foot into this venerable environment except on very special occasions. It was only on Guest nights and graduation balls that officers and cadets, resplendently attired in mess kits or dinner jackets, were allowed to escort equally elegantly attired females into the main college building for an evening of music, food, wine, and culture. On these rare evenings, the grand central foyer, the wide corridors, the anterooms with their polished wood paneling, the huge dining room with its massive oak tables, the silent, imposing library would all become accessible to females.

Despite this official concession granted to the cadets, one could always sense a presence of those who frowned on this intermingling. As these charming visitors graced the premises, life-size portraits of heroes of the past would look down imperiously over the eager young men who were aspiring to follow in their footsteps. The portraits would stare down disapprovingly on ecstatic cadets and their equally delirious dates. They would see flushed boys and girls, twisting, shaking, shuffling, shrieking with joy, jumping up and down as the deafening band played the latest pop songs. Lt. Gen. Baden Powell, Sir Robert, Lord of Gilwell, founder of a movement that spanned the globe would, from one corner of an imposing anteroom, see boys scouting and girls guiding.

Had someone peered into the dim corner one would have seen Rahul and his date watching the couples gyrating on the floor. Seated in Rahul's lap, her back toward him, his dusky date was tapping her foot to the music, rocking back and forth, eyes closed, parted lips half smiling. She was a pretty, doe-eyed female dressed in the "Choli Ghagra," a beautiful oriental dress that had a miniscule top with a plunging neckline that barely covered her bouncing breasts and terminated immediately past them, exposing her midriff fully. That wisp of an upper garment contrasted sharply with the billowing, heavily pleated full-length skirt. It was a dress of the harem of olden days, an enticing attire designed to arouse even the most flaccid of males. The dress enabled total freedom of action. If the situation demanded, a woman could even hide a man under the ample garment. Nineteenth-century Europe had its hooped skirts, the puritanical Muslim females had the burqa, Hindu women had their "Ghagra." A veritable tent tied together at the waist able to hide everything within

87

itself, portability perfected. Within its billowing folds, one could do whatever one desired.

She came dressed thus because Rahul's instructions had been extremely clear. She had a job to perform. She had to "meet a Pakistani cadet, chat him up, and then humiliate him." The horny heathen would be attracted to the "Choli Ghagra," and she was supposed to lead him on. Having aroused him, she would then exact Rahul's revenge. "Insult him, create a scene, embarrass the bastard." Rahul had been quite explicit. The gods had spoken, this was what had to be done.

Finding the Pakistani was not difficult. Even if Rahul had not pointed him out, she would have recognized him. Pity, she mused, this appeared to be a person whom she would actually have preferred to get to know better. Still, when one Brahmin sought help from another, the call had to be honored. And when it was against a Mooslah, it became a religious obligation, a duty. Pervez was standing at the bar, nursing a drink, and there was a decent-sized crowd around him. The setting was perfect; this would be easy. She excused herself as she slid into the group, indicating that she needed to get to the bar. People moved apart, a path opened, she squeezed in, making sure that her breasts rubbed firmly against the Pakistani's chest, her pelvis, thrust forward, grinding against his thighs. Once against the bar, she turned and faced him. The men had stopped talking and were now watching her.

"Oh, Hi. Sorry, I didn't see you. Are you from India also?" she asked innocently.

"No, no. Close though. I'm from Pakistan."

"Wow. That is fantastic. I know a lot of Pakistanis. I'm from London. We have a lot of Pakistanis there, you know. All the bus drivers, the conductors on the Underground, the sweepers, and the cleaning guys. All Pakistanis. Quite nice chaps, really."
"Well, it's pretty hard to tell, you know. We are all very much alike. They could be Indians, Pakistanis, Afghans, Sri Lankans, whatever. But I agree, there are a lot of us out there. If it weren't for us, the British transportation system would collapse." He laughed.

"I don't think so. We are not really alike at all. We are very different. Pakistanis are good at menial jobs. We Indians tend to be more artistic, more creative, more intelligent. I don't think we are alike at all." She smiled innocently. She had delivered the opening blow. She had insulted the Pakistani. She squared her exposed shoulders, waiting, hoping for a response.

P. K. remained quiet, not quite comprehending what had just happened. Everyone else was equally taken aback by the female, including Robert, who watched in fascination the scene that had unfolded in front of him. He wondered what was going on in his friend's mind. The trouble with the Pakistani was that it was impossible to tell if he was blushing or not. The color of his skin just did not show a flush too well.

Pervez appeared to be tongue-tied. As he continued staying quiet, saying nothing, she became a bit flustered. This was not the way it was supposed to be. He was supposed to say something rude and then she would deliver the coup de grace. But he said nothing.

P. K.'s mind was numbed by the female. She was beautiful. She was delightfully attractive. He just couldn't imagine why she was being so antagonistic. Unable to respond to the Indian's date, he kept quiet and then, to save himself further embarrassment, he decided to walk away.

"Excuse me, but I think I see someone over there I need to say hello to," he mumbled and tried to wedge his way out of the group. She stepped forward, raised her hand, extending it across his path. "I'm sorry. I seem to have upset you. I take my words back. We aren't that different, you and I. We are the same really. Quite the same." Sidling up to him, pressing her body against his, she continued, "and you are so good looking, so attractive. I would love to go to bed with you."

Robert was now able to see the Pakistani blush.

"There is only one problem. You're a Mooooslim, aren't you?" The word, drawn out and emphasized, was obviously sarcastic. A dumbstruck P. K. nodded his head.

"That's the problem."

"You Mooslahs don't eat pigs."

"Me. I don't fuck them!"

Tossing her head back, satisfied that she had really outclassed even herself, she strode off, fully aware of the incredulous group in her wake.

Mission accomplished, she sat there, in the dimly lit corner of the dance floor, under the portraits of the generals and admirals gone by, in the lap of Rahul, rocking herself back and forth, eyes closed, swaying to the music. She suddenly arched her back and then collapsed, head falling forward, her cascading black hair hiding the sweat breaking out on her forehead. Beneath her, Rahul continued holding her tightly, drawing her toward himself. They would continue sitting, stationary, not dancing, not moving, not tapping for a long time. It had been a most rewarding evening. Two males had been vanquished. A cocky Pakistani had been disgraced; put in his place.

And so too, a cocky Indian.

10

It was a typical English day. The weather was melancholy, a dismal air hung over everything. Intermittent rain, incessant drizzle. Pervasive dampness, sodium lamps bathing everything in a depressing glow, a glistening wet yellowness. People scurrying about, heads down, intent on reaching their tedious destinations. Drab outfits, glistening raincoats, dripping umbrellas, wet headscarves, rain-soaked hats. Harried, careworn looks.

Group Captain Niles Barrington walked across to the flight planning section. This was a special day, because today he would fly his last mission as an operational pilot. A career that had started over thirty years ago would now irreversibly change tack. Tomorrow he would depart for the United Nations to take up a desk job as an emissary of Her Majesty's government to the world body. From being a frontline fighter pilot, Niles would metamorphose into a planner and a strategist. Old age and promotions did that to everyone. The body would eventually refuse to be part of the man-machine union that fighter flying was. The man would soon become unable to withstand the rigors of the union; his body would no longer be able to endure the debilitating forces generated by the machine.

Niles studied the weather charts in minute detail. He found that the cloud cover extended from Wales northwards almost up to the border between England and Scotland. He therefore chose a route that would take him across England, into Wales, through Scotland, and back into England. After getting airborne, he would head west into Wales. He would then descend to treetop height and follow the A5 road toward the island of Anglesey. Flying low and fast, wings swept, he would hurtle through the A5 pass at breakneck speed, staying below the level of the road as it ran along the face of the mountain hurtling past his right wingtip. He would aim for the mountain facing him; a rock face rushing toward him at eight miles a minute. At the precise moment, he would roll the screaming jet hard right into a gut-wrenching, six G turn, racking the aircraft around the ninety-degree bend. A fraction of a second later, he would plow into the rock wall ahead; a fraction of a second earlier, he would impact against the canyon wall to his right. Done properly, he would negotiate the bend and head for the Menai Strait, making sure he stayed well clear of the bridge. He was not going to fly under it. That was irresponsible, illegal, and quite unnecessary, because he and already done that much earlier flying a Folland Gnat, while training at the nearby air base.

Instead, he would head north, dropping further down, skimming the waves, his exhaust hitting the water below and behind, churning it into foam. From there on to the Lake District, the beautiful countryside that he loved, the land that he had explored on foot, on bicycle, by car, by jet. He knew each and every nook and corner, every hill, every dale, every loch, every village. Staying well clear of populated areas, he would once more head out to sea, this time eastward, barreling over the North Sea, roaring across its gray surface, screaming past the oil platforms, once again skimming the waves, yet again churning the water behind into white frenzy as the Tornado streaked across the watery expanse, its engines roaring. Another turn to the south, toward the Wash, and then, turning again, he would race across the beach, pushing his afterburners fully open as he pulled up steeply to reach the altitude from where he would begin the sedate and boring descent. Back to a dreary, rain-soaked existence.

The excitement was already building up. He hurried across to the flight line to check the aircraft records and then sign acceptance of the machine. A recognition of Her Majesty's government entrusting him with 50 million pounds worth of hardware, his to operate, his to command. This was just a training mission for the more deadly, and hopefully never to be exercised, task of national defense. He approached the row of evenly parked machines, found the one assigned to him, carried out the preflight, checking and rechecking, and then climbed in, strapping himself to the ejection seat.

Starting the engines, closing the canopy, ensconced in a warm, comfortable cocoon, taxiing out to the end of the runway, commencing the takeoff roll, getting airborne. Locking his gaze on the bank of instruments, flying the aircraft by reference to mechanical, electronic, instruments, manmade replacements of nature's sensory elements. Entering clouds, entering a gray nothingness, where there were no references, no indicators, where sensory deprivation was the norm. Fighting one's own senses as they played cruel tricks on the mind. Knowing that if he heeded his senses, he would die.

And then, suddenly, in a blinding flash of brilliant glory, the aircraft broke through the dark clouds into radiant sunshine, into crystal-clear air, into visibility that extended for mile upon unending mile!

Nothing could ever compare with the powerful emotions he felt each time this happened. It was the breaking of chains, the shedding of the monumental burden of being bound to earth; it was freedom, it was "reaching out and touching the face of God."

Each time he came up into the brilliant blue sky, each time he broke out of the cloudy and dreary world below, he would feel exalted. He was an angel, a spirit unchained. He would dance above the earth with joyous abandon; he would soar above those unfortunate souls bound to the earth, shackled, confined.

He would be free.

And he would feel guilty. Unlike the earthbound millions, he could fly.

He could waltz with the angels.

He could be with God.

11

An individual that had touched the face of God, an earthling who had mingled with angels was now firmly grounded. A carefree, unfettered soul was now chained to a desk.

While it was definitely not a fighter pilot's dream, an assignment with the United Nations was not too bad. Working in the United Nations, flying the desk responsible for UN-UK coordination on military matters for peacekeeping was something Niles soon became fully involved with. Equally exciting on the social front was the presence of R. F. in Washington, now a brigadier general, assigned to the Pentagon and the frequent official visits to the United States of the program director of the Pakistan F-16 program, Air Commodore Pervez Khan. The three friends were able to meet regularly, most often in Washington. This charming city was the venue of choice, because it offered an opportunity for the three to savor the many delights it had to offer. The National Air and Space Museum, the Smithsonian, the National Museums of

American History and Natural History, the richly stocked national art galleries, the Corcoran, the Freer, the Phillips Collection. The priceless works in these galleries portrayed the exalted state to which human beings could soar; they documented the ascent of Man, while, at the Raoul Wallenberg Place, a somber institution depicted the descent of Man. The Holocaust Memorial Museum documented the history of the millions of Jews and other minorities who were affected by the Second World War and revealed the depraved depths to which those created in His image could descend. Yet elsewhere, the International Spy Museum recorded the ingenuity of Man, the lengths to which Man would go to be one up on fellow Man. One could also spend an enthralling evening at the Kennedy Center or take in a show or attend the National Symphony Orchestra or, as the three friends almost invariably had to do when they were together, visit Georgetown or Adams-Morgan. In one compact area, within walking distance, one had a complete spectrum of musical delights to choose from. Depending upon their mood, they could enjoy funk, rock, the blues, jazz, calypso, or reggae.

"Not this time," thought Niles. There simply would not be any time for entertainment during this coming visit by P. K. He would be lucky if he could make a quick overnight trip to meet up with the two. It was a particularly busy time, because the Americans were now pressing Great Britain for payback. And although Niles was at the UN, looking after peacekeeping operations, as a senior British officer, he was involved in the dialogue that was taking place. It had taken its time coming, but come it did. It had to. There were no free meals in the world of hardball politics. Britain was being asked to pay back for the American support it had received during the Falklands War.

"What a screwed up war that was! If only we could show such tenacity when it came to defending real human values, actual human rights," thought Niles as he glanced at the clock, realizing that P. K. must be landing in Washington, D.C., at about this time.

As P. K. emerged into the busy concourse, he saw the girl standing at a distance, holding the placard. He walked up to the trim, uniformed soldier, introduced himself, and the two walked out to baggage check area. He collected his suitcase and then headed out toward the staff car, which delivered him to the drab residential complex of the military base.

The visiting officers' quarters for general officers looked as boring as the rest of the barracks on the outside. However, that is where the similarity stopped. Inside, it was a comfortable, well-laid-out suite that was tastefully furnished and fully equipped. P. K. slumped into the sofa chair, leaned back, and closed his eyes. Although tired, he had to make sure that his program was on track. He picked up the phone and dialed R. F.'s number. Robert was now running the office that coordinated all military programs in the Middle East and South Asia. Brigadier general Forrester was obviously going places, destined for better and bigger things. This assignment had the added charm that he worked directly with P. K., who was the project director of the Pak-American military cooperation program. The two friends were now caught between the mercurial relationship of two flirtatious lovers, America and Pakistan. A spat that had lasted for over a decade was finally over and the two had decided, once again, to kiss and make up. America had offered the Pakistanis something irresistible to the military-controlled nation, and, as expected, it had eagerly hopped into bed with America. Everyone had their aphrodisiacs; for some it was cider, for others fried rice. For the Pakistanis it was weapons, military hardware.

Robert had clout and could move things. In his present assignment, he was fully involved in the Afghan crisis and had been instrumental in obtaining approvals for most of the highly classified hardware for Pakistan, such as the Limas, the all-aspect air-to-air missiles and the Stinger shoulder-fired surface-to-air missiles. P. K. was lucky to have him around. Not only was he a friend but Robert also cared for that part of the world. He was very keen that the region remain firmly under the influence of the United States.

"Hi, P. K. Good to have you here. Listen, no can talk. Am in for a long one with State; will take me all day. We're all set for tonight, though. See you at seven, your place. Stay away from the bar and don't screw the staff!"

While Robert was glad that P. K. was visiting, he was also unable to take too much time off. Niles would also be there for only a very short visit and therefore they would not be able to take any time off for their usual jaunts. There just did not seem to be enough time nowadays. The global situation was changing rapidly, and they had to spend a lot of time planning and replanning. As they had aged and moved up the promotion ladder, life had taken on a new meaning. No longer did it mean flying fast jets, burning holes in the skies, twisting and turning as they pleased. All that had now been replaced by negotiations, discussions, dialogue, arguments, and debate. The cockpit had been replaced by paneled halls, secure meeting rooms, dimly lit operations centers, and other esoteric settings. Fighter flying was now a memory for him, just as it was for Niles. P. K. was lucky. Being in an underdeveloped country did have its perks. One could continue flying fighters, and, if the nation happened to be fighting a surrogate war, one could do this for real, on the front line, flying operational missions. Robert knew that this could not last forever and eventually P. K. too would end up behind a desk. He would also have to graduate and become a planner charting the intricate world of military operations and combat leadership. Yet another unchained spirit soaring the blue skies would be shackled and made to face the hard realities of a cruel world.

This was the world Robert lived in nowadays. He was leading a very select working group that carried out all the military planning and force calculations. These were the elitist of professionals who would do the spade work and recommend a set of well-thought-out alternatives on weighty issues that the U.S. government needed to address. They were the ones who provided multiple options to commanders who then were supposed to ponder them and choose the best, based on their superior perception. Of course, everyone recognized the irony of the entire process. The superiors never mulled over anything. They hadn't a clue. It was always the staff that solved the problem. The boss only made cosmetic changes and signed on the dotted line. When things went right, the boss got the credit, and when they did not, the shit fell on the working group.

Robert knew that if the proposal he was working on presently failed, heads would roll and his would be the first one to go. As he hurried across the marble floor to the waiting bosses, he had a brief vision of his head rolling down the long corridor. He smiled at the thought, because he knew that it would not happen. They had got it right; his team had come up with the most sensible list of options for what was undoubtedly the most difficult and complex operation ever to be undertaken by the government of the United States of America. The plan had to hold together, it had to work.

For years, the United States had orchestrated a lingering war of attrition between two evil empires, Ba'athist Iraq and the Islamic Republic of Iran. R. F.'s office was fully involved in fine-tuning this venture, ensuring that no clear winner emerged, that as one gained the upper hand, the other was supplied weaponry to neutralize the threat and thus the imbalance was redressed. Using an exceptionally complex mechanism of material management and an intricate intelligence web, this plan ensured that the two nations were kept involved in the futile adventure, thus effectively preventing them from making mischief elsewhere. It was an enviable plan. Two errant regimes were systematically being destroyed by an expensive war, while the West raked in the dollars as it equipped both the warring parties. In addition to the United States, countries such as France, Britain, Italy, Russia, South Africa, and even Israel were selling billions of dollars of equipment at hugely inflated prices to both Iran and Iraq. The Israelis had even used the situation to their advantage and destroyed the Osirak nuclear facility that Saddam Hussein was building to achieve his avowed aim of becoming a nuclear power.

The payback that America was asking of Britain came in the guise of a U.S. "request" that Whitehall call off its impending sale of helicopters to the Iranian revolutionary guard. Britain was fully aware that the request was being made even as the Americans themselves were releasing spares for the grounded combat fleet of the Iranian air force. Britain would, however, drive a hard bargain and would, in turn, seek approval for supplying its deadly surface-to-air missiles to Iraq and request that the Americans channel more deals through British arms dealers. That would square things up, and it was Niles who had suggested this tradeoff at one of the high-level meetings. The mullahs of Iran and the evil dictator of Iraq both had to be stopped from acquiring any meaningful capability, and at the same time they were to be encouraged to spend their energies and petrodollars, bringing business to the West.

Getting to this stage of relations with Iraq had not been easy for America. Official relations between the two countries had been severed following the 1967 Arab Israeli War. It was President Ronald Reagan who finally decided to have a letter delivered to Saddam Hussein convincing him that the American government wanted to resume relations. America wanted to assist the innocent Iraqi people who were facing the evil Iranian onslaught.

The man chosen for this task, for being the envoy to Saddam Hussein and for coordinating the U.S.-Iraq rapprochement, was a former defense secretary, Donald Rumsfeld. He traveled to Baghdad, met the Iraqi dictator, and delivered the letter handwritten by the U.S. president personally. He tried his best to forge a close relationship with the Saddam and emphatically assured the Iraqi dictator that America's interests remained "in preventing an Iranian victory and continuing to improve bilateral relations with Iraq." Saddam had accepted the message but rejected the messenger, who he thought was weird. The American would ask a question, the interpreter would translate it, and Saddam would then figure out a response. However, before he could articulate his reply, the American would start answering himself! Saddam, who understood English perfectly, had been floored by this method of discourse. He dismissed the envoy summarily and instructed his staff that the next time the envoy came visiting, the "one man dialogue" was to be dealt with by the foreign minister.

The slighted emissary notwithstanding, United States was fully satisfied with the visit and its outcome. Soon afterward, Iraq bought over a hundred helicopters from America. This was just the first order of hundreds of millions of dollars' worth of military and commercial hardware that followed.

12

R. F. zipped open the chilled cans and handed them out before resuming his emotional tirade. "Do you really think we can forget the events of 1975? Do you actually believe the American mind can wipe out the horrible images of our ignominious exit from Saigon? A war that we could have won, we would have won, if only the damn politicians were not so pushed for votes. The world will never know how close the U.S. military came to a head-on confrontation with the politicians. You don't know how bitter the scene was right here in Washington. You think Nixon pulled the doctrine out of his ass? No sir, it was the soldiers, the sailors, and the airmen who told him exactly as it was to be. And that is why the politicians went around making the speeches. Never again would the United States be the policeman of the world. Never again would we fight with our troops for the free world. We would control events through diplomacy, through Washington and the United Nations, and if that failed, we would fight through proxy. No more American blood needed to be spilt over world issues. From Vietnam onward, we would use regional surrogates throughout the world."

They were discussing the current situation and how the military thought and actions were being shaped. Niles loved it when R. F. was worked up, as he obviously was now. He knew full well how strategy was evolving but was always delighted to hear R. F. put it in such simple and frank words. He knew exactly how America had handled the Middle East over the past decades; how it had used the two surrogates in the volatile region, Iran and Saudi Arabia. Both monarchies, both far removed from the principles of democracy, both oppressive and severe regimes, but both rich with oil and low population bases. While the oil companies made obscene profits as they pumped oil out of Iranian and Arabian sands, the royalties that were paid to these nations were also promptly sucked back into the U.S. economy through weapons sales, the need for which was created by fostering a sense of insecurity among the oil-rich states.

Weapons were sold to both nations to create a balance of power aimed at keeping the region free of strife. The massive might of the Iranian armed forces, equipped with the latest weaponry from the United States, ensured that the regional aspirations of Iraq were kept firmly contained. The kingdom of Saudi Arabia was armed to the teeth to ensure that Iran did not expand into the Arab lands as it had historically done. Just as a rebirth of the Persian empire was forestalled, so was the possibility of a Pan-Arab state kept in check. On more than one occasion, Iraq was made to eat humble pie and its ideological vision of the Arab nation was thwarted. And more than once was the Iranian desire to go back to the boundaries of the mighty Persian empire frustrated by arming the Arabs.

Now, once again, the Arab desire to tame Iran had surfaced. Within a year of taking over control of Iraq, Saddam Hussein had plunged the nation into a war with its eastern neighbor. This was tragic both for the Iranians who were still recovering from the aftermath of a bloody revolution and for the Iraqis who had hoped for a betterment of their lives under the Ba'ath Party. It was, however, extremely fortunate for the arms manufacturers of the world, because it overcame the slump in sales caused by the cessation of the war in Vietnam.

"So how come you guys missed out in 1979? How come you did not figure out that the mullah, the imam, the Ayatollah Khomeini was going to take over in Iran?" P. K. asked, feigning a quizzical look.

"That got us; it really got us. Quite simply, we were let down by the system. This is our big weakness, I have to admit. This is where the Brits have us beat by a mile. Americans are not bold enough or adventurous enough to get out there and mix with the crowds. We prefer to buy information in backrooms, in darkened alleys, or in ritzy casinos from disgruntled and disenchanted locals who are always willing to sell out their country and its people for a price. Greedy sonsofbitches, clever little bastards. They never tell it as it is. They tell us what we want to hear. Most of the time they succeed; they suck us in. They told us that the imam would not be welcomed in Iran, that his following would be minimal, that we had no problem. And you saw what happened?"

They knew. Each one of them knew very well the panic that had ensued. It had sent a ripple of fear across the world. From the penthouses of Manhattan to the pleasure spots of East Asia, millions watched, transfixed to their television screens, the spectacle that was unfolding in Iran. They saw the seething mass of humanity, the chanting sea of bodies. They saw frenzied, emotional chest-beating scenes of a nation welcoming its leader, its imam. For the very first time in modern history, the entire world saw a religion rear its head. They saw the Muslims; they witnessed the power of Islam. The mightiest of the mighty, the King of Kings, the Shahinshah of Iran, the Arya Mehar, The Light of the World, the Dispenser of Justice, the Provider for Mankind, the Keeper of the Keys, the invincible emperor from a dynasty that had ruled Persia for over twenty-five centuries was toppled from power by a bearded old man in a cleric's robe.

Islam had brought the House of Pahlavi crashing down. A religion had arisen. Iran would henceforth be an Islamic republic, ruled by the mullahs.

While this scared everyone, it scared some Muslims the most. It specifically scared the House of Saud and the House of Hashim. The Kingdom of Saudi Arabia and the Hashemite Kingdom of Jordan were petrified. They recoiled at the strength shown by a brand of Islam that was different from theirs. Docile Sunnis saw aggressive Shias on their borders. Horrified, they saw a theocratic regime establish itself in their midst, propagating a version of Islam that was in direct conflict with their beliefs. They therefore reacted in a manner that they had been conditioned to react. They called up the United States of America. They knew that America could not have its two allies in the region so threatened. More important, they knew that America needed the Saudi Arabian oil. It would do something. America would develop a counter to the Iranian threat; it had to. America would find a surrogate to fend off the Iranians.

Jordan could not be that counter; it was a small nation embroiled with problems on its borders, both with Israel and Syria. Jordan could not therefore be employed as a regional surrogate for America. Saudi Arabia likewise was not suitable. It had never been willing or able to take on the role of the regional bully. It was a monarchy, with its rulers having an ingrained aversion to aggression. Its population was small, its armed forces largely ceremonial, but, most important, the Kingdom of Saudi Arabia was the seat of Islam. It was not in the American interest to see a powerful Saudi Arabia. If a Shia leader could emerge and topple the monarchy in Iran, it would be a global disaster were a Sunni leader to arise and overthrow the House of Saud.

For a fundamentalist Iran to be restrained, new candidates had to be found. New alliances needed to be formed. There were two possible candidates; Iraq to the west of Iran and Pakistan to the east. Pakistan was already fighting a low-intensity proxy war for the Americans in Afghanistan. That nation was already dancing to an American tune and could be used as and when necessary to assist the American endeavor in controlling Iran. Iraq was also already engaged in a war with Iran and this conflict provided America the means it needed to check Iran. The State Department decided to focus on Iraq as the primary means to rein in the Islamic Republic of Iran. To hedge its bets, it further boosted its cooperation with Pakistan, planning to use it as and when necessary should the Iraqis be unable to deliver.

Iraq was befriended based on the sound principle of "the enemy of my enemy is my friend." The dictator of Ba'athist Iraq , Saddam Hussain, was cultivated and wooed to combat the mullahs of Tehran. Iraq was supplied with sophisticated weapons, both conventional and unconventional, and considerable technology, intelligence information, and specialist advice for its war against Iran was transferred. Pakistan was declared a frontline state and an important ally of the free world in combating Soviet adventurism in South Asia. It was offered a substantial military package that helped bolster the

111

military regime in that country. The overt military assistance came in the form of F-16 aircraft, Cobra helicopters, and associated weaponry, while covert assistance came in the form of funding and equipping the Mujahedeen.

A considerable amount of this work had been carried out in the offices where Robert worked. He had provided considerable input to the plan and had actually drafted the final text himself. The proposal and methodology for containing Iran had been accepted; the concept had been implemented.

Operation Staunch was launched. While its stated aim was to ensure that Iran would not get any military hardware from any other country, the actual aim was to ensure that Iran was provided with weaponry in extremely calculated and metered doses to ensure the very explicit but unstated American aim that the Iran-Iraq War was to end "without there being a victor or vanquished." Robert had specially emphasized the point that, following the Iranian debacle, "We, the American people must resolve never again to make any surrogate so strong, to empower a nation to such an extent that it becomes powerful enough to threaten America itself by taking on a larger than intended role." No nation, not even Israel, was to ever be made all powerful. Everyone had to be kept in check. The paper had been warmly received and approved at all levels, even by the far-right, pro-Israeli lobby within the United States.

The mullahs of Iran, not surprisingly, were fully aware of this intent, because, while America was publicly condemning Iran and publicizing Operation Staunch, it was actively involved in large-scale shipments of arms to both countries. Middle Eastern arms merchants, Pakistani bankers, South American drug dealers, Israeli agents, and myriad other shadowy personalities were involved in planning, brokering, financing, and executing these transfers. Iran and Iraq were both getting weapons and yet, simultaneously, both were being restrained to ensure that the two countries remained locked into a stalemated war. Meanwhile, on the eastern front, the myopic Pakistanis were reveling in their newly acquired weaponry and ratcheting up their confrontation with the Soviets in Afghanistan. Both Robert and Niles were well aware of the intense activities that were going on across the Pakistan-Afghanistan border. Robert always felt a twinge of remorse whenever he thought of his friend's country. Pakistan was actually a nation with some horrendous problems. Corruption, poverty, illiteracy, a large population, an errant attitude toward the West. And now it was also saddled with a proxy war against the might of the Soviet empire. He was saddened by fact that the Pakistani nation was drifting aimlessly in the world of global politics. It was a nation that had everything going for it: climate, geography, manpower, location, everything except leadership.

The country remained trapped under martial law; it was a nation where the army ruled with an impunity that was resented even by its own sister services. It was an army that was the law unto itself and now, to add to the immense problems of this hapless state, it was entangled in the mess that was the Soviet occupation of Afghanistan. The military leaders were keen to reap the rewards that came with the status of a proxy fighter for the United States of America. This meant weapons, dollars, shopping and sightseeing junkets to the United States. It meant Western approbation and indulgence. They were not too concerned with the burden that accompanied this relationship. Refugees, drugs, guns, prostitutes, murderers, thugs, bandits, religious zealots, fanatics, killers were being created, and the fabric of Pakistani society was being ripped apart. An unwitting nation was being raped.

Fortunately for the world, Pakistani involvement in the Afghan war gave its military no time or occasion to start messing with India once again. They were fully committed to acting as American "frontliners" to contain the Soviets in Afghanistan. However, the Pakistani military was very clear that the eventual aim of inducting all the modern equipment and optimizing its use was to give it the desperately needed operational advantage over the traditional enemy, India. Blinkered by this passion, the Pakistanis remained true to form, displaying their childish pettiness and naïveté, gaining nothing substantial from the frontline status. Little did they realize that the United States was very much aware of this sentiment and that any capability buildup would be neutralized at an appropriate time.

The grand American design was working well. The Soviets were mired in Afghanistan, never to be allowed entry to the Indian Ocean or the Persian Gulf. Iran and Iraq were locked in a no-win situation. Saudi Arabia, Jordan, Pakistan, Egypt—all were pliant and manageable. The entire region was firmly under American influence. Middle Eastern oil would always remain firmly under U.S. control. Regional states would never be allowed to be independent; they would never be able to determine their own future.

Not even a greedy arms merchant.

Robert winced as he recalled the greasy haired individual who, apparently not content with his share of the pie, decided to tell the story to his reporter friend. The reporter friend told his boss, and the boss published the story. The Lebanese journal splashed details of the mind-boggling transactions across its pages. It was immediately dubbed the "Iran-Contra Affair." Heads would roll; scapegoats would be found. The work however would go on.

13

R. F. was outraged. "I can't believe that we're still screwing around with this one," he said angrily. The Kuwaitis had asked the United States to provide them protection for their shipping. True to style, the request had been bounced around from one office to another as the nation tried to prepare its response. And as the Americans debated and vacillated, the nervous Kuwaitis turned to the Soviet Union.

Russia responded immediately, positively, and from the very top—from Gorbachev himself. Soviet warships entered the Gulf—warships that had, until then, been firmly kept outside the Persian Gulf. Russians were now patrolling Arab territorial waters. Washington had spent the last fifty years keeping the Soviets out of the region, and now they were sitting inside the waterway that contained the American lifeblood, Middle Eastern oil.

Robert Forrester desperately believed that the United States had to move into the Gulf immediately; there just wasn't any time to delay matters further. It was essential that the Soviets be forced out of the Gulf. "We have fine-tuned the Iran-Iraq War. For seven years we have made the sons of bitches fight each other, ensuring that neither party wins. It would be disaster if the Soviets were allowed to establish a presence in the region. The balance of power would change irrevocably. We would end up confronting the Soviets in the constricted watery space of the Persian Gulf. This must not happen. It cannot be allowed to happen. We have to pressure the Kuwaitis to change their mind; they need to stop messing around with the Soviets."

An agitated Robert was explaining the fragile situation to his superiors.

"What exactly do you have in mind, Bob?"

"It's simple, Sir. We have to use American tankers to move Kuwaiti oil. No one would dare attack the American flag."

"You've got to be kidding, general. This has got to be the dumbest statement of the year. We simply do not have the capability. You should know damn well that there aren't enough American tankers available for this huge task."

"I know, Sir, I know perfectly well. However, there is nothing to stop us from acquiring more tankers." And before the superior could start speaking again, Robert continued, this time with emphasis, "There is nothing stopping us from taking charge of those tankers that are currently being used to move oil out of Kuwait. We take them over and reflag them. We put the Stars and Stripes on all tankers moving Kuwaiti crude. No one dare touch a ship flying the American flag."

The meeting had adjourned; this was a decision that would need to be taken by the president of the United States of America.

"The president will not do it. Why? I'll tell you why. Because the man in the street won't approve it. More important, the woman in the street would not allow it. Americans would never allow it. They would view it as a blatant reversal of the Nixon Doctrine," said P. K., as the friends debated the situation that evening.

"What's with this 'woman in the street' crap?" asked Robert.

"Listen, fellas, it is no longer the man in the street. It is now the woman. She is the one who calls the shots; it is the female who has got us by the balls. Women are everywhere—running countries, leading corporations, driving trucks, working on construction sites, manning oil platforms in the North Sea, jumping out of aircraft, freefalling from the skies; women across the world are taking over all the male roles. Even in our domain. Women are now sitting in fighter cockpits, pulling 'G's wondering what their nipples are doing on their knees. Hell, pretty soon they won't even call it the cockpit anymore. There used to be a time when behind every successful man there was a woman. Now, she is no longer behind. She sits atop him, riding him, fucking his brains out. And, he, in turn, staggers out each morning with a delirious smile on his face, drained of all body fluids, spent emotionally and physically, and in turn, screws the world to the best of his ability. I kid you not; pretty soon the women will have us popping babies!"

"Thank you, Oh Enlightened One, thank you, Oh Mystical Khan, for that wonderful insight, for such inscrutable logic. You of all people. You have some nerve, speaking like this against women. You bloody ingrate. How could you ever be so critical of females? Have you forgotten it was a woman who won you your personal battle? Have you forgotten Sandra?

Sandra.

Young, pretty, vivacious Sandra.

14

She saw the foreigner walking up to her; her heart missed a beat. She had not come prepared for this. All she had wanted to do was meet an average guy, talk, have a couple of drinks, dance a bit, and call it a night. This was the done thing, a standard routine for a normal weekend. It had never occurred to her that she would do this with a foreigner. This was uncharted territory, strange and uncertain, something she had never done. But he appeared to be nice, he was good looking; it would not hurt to find out more. She would have to be very careful though. She had heard of other girls who had gone out with foreigners and some of the stories were pretty scary. The stuff they said about their physical endowments and their immense stamina was unbelievable. This, however, would not be an issue for her, because Sandra had a very firm rule. There was no question of her going the distance with anyone. She was saving herself for her husband.

She had however learned, fairly early in life, that boys were interested in girls for one and one reason only.

Sex. This foreigner would be no different. There was absolutely no way she would engage in any such act with the dark-skinned foreigner. All she would do is talk to him and dance. Once. Well, maybe she would allow him a second one. Maybe.

They were the only couple on the floor when the band finally stopped playing for the night. Sandra was saddened that the evening was over so soon and that it was time to head back home. She allowed P. K. to kiss her good-bye. She also agreed to meet him the next day. She had enjoyed herself thoroughly and wanted to do it all over again. This dark skinned person was definitely worth getting to know better.

They met the next day. And the weekend after that. And the following weekend. They started going steady. Their liaison was now turning into something special, and she began thinking that maybe this was the man she was destined to wed. Her parents had spent a considerably long time in the Indian subcontinent and had always talked fondly of their stay in India and the natives of that distant land. They had met and liked P. K. She had become immensely fond of him and did not want to lose him. At the same time she was mindful of other females who spared no occasion to make a pass at the foreigner. It was only a matter of time before P. K. would fall prey to the sexual advances of one of these predators who had openly stated that they "had the hots for him." Yet, she had to remain resolute; she would never go the whole way before marriage. She would therefore have to do something more to keep P. K. interested in her. She would have to come up with a solution. She would have to put on her thinking cap. She would have to use her head.

She did. She put on her thinking cap and found a solution. She would use her head.

Unknown to her at the time, this momentous decision would form the basis of the ultimate revenge.

It was the final event; the Graduation Ball. Cadets had become officers; they had been awarded the Queen's Commission that morning and would now leave the college. P. K. and Rahul had spent three years in illogical animosity, each trying to outdo the other. A clear victor had not emerged but it was quite apparent that the Indian had had the upper hand. This was of course not acceptable to the Pakistani Strategy had been devised, a plan conceived. Sandra was recruited to deliver the coup de grace in the battle between the two sub-continental warriors.

 She sat at the table with P.K., sipping her drink waiting for the signal which did not take long in coming. Sandra's eyes widened mischievously as she slid under the table. A few minutes later she emerged, her face flushed, lips pursed, eyes alive. She winked at P.K., smoothed her dress and walked towards Rahul with a purposeful, seductive gait.

Rahul had no difficulty recognizing P. K.' s girlfriend; she was a fine-looking woman, he mused wistfully. "If only I could have a girl like the one P. K. has; if only I could once be with someone like her." He realized that Sandra would pass very close to him and he stepped forward impulsively ensuring that she would have to brush against him. Sandra came close; she was looking straight at him and as their eyes met, RSOL put on his most winsome face. The face he had studiously practiced in front of the mirror for hours on end. A look that conveyed a message that he was an intelligent, caring, healthy, virile male, fully versed in the intricacies of Oriental love, the art of Kama Sutra.

Sandra had no problem recognizing the leer of a horny male. She continued smiling; her eyes still had the twinkle, her perfect red lips still pouted enticingly, her cheeks were still flushed. As her blue eyes locked into his wide-open brown ones, Rahul was dumbstruck as he saw Sandra sidle up to him, raise her hands, caress his cheeks and then run her fingers through his shiny black hair. Sandra then grabbed hold of his head in both hands, pulling it toward her and, holding him thus, pressed her full, warm body against his.

She then kissed him squarely on the lips.

It was a long, sensuous kiss, full lips crushing wetly against a startled face, an alive tongue parting nervous lips, forcing wetness into a drying mouth.

And then, just as suddenly as she had kissed him, she drew back, the full red lips now fully parted; bright, wet, white teeth showing. Still smiling, eyes still sparkling, she turned and walked back in the direction she had come from, her firm behind swaying provocatively.

Startled eyes tracked the receding female even as a brain raced furiously, trying desperately to analyze the events of the last few seconds. This had been a unique experience. It should have been unadulterated delight, but something was terribly amiss. There was delight but there was also plenty of confusion. How? Why? What? The mind boggled and it forced the body out of its stupor, ordering all senses to feed information afresh as it attempted to make sense of the situation.

"OK guys," said the brain, addressing the senses. Let's take it from the top again."

Once again the senses reported their experiences. The eyes reported a pretty woman. Walking up. Coming close, staying close. Nerve endings from all over the body sent in their signals. Nipples, ears, cheeks, hair, lips, arms; from all over the torso, the message came in loud and clear.

Contact, close intimate contact, both external and internal had taken place. Nature of contact; definitely erotic, endorsed by a rising, throbbing member down below. The olfactory senses reported the fragrant blend of heady perfume, freshly shampooed hair, the scent of a woman. The mouth reported a warm, wet, deeply intimate kiss.

And then the brain hit its first bump. The nose was reporting an unidentifiable, musty smell. This particular smell did not compute; it was completely alien.

A second bump followed. The taste buds now reported a taste that also did not compute. The brain scanned these two inputs against its entire library of stored smells and tastes but could not find a match. More information was needed to complete the picture; more information was required to comprehend.

It was the eyes that provided that vital detail. As he looked past the retreating female, he saw P. K. in the distance, standing tall and looking straight at him. And he was patting his crotch suggestively.

"Ka-ching!" The sound of a cash register opening.

"Ding, Ding, Ding." The sound of a jackpot being won.

"Boiinnnng!" The sound of a restrained spring being released.
"Aarrrgghh." The sound of anger venting.

To this interesting lexicon, RSOL added a new word as he raced toward the doorway.

"LLLLIIIIAAAAEEEEECCCCHHHHH."

The sound of a man violated in a most obscene manner.

Rahul was violently sick. His insides heaved, his gut strained. He emptied the entire contents of his stomach but he could not lose the creamy feeling inside his mouth; he could not get rid of the bitter, salty, fishy taste.

He would be sick many, many times. He would empty bottles upon bottles of mouthwash. He would rinse and spit, spit and rinse until exhausted. He would gargle until he choked. He would chew the strongest of gums. He would eat the foulest tasting foods to swamp his taste buds. Sadly, the taste would not go away.

Niles was right. P. K. could never forget Sandra.

Neither indeed could Rahul.

15

The reflagging proposal was accepted and implemented. Vessels that carried oil out of the Gulf started flying the American flag. With these reflagged ships came an armada of escort warships, AWACS aircraft, carrier battle groups, submarines, combat air patrols. Not only did the United States move into the Gulf, but it also came in full strength.

All was not, however, well. The administration still had to contend with the reluctant public. For American troops to go fight in the Gulf, the American public had to be involved. They had to be made supportive of this drama. The ruse of an oil crisis would not work; it had been tried earlier, and the public had responded by conserving and by questioning the nonuse of America's own vast oil reserves. Something more drastic needed to be done. A sacrifice needed to be made. Friends needed to be called in to help out.

On May 17, 1987, the USS Stark, a modern, fully equipped, highly capable Perry-class frigate, patrolling the waters of the Persian Gulf, turned its sensors off, put its fire control systems in a standby status, and ordered its crew to stand down. The ship went into a "possum" mode as directed by higher authority. It played dead. The captain was following orders that had come in on the secure communications system. He was comfortable doing so, because he knew that the ship was well away from any threat and was sufficiently covered by other friendly sensors that were monitoring the area. Adequate early warning was available. There were other radars, other ships, an AWACS aircraft was airborne, combat air patrols were being flown. The entire Gulf was under the watchful eye of the American military machine. The ship was quite content to remain "possum" until ordered otherwise.

A lone Mirage aircraft, flying at a high altitude at which even the most basic of radars would be able to detect it, navigated over 200 miles through the AWACS cover, through the combined and overlapping coverage of at least six surface based radars, and fired two French-built Exocet missiles at the defenseless ship. It then turned around leisurely and returned to base without provoking any response. No weapons were fired in defense of the vessel. The Mark Thirty Six Super Rapid Bloom Offboard Chaff Countermeasure system was not activated. The Phalanx Close in Anti Missile Weapon System capable of firing one hundred rounds of 20 mm ammo per second against any incoming projectile was not armed. The Separate Target Illuminating Radar was switched off, preventing the firing of the Standard surface to air missiles.

The first Exocet impacted on the port side of the ship and tore a fifteen-foot diameter hole in the steel hull. The second exploded in the crew's quarters. Thirty-seven U.S. sailors died. High-definition cameras recorded, in Hollywood-quality still and video photography, the kaleidoscope of human remains splattered across twisted metal. These brutal pictures and the graphic scenes hit the American airwaves shortly after the incident.

The American public was outraged. Iraq and its evil dictator, Saddam, had killed innocent U.S. sailors. Street opinion swayed wildly in favor of a larger and more aggressive U.S. presence in the region. The vacillating Arab states of the region were forced to reconsider their aversion to the presence of U.S. troops on their soil. Until now, the nearest base that America could use had been the British island of Diego Garcia, some 3,000 miles away. This handicap could now be redressed. It now became possible to convince the Arabs that they needed to allow U.S. military assets into the Gulf, on Arab land, on Arab bases. American troops arrived, bringing with them surveyors, engineers, construction crews, equipment, and hardware. Combat squadrons followed. The Rapid Deployment Force moved in. Central Command was now firmly in command of the center of the world.

The Middle East.

It had been a very long flight for the Mirage. The round trip had required flying at high altitude using extra-long-range ferry tanks. The last time a Mirage had attacked an American ship, it had been in a much shorter trip for a formation of two aircraft. On a clear, sunny day, June 8, 1967, the fourth day of what would become known as the Six-Day War, two Israeli jets had attacked the USS Liberty in the Mediterranean Sea and return to base unharmed. The first Mirage had strafed the ship and the second had dropped a napalm bomb on the deck of the undefended vessel. The stricken ship had radioed for help, and two aircraft carriers patrolling the Mediterranean had responded immediately by launching fighter aircraft to engage the raiders. President Lyndon Johnson had personally ordered the American fighters back. Subsequently, Israeli patrol boats had fired five torpedoes at the stricken ship and strafed its decks.

It had taken two Mirages to kill thirty-four Americans aboard the USS Liberty. The attack on the USS Stark was considerably more successful. In this attack just one aircraft killed thirty-seven Americans. The French had always claimed that the Exocet missile was the best anti-ship missile there was and, sure enough, it worked better than guns or napalm. For the pilot, it was a simple, routine mission. It had been done earlier, and, as before, there never had been any threat to the launch aircraft.

The Stark affair, like that of the Liberty, was investigated and closed promptly. No major actions were recommended; none was taken. Cmdr. William Loren McGonagle, the officer commanding USS Liberty had been awarded the Medal of Honor. The ceremony had taken place quietly in a naval yard instead of its normal place, the White House. The medal was presented by the secretary of the navy rather than the president.

Cmdr. Glenn Brindel, the officer commanding of USS Stark, was retired with full benefits.

The Kuwaitis however continued to be awkward. Not only had they invited them into the Gulf, they had also entered into negotiations with the Russians to purchase aircraft, missiles, and other military hardware, thereby providing the Soviet Union a major foothold in the region. They had also built up huge cash reserves and were now beginning to exert their power in the field of international finance. The Kuwait Financial Company now posed a major threat to the established financial dominance of the West. To boot, the Kuwaitis were an arrogant and pretentious lot! This miniscule country and its obnoxious people needed to be tackled. Their economic independence and their desire to pursue an independent foreign policy needed to be curtailed. Their billions needed to be spent.
Kuwait needed to be made poor.

Iraq needed to invade Kuwait.

April Glaspie, the ambassador of the United States to Iraq was a welcome guest at the presidential palace. She got along quite well with the dictator, Saddam Hussain. This was just another of their regular meetings and both had no way of knowing that it would be the last. April informed the president of Iraq that America was interested in having better relations with his country. "I have lived here for years. I admire your extraordinary efforts to rebuild your country. I know you need funds. We understand that and our opinion is that you should have the opportunity to rebuild your country. But we have no opinion on the Arab-Arab conflicts, like your border disagreement with Kuwait. I was in the American embassy in Kuwait during the late sixties. The instruction we had during this period was that we should express no opinion on this issue and that the issue is not associated with America. James Baker has directed our official spokesmen to emphasize this instruction. We hope you can solve your border problem with Kuwait using any suitable method.

Saddam smiled. He understood clearly what the diplomatic female was saying. As he personally escorted her to the door, he thanked his charming guest for the message she had delivered from her government.

One week later, on the Second of August, Iraq invaded Kuwait.

Kuwait would now be turned into a pauper state. Its oil fields would be set alight, its citizens sent scurrying for safety across the globe. Its wealth would be squandered; the Kuwaiti dinar would become worthless. American forces would move into Kuwait and establish major bases in the tiny country. A new killing field would be established on the Iraq-Kuwait border. A new highway would be created.

A Highway to Hell that was to be paved with the bodies of Iraqi soldiers.

16

TV-guided missiles are incredibly accurate weapons. They carry a high-resolution camera in the nose, a specialized radio link in the tail, and, sandwiched between these two, a powerful explosive charge designed to knock out bridges, tanks, bunkers, and other similarly hardened targets. As the missile homes onto the target, the camera relays the picture of its flight path to the launch aircraft. Seated comfortably in the cockpit, well out of harm's way, the pilot receives a very clear, high-definition video image of where the missile is aimed. Using a little joystick controller, the pilot can place a set of crosshairs on any object within the image. The cross marks the place where he wants the missile to impact and, as the crosshairs move, so do the missile control surfaces. The missile alters its flight path to arrive at the point of desired impact. A competent pilot can put a TV-guided missile into a garden bucket from forty thousand feet.

Blue Fox Leader was a competent pilot. He identified the bridge and placed his aiming index squarely in its middle and then pressed the button to launch the missile. A flash lit up his starboard wing as the deadly weapon took off, trailing thick white smoke. Within seconds the Heads Down Display started showing the video being transmitted by the missile as it hurtled toward its target.

As he watched the display, waiting for missile impact, Blue Fox Leader saw a tractor entering the bridge from the far end. The driver was blithely ignorant of what was about to happen; he could not have known that the bridge was about to disappear under him. "The poor sonofabitch is not going to make it across," thought Blue Fox leader as he decided to tweak an already perfect aim. He raised the crosshairs and brought them up to the engine of the tractor, which was now almost halfway across the bridge. He could now read the name of the American manufacturer on the tractor. "God, the resolution of these motherfucking missile cameras is amazing. I can even count the frigging rivets on the hood." And then, on an impulse he was to regret for the rest of his life, he tweaked the crosshairs again. The face of the driver appeared center screen; a weather-beaten, unshaven face of an Iraqi peasant with blackened teeth and cracked lips. As the missile approached the end of its journey, the face continued to expand, the screen eventually filling up completely with the eyes of the farmer. Wide-open, disbelieving, staring, confused eyes into which the powerful camera of the missile drove deeper and deeper until suddenly the screen went blank and filled up with static. The missile had exploded and destroyed everything around it. The bridge, the tractor, the driver, the TV camera; everything disappeared in a huge ball of fire and smoke.

Denied the TV image, the display on board the aircraft reverted to its earlier function; it switched to displaying the radar image in ground-mapping mode. Where a road had once crossed a river, there now appeared a distinct break. The bridge was no more. No more too the tractor and its driver.

Although the bridge had been destroyed, although the mission was an obvious success, the pilots had to go through a detailed post-attack damage assessment process. It was necessary to go over the video, frame by frame, over and over. They had to review the tape for weapon accuracy, aiming accuracy, and missile performance. A host of other parameters also had to be measured and recorded. The final frames leading up to the moment of impact had to be studied in detail and, using the sophisticated controls of the playback device, they did so. The first time Blue Fox Leader played back the tape that had recorded the missile hit, everyone broke out in spontaneous laughter when the driver's face appeared on the screen. "That should give him one helluva headache," Blue Fox Four remarked.

The tape was paused, shuttled forward, then reversed, replayed in slow motion, switched to frame-by-frame display and then again in quick motion. Time and again they watched the Iraqi farmer's face as it filled the screen of the monitor and, as every time they reached the end of the recording, they found themselves staring into the wide eyes of the illiterate Iraqi farmer. There was no more laughter, no flippant comments. They sat mesmerized, gazing at that haunted look, those wide-open eyes for what seemed like eternity. Blue Leader finally stood up, turned the machine off, and went back to his tent, intent on catching some sleep because he had a dawn mission the next day. He tried his best to sleep, but failed. Every time he closed his eyes, he would find the farmer looking directly at him. Unblinking, wide-eyed, puzzled.

In countries where capital punishment remains in vogue, executioners are well versed in the procedures involved in the discharge of their duty. While they meticulously follow all the laid-down rules for execution, they are especially mindful to ensure that they never violate the cardinal rule. They have to cover the eyes of the condemned prisoner. This is an essential requirement. This is the law, laid down and practiced since time immemorial. This is an absolute must. Whether the execution is by a firing squad, the guillotine, the gas chamber, the noose, the swinging sword. Whatever the method, the eyes of the one being executed have to be covered. The commonly held belief in the West is that it prevents the condemned person from recognizing those watching him die. Despite the fact that such recognition serves no meaningful value and despite the fact that modern day executions are conducted through remote control with the executioner and spectators separated by one-way mirrors, most people in the West believe this. Not so in the East. Not so the executioners of the East. They know the real reason for the blindfold in that part of the world. The sword-wielding executioners who chop off the heads of drug dealers in the town squares of Saudi Arabia after Friday prayers know the reason. The executioners who dispatch the condemned to the next world on the gallows in Pakistan understand the absolute necessity of the blindfold. The executioners of Iraq know it; those of Iran understand it clearly. Every executioner of the East knows why the condemned must be blindfolded at the time of execution.

Clerks fill forms, technicians operate machinery, bosses boss, farmers farm, brokers broker, judges judge, writers wrong. Executioners execute. Executioners kill people. It's just a job. Chopping heads off, slipping nooses around necks, pulling trapdoors, pressing triggers, swinging swords, they do their job. It puts food on the table, but, as jobs go, it's a pretty dull one. The pay is lousy, there is not a lot of room for advancement, and there are very few incentives. You don't make too many friends at work. The guys you deal with are usually a pretty nasty bunch. Being an executioner can be quite frustrating. And when people are frustrated, tempers rise. When tempers rise, they fight. They call each other names, they abuse, they swear, they curse. They use foul language, evil words, disgusting invectives, each expletive more graphic than the other. And in the executioner community of the East there is one curse that tops all others. The mother of all curses.

"May Allah uncover the eyes of your prisoner as you kill him. May you look into the eyes of your victim as he dies!"

It is a chilling curse. A curse that sends shivers down the spine of those who hear it. A curse that prompts an instant prayer. A prayer of forgiveness, a begging of His mercy, a desperate prayer pleading that they be spared the experience. It is a curse that is never uttered frivolously, never voiced in jest, and when uttered, the fighting invariably stops; the one cursed invariably hastens to remedy the wrong he may or may not have done.

Because, for the executioners of the East, it is terribly important that the blindfold never slips. Many reasons are put forth for this, but all is conjecture. Some say that were the eyes uncovered, they would see an indescribable agony, an unbearable torment. Others talk of experiencing physical pain, the nature and intensity of which one cannot explain. Some talk of a feeling of one's insides being ripped apart as a soul is ripped violently from its earthly bond. Others speak of an immense hollowness, an emptiness that is bigger than the darkest night sky. Yet others say that the viewer sees what the dying person sees; his or her complete life flashing across the eyes of the condemned. While there are many opinions of what actually happens if the condemned eyes are open, everyone agrees on one point.

Whatever it is, it destroys the mind.

In the East, they know that the eyes have it all. They know that the eyes are the most powerful of sensors; the most wonderful gift of God. They believe that these organs not only see, but they also sense, they feel, they touch, and, above all, they speak. They speak a language that is universally understood by all of God's creation — man and beast alike. A language that overcomes all barriers, a language that transmits sentiments and feelings straight from the heart, from the soul.

The eyes are windows to the soul. Look into a person's eyes and you shall be able to see the innermost depths of character, you can see the soul. Gaze into the eyes of a loved one, see the beauty of love; relish the innocence of the soul. Look into the eyes of a doting parent, see the overpowering mantle of warmth, protection, kindness, possessiveness; bask in the strength of the soul. Stare into the eyes of a child; wonder at the purity of a soul. Peer into the eyes of a criminal; experience the evil of the soul. But never, never look into the eyes of Man being killed by fellow Man. Never witness the agony of a soul as it is forced out of the body, for you shall see something unendurable; you shall not be able to live with that vision.

Blue Fox Leader was not flying a surface attack mission the next morning. This time it was an air superiority mission, the aircraft configured to carry out high-speed dashes across the sky, intercepting any hostile aircraft that approached the Gulf. He sat back in the cockpit, relaxed and comfortable, talking to the ground controller periodically over his radio. Nothing much ever happened on these missions. Rarely, if ever, was there any enemy activity. Neither the Iraqis nor the Iranians had any air power worth mentioning. As he looked below, he could see the blue waters of the Gulf, contrasting sharply with the brown sandy waste that was Saudi Arabia. An inhospitable desert floating on a sea of black gold and, painted on that brown canvas, he saw them again. Wide-open eyes, staring at him from down under, unblinking, unrelenting.

And, as before, he could see inside them. And as before, he could see the images inside those wide-open eyes. As before, he forced his mind elsewhere. And, as before, he failed.

Once again he saw those images. He saw primordial ooze jelling. Mountains rising, forests blossoming, rivers forming, seas churning. He saw Man being born. He saw a woman in labor, legs spread; he saw the magic of birth. He saw a child running along the bank of a lazy brown river. Men praying, women

141

cooking meals. Laughter, happiness, hope. He saw the child-turned-man herding sheep, a husband deflowering a bride, the bride turning mother, the mother dying slowly, painfully. A lingering disease, lonely children, weeping orphans, mud huts, man tilling land, land turning green. Land oozing blood. Sad children, somber graves, sweet sugary tea, gold-covered minarets. He saw it all flashing past in double quick motion. He saw happiness, he saw pain, he saw agony. Transfixed, unable to move his gaze away, Blue Fox Leader continued looking into the eyes of the distraught Iraqi peasant.

He saw bloody nails piercing innocent flesh. He saw metal shattering bone, impaling limbs. He saw a man on a cross, head hung, a tear in his eye, a wistful smile on his radiant face. He saw women being butchered, men being beheaded, he saw an angelic child floating down a river in a wicker basket, he saw a gentle old man leaning on a staff as those around heaped abuse upon him; he saw a river parting. He saw daughters being raped, sons being slaughtered; he saw young girls being burnt at the stake. He saw a tall Arab in a black mantle being stoned by a jeering crowd even as he blessed his attackers. He saw innocent bodies hacked to pieces; writhing children carried aloft spears. He saw tender loins ripped apart, virginity bleeding, flesh rotting, limbs decaying. Man laughing, evil gloating. He saw a frail old woman moving among incomplete bodies, alive, writhing in pain, flesh dripping. He saw vicious dogs ripping apart black bodies, he saw screaming flesh dissolving in acid baths. He saw grinning B-29 pilots discharging their deadly loads over unsuspecting cities. He saw mushroom clouds, bodies vaporizing, jubilant individuals backslapping each other. He saw a naked girl running down the winding village road, her skin removed, charred flesh propelled by obscenely exposed bone. He saw trainloads of emaciated bodies, dark chambers, naked bodies, huddled masses, airtight halls, choked lungs gasping for elusive breath. He saw frantic, futile nails scraping against unyielding metal. He saw giant incinerators; flesh burning, rakishly perched, peaked caps crowning gloating faces.

And then, as he continued watching in immobile fascination, he saw that which would destroy his mind. In the frantic eyes of the peasant farmer he saw the ultimate torment for Man.
He saw Him.

An indescribable radiance; an overwhelming sadness.

He saw God.

Weeping.

Blue Leader realized that he had to shut the farmer's eyes. And, that there was only one way he could do this. He rolled his sleek machine over and pointed the beautiful, deadly dart of steel directly at the questioning eyes. He then ramped the throttle to the forward stop.

Not much of the aircraft was found in the surprisingly compact hole in the ground. The Accident Investigation Board did however recover the flight recorder and from the 'black box' and determined that the aircraft was in full afterburner, pointed vertically downward when it impacted on the ground. All systems were working fine; there were no failure indications. There were no recorded malfunctions; no adverse operating condition. The pilot had not made any announcement on the radio. They listed the cause of accident as Undetermined."

Brig. Gen. Robert Forrester closed the accident investigation file with a shudder. He had seen it all; the cockpit video recording of Blue Fox Leader, the post attack damage assessment reconnaissance photographs, the statements, the final verdict of the investigating team. As a senior field commander during Desert Storm, he had to see it all. He was an integral part of "The Mother of All Battles" and had seen the havoc that had been wreaked on the Iraqi nation. He had seen the calamitous rout. He had seen the force and fury of the coalition forces as they beat back an aggressive dictator. Thousands upon thousands of fleeing Iraqis were killed on the Highway to Hell. All weapons, legitimate and banned were employed to vaporize the retreating force. Hundreds of Iraqi soldiers waving white flags were gunned down simply because there were no provisions to handle prisoners of war. It was a brutal victory.

R.F. stopped sleeping the sleep of the innocent. He would lie awake at night, tossing and turning. He would pace the floor, raid the fridge, stare blankly at late-night shows on television. When sleep finally came; it was always fitful. He understood that this was the penalty for him being different, for caring, for feeling. He wanted desperately to be as casual as the others. If only he could brush it off, just let things happen and watch from the sidelines. But he couldn't, there was too much wanton killing, far too much suffering and pain. Too much blood was being spilled.

And, as time progressed, Robert became aware of another horrible truth. He realized that, in his desire to bolster the morale of a beleaguered force, the phrase that Saddam Hussein had come up with was amazingly insightful. Of course, the dictator could never have realized the profundity of the phrase he had coined as he urged his troops onward; he did not have the brains for such sensibilities. To Saddam's crude and simple mind, it was just a catchy and emotional term that, to his dismay, could not prevent the war from being short, swift, and considerably humbling. In his self-seeking endeavor to coin a jingoistic phrase, Saddam had unwittingly managed to find the most fitting, indeed the perfect, label for that misadventure.

The first Gulf War was definitely the Mother of All Battles; only it was not a mother in the figurative sense that Saddam intended. It was the Mother of All Battles in a literal, procreative sense!

The events that unfolded since Saddam's misadventure of 1990 were now proving that the first Gulf War was a horribly evil, fertile, gestating mother that has spawned a litter of equally evil and horrific children. It was the parent whose malevolent progeny now dominated world affairs and wreaked untold havoc across the globe. These iniquitous children begotten by that evil Mother created a veritable web of disaster and tragedies across the globe. Seeds had been planted by the fertile mother all over the world. Their presence ranged wide—from the poverty-ridden ghettos of Sudan to the pleasure spots of Bali, from the blue water piers of Oman to the steel and glass skyscrapers of Manhattan, from the rocky caves of Afghanistan to the leafy jungles of the Philippines. Each progeny more devious, more horrific, and more deformed that the previous one.

And she was breeding yet again. Other malevolent spawn were nearing maturity. More evil was in the process of being delivered onto a helpless world. Syria, Iran, Korea, Pakistan, Cuba. Multiple delivery rooms, multiple theaters. Evil was in labor; the horrific mother would bring forth one wicked child after another as a tortured world watched with resignation.

17

The aircraft winged its way across the blue waters of the Adriatic Sea. Dipping low, it turned east and commenced its approach into Split. Seated in the jump seat of the chartered freighter, Niles could see the islands that dotted the water below and the white wake of the ferries plying between them. In the distance he could make out the picturesque city and the fertile, cultivated fields surrounding it. He could also see the large chemical factories and the metallurgy plants that dotted the verdant landscape. From this distance Split looked very beautiful, calm and inviting. It appeared just as it did in the travel brochures; a city of superb landscapes and unparalleled seascapes; a tourist's wonderland. A city twinned with another port, somewhat larger, somewhat distant, 6,386 miles away, a City of Angels, Los Angeles.

On ground, it was a different story. The city was tense, the air completely hostile, and the environment absolutely military. The much–sought-after tourist spot was now a major staging post for the United Nations peacekeeping forces in Bosnia.

Split, Croatia, was in a war zone.

Air Commodore Niles Barrington had completed his tour of duty with the United Nations and was now back in the UK, posted to the Ministry of Defence in Whitehall. However, he still remained associated with the world body because of his new assignment as the officer in charge of UK peacekeeping activities across the globe. It was a posting of his choosing, because it gave him yet another opportunity to contribute toward the progress of humanity and participate in the global effort to eradicate hunger, poverty, disease, and illiteracy. This was a sentiment that had taken root and strengthened over the years and that had especially been reinforced during his tenure at the United Nations. In that period he had seen untold human suffering and witnessed firsthand the deviousness of the bureaucrats and politicians as they argued and bickered over petty issues while humanity suffered across the globe. He had vowed to himself that he would strive to make the world a better place, and, despite knowing full well that this was almost impossible to attain, he remained fully committed to this cause.

The United Nations was, for Niles, "a real eye opener." While on the one hand he was thrilled by the noble efforts and aims of the world body, on the other hand he was deeply disturbed by its failure to

148

implement its goals. He had been appalled by the crass behavior of some national representatives fighting for petty, personal gain, not caring a damn for the teeming millions they represented and on whose monies they were leading a life of luxury and indolence. Individuals sent as ambassadors to the United Nations to espouse the cause of their impoverished, underdeveloped countries were living in obscene splendor, applying for American Green Cards, seeking U.S. citizenship. He saw national missions whose sole aim was to make money for their staff and serve the interest of their masters back home who had sent them to the UN for that specific purpose. He saw diplomatic privilege being grossly misused. He saw third world representatives openly abusing the third world. He also saw the rich nations undermining the efforts of those that were intent on doing good. He saw the first world paying lip service to the efforts of the United Nations. He saw them defaulting on contributions, avoiding payment of dues, and procrastinating on important issues that needed immediate resolution. He saw the Security Council being used to further national aims in direct conflict with the Charter of the United Nations. He saw the weakness and ineffectiveness of the General Assembly as it passed resolution after resolution that were then openly flouted by all. Spread across the globe were glaring examples of Man killing Man. Africa, Asia, Europe, Australia, America.

And it was now happening in Bosnia. Bosnia the beautiful was now Bosnia the battered, the bullied, the bleeding. A land with a political and cultural history unlike any other in Europe; a land where great powers overlapped, where the empires of Rome, Charlemagne, the Ottomans, and the Austro-Hungarians merged, was now a war zone. A land where the major religions of the world had historically existed side by side, a land where Roman Catholics, Orthodox Christians, Jews, and Muslims had lived together, each worshipping the same God in their own manner and form, was now a religious battleground. Bosnia of the idyllic towns with beautiful names was now a land where every single town's name evoked memories of horror and untold atrocities. Sarajevo, Mostar, Banja Luka, Tuzla, Srebrenica. Towns where once, during the Ottoman period, the nobility had been Muslim and the peasantry Christian and where both coexisted peacefully, were now killing fields that defied description. The erstwhile nobles were being forced out of their homes and systematically murdered through a process termed "ethnic cleansing." It was an activity to which the leading nations of the world—the United States, France, England, and Russia—had not only elected to turn a blind eye but had actually also empowered the Yugoslav army to use military force for this purpose. And as these forces raped, looted, plundered, maimed, and killed, the United Nations, the European Community, and the United States discussed, debated, and negotiated. Everybody stalled for time, waiting, hoping, and wanting either nature or the Serbs to render any action on their part unnecessary!

The champion of the free world, the world's most advanced and well-equipped armed forces, remained unable to tackle the modest military strength of the Serbian armed forces. The most powerful nations of the world watched from the sidelines as a motley force of 90,000 soldiers backed by 21 fighter aircraft, 30 helicopters, 300 tanks, 200 armored personnel carriers, between 500 and 1,000 artillery pieces, and an undetermined number of mortars were allowed to spread destruction and carnage. Worse, by imposing an arms embargo through Resolution 713, these world powers used the UN Security Council to effectively grant a monopoly on heavy weaponry and air power to the aggressors. Bosnia was a land that was to be destroyed, its rich past obscured by violence and war, a war that the developed world desperately tried to keep shrouded in a fog of ignorance and misinformation.

It was only after television news reporters had showed the world public graphic videos of the rape, the wanton killing, and the appalling treatment of prisoners in Serbian-run camps that the UN and the world leaders were forced to take action.

Niles had been following the crisis in Bosnia closely. It had made him realize the abysmal level of depravity of the political process. The more he studied what had happened in Bosnia and Kosovo, the more he could appreciate the selfishness of nations, the cruelty of Man. Unlike many, Niles knew well the significance of Bosnia. He knew that the trigger that caused the death of almost 30 million human beings originated in Bosnia. Niles knew of Gavrilo Princip, the Bosnian Serb who had assassinated the Austrian archduke Franz Ferdinand in Sarajevo in 1914. It was a murder that had started the First World War, a war that would be remembered only for its futility, its depravity, and its wanton destruction. It was a war that would lead to another, more vicious one, a couple of decades later. Niles could not help wondering whether Bosnia was now becoming the setting for yet another global conflict.

As the aircraft came to a stop, the jeep was already pulling up alongside it. Niles was greeted by the smartly dressed Pakistani brigadier commanding the contingent of UN peacekeepers from the Pakistan army in Bosnia. The brief welcome over, they climbed aboard and sped off toward Bosnia. The brigadier was a talkative individual, bent on impressing the visiting dignitary, both with his professional knowledge and his command of the English language. In fluent Queens English, complete with a perfect Peter Sellers accent, the officer gave his guest a complete rundown on the mission.

"Here we are, Sir, in Bosnia," he said as they crossed the border from Croatia into Bosnia. "Actually, to be precise, we are in Herzegovina and are headed for Mostar, its main city. Herzog is German for duke, and the former rulers of this part carried the title of Herzogs. Everyone here is Slavic, they all speak Serbo-Croatian, but they differ in religion. A mixed lot here,

Sir. Followers of Islam, Roman Catholicism, and Eastern Orthodoxy."

Niles remained silent as they drove through the countryside. He took in the streets filled with rubble, collapsed houses, burned buildings, charred rafters, hastily constructed graves, a bleak and desolate countryside that had once boasted a thriving economy. Factories and buildings built over years, capital accumulated over years of toil and investment now lay destroyed. A land ravaged by war, by mass killings of civilians, systematic rape of women, the forced displacement of millions; Bosnia had created the largest flow of refugees in Europe since the Second World War. He knew the figures better than the Pakistani brigadier did. His office had recently updated the figure to 3.5 million refugees. Almost half a million Bosnians had been killed. Others were incarcerated in prisons that were much worse than the concentration camps of Nazi Germany. The number of rape victims was difficult to estimate. It was believed to be in tens of thousands.

The United Nations Protection Force, UNPROFOR, was now up to almost forty thousand persons. This had turned out to be the largest peacekeeping operation in the history of the United Nations. The annual budget of about $1.6 billion was contributed by member states. As always, some states were delinquent in payment, and approximately $1 billion was outstanding. As always, the largest chunk owed was by the richest nations.

For Niles, the tour was a blur of powerful emotions. He had never seen such needless destruction, so much pain and so much suffering. Reading about war, seeing it in photographs, in museum exhibits, even in live footage could never arouse the feelings that this tour of the Bosnian countryside had done. Here, in the Balkans, he came face to face with the dark side of Man. In Bosnia, Niles saw the evil that man is capable of.

It was soon after his return that he realized that remaining silent was a crime in itself; perhaps even a bigger crime than being the looter, the arsonist, the rapist, the murderer. He could not stand idly by as the world was steered toward destruction.

Niles also started having problems sleeping. He would lay awake at night, reliving the Bosnian horrors, appalled at the direction in which the world appeared to be headed. Sleep, whenever it came, was short, fitful and full of disturbing dreams from which he would wake up suddenly, his body bathed in a cold sweat, his nerves taut, his muscles tense, his senses alarmed. It had been a long while since he had nightmares.

Niles recalled the time when, as a youngster, he had problems going to sleep. He was very young; just a little child and he had a nanny to help him overcome his fear. It had not taken him long to get over those nocturnal apprehensions.

There was no nanny now to comfort him. More importantly, this was no childish fear.

This was adult dread.

18

"The—Pet— Goat.

"A—girl—got—a—pet—goat.

"But—the—goat—did— some—things—that—
made—the—girl's—dad—mad".

Slowly, carefully pronouncing each syllable, George
read on, totally immersed in the book, delighted by its
beautiful illustrations, thrilled by its understandable
text. His mind worked furiously as it raced ahead,
trying to figure out what were the things the goat did
to make the dad mad. This was a deeply complex and
immensely intriguing situation and he would have to
get to the bottom of this. There was nothing in the
world that could stop him from unraveling this
mystery.

Not even the fact that almost half an hour earlier, at
twenty-six seconds past eight forty-six that morning,
the fateful day of September 11, 2001, American

Airlines Flight 11 had slammed into the North Tower of the World Trade Center in New York.

Not even when someone whispered in his ear, "A second plane just hit the other tower and America's under attack."

It took another twelve minutes for George to reach the end of the story. Having found out the goat's problem, he could now turn to that of America. The president of the United States of America could now assume his role as commander in chief of the Armed Forces of the world's only superpower.

Terrorists had hijacked commercial airliners and were flying them into American symbols of authority, power, and prestige.

Terrorists, Islamic fundamentalists, Jihadis, third world citizens who hated America and all that it stood for had breached Fortress America.
A carefree, happy-go-lucky, fun-loving people had been violated.

The president of the United States of America could now launch the most powerful military machine the world had ever seen into battle. He excitedly jumped into the driver's seat and threw the gears of this potent force into full forward. The world heard an evil, rasping sound. It was the sound of fury grinding against disbelief. It was the sound of emotions being driven by grief.

The world changed direction. A fragile blue planet, carrying with it hapless billions of His finest creation, was now pointed on a new, disastrous course.

He could be frank with P. K. With his childhood friend he could be direct and completely candid and could therefore ask him point blank, "What is it with you guys? What exactly is your reason? Why do you people hate us so?"

P. K. had tried to wiggle out of the answer, but Robert had insisted. "I need to know, I really need to know, Pervez. Tell it to me as it is. No fucking bullshit."

P. K. realized that he had to be truthful. He had to explain. "No one hates the Americans. On an individual level, the average American is easily more likeable than any other nationality. The problem is with your collective actions, your government, your policies. Your lack of human warmth in your dealings. Your total aloofness, your imperial attitude that whatever you do, you are right. That no one else can have a better plan or a better idea. What people hate is your philosophy. Live and let die."

He waited, allowing this to sink in. Robert remained quiet. "And you know what the worst part is, Robert? You guys actually do not have this attitude. It is just one big façade. I know it because I know you. I have lived among you, seen you, heard you. I understand you. You guys are really very soft on the inside. You have to put up this front because that is the way it has been done, that is the way you have been taught. Grown men don't cry. What you don't see cannot hurt you. Hearts can be broken. People can hurt people. Pain is not acceptable. Failure is not an option. So let's put up a stern front. Let us not show any weakness. Tenderness, love, emotion, this is sissy stuff. Walk away, don't look back. I don't want to know. Whenever there is an occasion for you to act like a normal human being, you take off. You don't like being human. You think that you are goddamn paramecium. Single, independent cells, aloof and complete, by yourself, on your own, not needing anybody, not requiring anyone else. Actually, you are not too far off the mark. You are goddamn paramecium. Just like that organism self replicates, you always end up screwing yourselves.

"You wonder why the world hates you so? Trust me when I tell you that the world does not hate America. It was not the world that is screwing America. It is you, yourself who are bent on destroying yourselves and your wonderful country. In the desire to do good, you are actually doing pretty bad. Because you think that you are smart. That you know it all. You are so bleeding smart that you are regularly suckered by the most dubious of characters, the shadiest of individuals. You make fun of blondes being dumb. Buddy, you are so damn blond, it just isn't true. You are so gullible it is pathetic. Why? Because you are actually more honest, more straightforward, more fair than most others, and you think everyone else must be like you."

159

And P. K. carried on. Now, agitated, excited, he told an incredulous Robert things that made sense in a twisted way. Honest Americans, in their efforts to emulate their president who could not tell a lie, boldly stating the truth only to be taken in by the most blatant of lies that even an intellectual midget, a moron would be able to see through. Not the Americans. They would willingly accept into their midst, individuals who came begging for refuge, seeking protection from a despotic regime, from a dictatorial ruler, from religious persecutors. The Americans would believe them, protect them, shelter them, and then help them get back their country — only to find that those they were assisting were actually much bigger and worse thieves and scoundrels than those who had turned them out. Opportunists all, having lived off their homeland, having sucked up its wealth, they had taken off when the shit had hit the fan, departing the nation they had bled dry to a refuge provided by the gullible Yankees. People who readily believed that they were protecting and sheltering victims, refugees, political asylum seekers. Having arrived at the shining shores, these unscrupulous individuals immediately started screwing their protectors, taking full advantage of the American desire to be respected, believed, and loved by the world.

"You guys have been brought up believing in Hollywood and Roswell. You guys are really messed up. You hate violence and crime but revel in Hollywood blood and gore. You are reluctant to strike

160

a relationship with a foreigner but are desperate to establish a relationship with some freaky creature from outer space. I have to give it to you. You dispatch serial killers and mass murderers to the next world but have to ensure that the execution is humane, that the lethal injections are painless. You are so brainwashed that you actually believe that it really washes whiter, that a frigging rabbit goes further, things run faster, stuff lasts longer. That it is cheaper, harder, softer, better, worse, good, bad, evil; whatever the media tells you, you believe. You don't mind making a complete fool of yourselves on national prime time television just to please the show host who really does not give a rat's ass who you are and what you do. All he or she is interested in is the ratings your stupidity generates.

Robert reacted angrily at this. "How dare you. How dare you, you, you, you," he stuttered and, unable to find the right word, he continued, "pass judgment on us. How dare you demean our achievements? You forget where you live? You frigging third world citizens. You forget that you owe us big time. We are the ones that work our butts off, we produce food for the world, give our wealth to the rest of the world to help them improve their lot. Do you forget that it is the Americans that slave away, commuting miles upon endless miles to generate the money you get and what do you do? You squander it. You abuse our largesse. You are right my friend; it is us, the Americans that are the suckers. You are the smart ones. Hell we are even stupid enough to put our lives on hold so that we can take care of the world. We would be better off, screwing around like you, the third world does, producing kids, causing a population explosion while we deny ourselves a family, kids, everything."

"You do not have children because they would interfere with your work. But then, when you do need kids, where do you go? Back to us, the third world. The same place you go to buy kidneys, eyes, organs. You go out into the third world and bring back orphans, destitute kids, homeless wanderers. You adopt them and rear them as best as you can, only to be challenged in a court of law by greedy money-seeking parents and relatives who suddenly surface one day. You go to war and bring back war brides; hell, you even order wives through the mail. You seek out life partners on the Internet, and having found them, you watch helplessly as they take off with your hard-earned assets. Now you have to work twice as hard to make the alimony payments."

Both friends realized that the conversation was getting nowhere. It was Robert that decided to put an end to it. "Hey, all I asked was a simple question. You could have kept the answer equally simple. I really don't need this kind of shit. This is what we are and this is the way it shall be. You cannot change culture. We do what we think is right and we shall continue doing so."

"And my friend, so shall you continue to be hated. Because of what you do in the belief that you are right. You screw things up. The way you are messing up in Iraq."

Robert agreed reluctantly. He knew that the obscene assault was unnecessary. Iraq was no threat to his homeland, his America. He knew because it was his duty to know. As one of the senior members on the intelligence task force that dealt specifically with the threat from the volatile region of the Middle East, he had an extremely informed knowledge of the actual conditions that existed in Iraq. He was fully aware how that nation had been transformed into a pauper state with over $120 billion of debt. An oil rich nation was now an economic disaster where its people spent their entire waking lives trying to scrounge a decent meal. Iraq was a nation with a devastated infrastructure, ill-equipped hospitals, insufficient power supply, inadequate drinking water. It was a nation in despair. Ten years of sanctions, ten long years of its oil revenue being managed by the United Nations, ten years of being dependent on that world body for spending its own wealth had reduced a country that had the world's second largest oil reserves to an impoverished third world state. A nation with over a hundred billion barrels of oil below its land was going around with a begging bowl. He knew the reports, the intelligence probes, the overflight records, the satellite reconnaissance. The country had no weapons of mass destruction. It was clean. To this pathetic nation, America presented shock and awe. To its miserable citizens it offered overwhelming force.

Robert had wrestled with his conscience for weeks on end. Where did we go wrong? How did our wonderful philosophy mutate into this arrogance? How could we go into a country and blow it to bits, without any evidence, without any moral justification? He agonized over the remark made by the secretary of defense, Donald Rumsfeld, that it was "utter nonsense" that the United States was in Iraq for its oil. The secretary had gone on to say that "we don't take our forces and go around the world and try to take other people's real estate or other people's resources, their oil. That's just not what the United States does. We never have, and we never will. That's not how democracies behave." Robert knew that the secretary was lying through his teeth. It was the oil. It was America's lust for oil that made it act in such a depraved manner. And Robert was mortified. This was not why he had opted to be a military man, a fighter pilot. He had not signed up to kill so that he could fill up his gas tank. How could it happen? How had this proud nation allowed itself to drop to this level?

He understood the hurt of Vietnam; he recognized the military debacles such as Desert One, but he could not understand why, rather than attribute fault where it belonged, rather than blame incompetent leadership, why the nation had decided that it was far more palatable to change the rules. In Vietnam, it was definitely not the fighting men and women that were responsible for the American rout; it was simply a case of poor leadership at all levels; from the Washington top down to the My Lai bottom! Sure, there were individual acts of bravery and some superb examples of sound military planning, but Vietnam had to be appreciated for what it really was—a vague, ill-defined campaign with an elusive aim orchestrated by a vacillating leadership. Rather than place the blame where it lay, it was considered more expedient to dish out medals and rewrite the national doctrine. Worse, the nation revised the established principles of war. In an attempt to prevent America from being bogged down in a war the nation had no heart to win, economy of effort was replaced with overwhelming force.

Operation Desert Storm, the attack on the Iraqi forces invading Kuwait in 1991, was the first spectacular display of such a philosophy. Against a small third world country, a massive military coalition, equipped with cutting-edge weapons and technology, used amazingly disproportionate force. This was no "hammer against a fly" operation; it was an outlandish display of overwhelming force. This crude and patently horrific maneuver was refined and made even more disproportionate over the decade that followed and the next display of this concept was seen in Afghanistan. This was a truly awesome use of force. The Americans used the most powerful conventional weaponry available to man against an opposition that carried AK-47 rifles and lived in holes in the ground.

Robert winced as he remembered the meeting held at the Pentagon where it was proposed that the nation use tactical nuclear weapons against the caves of Tora Bora. Luckily, sense had prevailed. But only just.

The results achieved in Afghanistan were spectacular; they had to be. Unfortunately, this success generated a new level of arrogance and recklessness in the politicians. It made them extremely comfortable and willing to use the military solution as a more practical, more rapid, and indeed more adulatory means of securing the leadership of the world. And, when the president happened to be a wannabe military officer, it was incredibly simple to motivate him into using this powerful tool and establish his credentials as the victorious commander in chief of the armed forces of the United States of America. An individual who had sadly been unable to lead a flight of two aircraft on a routine training mission while serving in the Air National Guard would now lead the combined might of the United States military machine to victory against cave dwellers. Worse would follow. Emboldened by the Afghanistan adventure, that frivolous individual would wreak havoc on the impoverished but yet proud and defiant nation of Iraq. A population already reeling under sanctions, laboring under an oppressive government, straining under a miserable yoke would soon be subjected to overwhelming force.

In his keenness to redeem his family pride, the president of the United States of America elected to play irresponsibly with deadly force. A commander in chief, charged with an onerous duty, violated all established principles of war. He opted to behave in an extremely casual and flippant manner. He did not know the basic fact that a military machine could never be launched into battle without having very clear intentions and objectives.

By attacking Iraq, America was forced into an open-ended commitment for a dubious cause. Worst of all, in invading Iraq, the commander in chief of the American armed forces did something incredibly disastrous. He put the world's best-armed and superlatively equipped military machine under the control of mediocre political aides. Mental midgets, militarily illiterate, combat-shy draft dodgers were given control of deadly force and they promptly began cobbling together unsound military operations in the back rooms of Washington. Crazy notions became policy. Through their irresponsible actions, the American public would be forced to once again relearn the lesson that it is much easier to get into a fight than to get out of one.

Sadly, the actions of these backroom planners were nothing original or creative. Theirs was not a new concept, there was no pioneering vision. It had all been done earlier. In the early part of the twentieth century, a similar set of pseudo intellectuals, an equally perverse group of backroom planners with evil minds, had put their heads together and formed a new group. They had called it the National Socialist

Party of Germany. A corporal with a funny mustache would lead the party. He would also lead a brilliant nation into war, disaster, and unconditional surrender. In the process he would wreak havoc with humanity. He would kill six million Jews and give the remaining six million an impassioned desire to survive. Ironically, the tactics used by the evil corporal would become reference standards for ensuring survival.

Kill or be killed. Kill with us or be killed by us.

The events of 9/11 were used to inflame the public and seek their approval to use force. The horrific attack on American soil was, in the average American's perception, completely unprovoked and unwarranted. The American public was blissfully unaware of U.S. policy, its actions and machinations the world over. No one knew the Mujahedeen, no one recognized the name Osama, no one particularly knew about the Muslims. No one really cared. For the average American, everyone was OK, foreigners were welcomed, helped, encouraged and assimilated into the melting pot of American culture. The nation was grievously upset at this terrorist incursion and the knee jerk response was understandably that of "kill." Opportunistic politicians ably aided by self-serving Iraqi exiles jumped at the chance. This was what they had been waiting for. It mattered not that Iraq had absolutely nothing to do with 9/11.

Operation Iraqi Freedom was launched.

Overwhelming force had by now been partnered with precision strike capability. New exotic terms were coined. "Decapitation strikes," "shock and awe," "bunker busting." The eloquent nature of these phrases hid behind them devastating and morally reprehensible actions. Spectacular attacks on centers of population were beamed across the world in live stereo sound and true color video, the whole affair being elaborately stage managed through embedded journalists. Not only did the Americans use overwhelming force; they also sent out a clear and highly explicit message using round the clock global radio and television broadcasts.

"Fall in line or else"

The devious planners in the backrooms of Washington were working on the premise that whenever stupendous odds are created against an adversary, failure must logically be overruled. For them, this concept also incorporated the desirable erosion of the importance of the military. It automatically meant that the art of generalship could be assigned a backseat. Brute force and technological wizardry could now make the professional warrior unnecessary. Military operations no longer required innovativeness, ingenuity, leadership, tenacity, courage, or resolve; these were now outmoded values. One did not have to be a Hannibal, an Alexander, a Churchill, a MacArthur, a Rommel, a Guderian. A moron empowered with an ability to generate overwhelming force could perform as well as any brilliant military mind and achieve the objective. Teddy Roosevelt's sentiments could now be taken a step further. His belief that by carrying a big stick one could speak softly could now be modified. By carrying thermobaric bombs, JDAMs, and precision-guided munitions, one could speak utter nonsense and yet command respect. The setting was not important nor was the concept limited to the military; this perverse philosophy remained valid whether it was Waco, Texas, or Baghdad, Iraq.

19

He had to find a counter to this madness. Robert had to come up with a solution that would put an end to the monster that had been unleashed by the evil planners. He had to find a solution. He simply had to. He was, after all, a thinker, an accomplished strategist. He would have to cleanse his mind, stop thinking, and then start the thought process all over. He would need to think laterally, tangentially, imaginatively. As he paced the floor, his eyes came to rest on the plaque that hung on the wall. A message from P. K. when Robert was detailed to attend the war college. He stared at the intricately carving and once again read the inscribed verse of the great Persian poet, Omar Khayyam.

The Moving Finger writes, and, having writ,
Moves on: nor all thy Piety nor Wit
Shall lure it back to cancel half a Line,
Nor all thy Tears wash out a Word of it.

And below it, in an almost comic font, was P.K.'s message:

So pull your finger out and do what the Poet says: WRITE, my Friend, WRITE!

"A Proposal for Integrating the Defense Department and the Services into a Unified, Interoperable Force Structure, Sharing Resources with Specific Emphasis on Intelligence, Surveillance and Reconnaissance"

Fifty extremely well-written pages of text, marked "For Official Use Only" presented the case for a major overhaul of the capabilities of the Department of Defense. Its arguments were convincing. After all, it was Maj. Gen. Robert Forrester who had written it. His arguments were, as always, precise and persuasive.

The cold war was over; an erstwhile enemy had been cut to size and befriended. The threat had changed completely. The new adversary was different, amorphous, difficult to track, and it used weapons and tactics that were not easily countered by existing arsenals.

Operation Enduring Freedom in Afghanistan had firmly driven home the point that the military needed to revamp its intelligence-gathering and analyzing ability. HUMINT, the jargon for intelligence provided by actual people observing things, events and places, was terribly lacking. So was SIGINT, or intelligence gathered from electronic signals such as communications, telephone lines, wiretaps. So too was IMINT, or intelligence gathered from photographs and other image-recording devices. Methods now existed to derive data from technically measurable aspects of any target, such as vibrations or hyperspectral emissions. Measurement and Signatures Intelligence, or MASINT, had been perfected to an exact science. It was rumored that MASINT experts had created an impressive database through fair means and foul and could identify all individuals accurately by their breath, body odors and farts. The sad part was that although technology was available to provide a level of detail that had hitherto been impossible, there remained a general deficiency in the analysis and dissemination of intelligence data.

The major contributors to the overall intelligence picture were the traditional ones, the Central Intelligence Agency and the State Department and, a fact largely unknown to the public, the Departments of Energy, Justice, and the Treasury. Not too many people knew that these relatively innocuous agencies were also part of the overall data collection and tracking system but were unfortunately not linked to other civilian or defense intelligence systems in any meaningful manner. All departments used different computers with different operating systems; they followed different procedures and worked in total isolation from each other.

The paper forcefully and brilliantly argued for a complete revolution in military affairs. It proposed that the military commanders be made fully aware of all that happened within each and every level of government. To enable this, a complete overhaul of the intelligence systems was needed. The primary component of the revised structure would be the Department of Defense's intelligence, surveillance, and reconnaissance capability. It stressed an unfamiliar term, "interoperability." Not only should the systems within a particular service be completely interoperable, but also each service, or more correctly, its computers, needed to be able to talk effortlessly to the others. It was essential that all civil and military systems be restructured so that they could function with each other across platforms, across states, across continents, overcoming barriers of language, operating systems, differing data formats, different hardware. That every piece of intelligence data, irrespective whether it came from HUMINT, SIGINT, IMINT, or MASINT, was to be merged into one unified or "fused" form.

The secretary of defense loved the paper. This was exactly what he had been looking for. He desperately needed something to pull over the generals who thought that just because they had a few brilliant campaigns under their belts, they were superior to him. He knew that the generals knew that he had weaseled out of Vietnam. He knew that most were aware of the contents of his short and somewhat pedestrian naval service record. Nevertheless, no frigging general, especially no damn immigrant, no slum dweller, educated, hah, educated in the New York City public school system, no sonofabitch rockhound with a bachelor's degree in geology would outsmart a Princeton graduate. No way. This paper was his big chance. He could now give the president something to think about, something that would make him the darling of the services, the favorite of the military industrial complex, adored by big business, loved by everyone. And because of the mix of classified and unclassified funding, euphemistically called black and white in budgetary jargon, the inquisitive public would never be able to quantify the expenditure on this account. It would be a breeze to get this past Congress. Yes sir, what America needed was a complete overhaul of its military system. He liked the concept. In fact, he loved it, but there was no way he was going to give this subordinate, this self-assured, over-decorated, smart-ass fighter pilot the satisfaction of knowing this.

"Hmmm. Sounds a bit grandiose." The secretary lapsed into his ludicrous question and answer style of speech that had become the staple of all jokes within the administration. "Do I like it? I don't know. Will it work? I'm not sure. Is it a crude idea that can be polished, refined? Definitely. One thing for sure, the name you have chosen is obtuse, confusing. What were you thinking when you gave this paper this convoluted title? Sounds something that those assholes in State would come up with. You guys need some Princeton brain to put this whole thing together.

What we need here is something more appropriate, more catchy, more modern, more educated. Hmmm. Wrinkled brow, index finger rubbing his left eyebrow, the secretary thought for a moment.

"Should we call it "Force Transformation"?

"Yes we should."

20

Force Transformation took off in a spectacular manner. A whole array of groups, teams, and cells were formed. Each service created a transformation senior steering group, which in turn created a complete set of junior steering cells. Working to strict deadlines and with considerable haste and egged on by the indefatigable secretary, each service came up with its own recommendations, which the Department of Defense integrated into a workable whole called ' "Master Document."'

To the delight of all military men and women, the Master Document contained a plethora of acronyms. SBR, UAV, ISR, AEHF, KC-X, Link 16, CITS, MC2AC, AWS, JTRS, GPS, SIAP, AFSCN; the list was endless. The military loved its acronyms.

The USG established the OFT within the DoD—the Office of Force Transformation within the Department of Defense—putting a retired naval admiral in charge who reported directly to the secretary himself. When it was realized that funds may take a while to materialize, the department reduced or canceled such major weapons programs as the F-22 fighter and the Comanche helicopter and redirected the funds to the newly formed organization. Huge funds were allocated, the exact extent of which was never to be known. The secretary of defense's choice of the team that was to form the nucleus of the Office of Force Transformation was driven by his deep-seated resentment that the military services always placed their greatest trust in people who were combatants— top-quality professionals trained to directly attack the enemy with deadly force. Those found lacking in combat skills invariably found themselves in less glamorous assignments such as logistics, administration, intelligence, and so forth, and these were rarely selected to be senior leaders of their services. Consequently, the most senior uniformed members of the military continued to be people who were thoroughbred professionals, fighting men, most familiar with the employment of lethal force. These officers were competent, self-assured, knowledgeable, and outspoken. Such officers were those who had exposed him and his lack of military talent in the sixties. Such were the officers that had forced him to slide out of the navy into the reserve. Such were the officers who had continued to irritate him in the ready reserve and had continued to hound him even when he had transferred to the standby reserve. He would make sure that no such wiseass professional combatant got to lead the team that managed this new and extremely important office. He would personally select the small, restricted group of about twenty individuals both from within the services and within the civilian ranks who would form the nucleus of the Force Transformation team. He would personally brief them and task them to focus on five broad areas, the most important of which was to be technology. The group was to identify gaps and make recommendations to increase efficiency, improve existing capabilities, and recognize and change outmoded paradigms like the one that it was the most decorated soldier who made the best leader. They were given a total of one year to have everything in place.

The air force, being the largest military provider of surveillance and reconnaissance and also the department's' executive agent for space, became the lead player in Force Transformation. It had already formed a center known as the Aerospace Command and Control and Intelligence, Surveillance, and Reconnaissance Center, which was busy standardizing command and control as well as the entire intelligence processes not only for itself but also for its joint and coalition partners. The Checkmate analysis cell that had helped plan the air operation for Desert Storm had been integrated with the Joint Warfare Analysis Center, which consisted of a completely different set of experts tasked with conducting engineering-level analysis of potential target systems such as power grids and transportation systems to find the linkages and vulnerabilities in them. Force Transformation was to tie together not only all the arms of the military, the army, air force, navy, and marines but also civil departments, quasi-military organizations, big business, the politicians. Even the coastguard!

Operation Deepwater was initiated. This was a very ambitious program aimed at fully fusing and analyzing the vastly increased amount of intelligence while coordinating with law enforcement within the coastguard community. Deepwater, like all other information and intelligence systems, eventually linked to the master database pool controlled by the Department of Defense. The master database used by military intelligence had inputs from the entire intelligence community, not just the military services. The Defense Intelligence Agency, the National Security Agency, and the National Imagery and Mapping Agency all were linked together in an impressive array of computing power.

A command and control battle lab with the catchy acronym C2B was created and located with the Command and Control Training and Innovation Group at Hurlburt Field, Florida. SeeTooBee was designed as a small, highly focused organization whose mission was to rapidly identify and prove the worth of innovative ideas for command and control that improved the ability of the United States Air Force to execute its core competencies to support joint warfighting.

Another battle lab, the Information Warfare Battle Lab was created within the Air Force Information Warfare Center and Air Intelligence Agency at Lackland Air Force Base in Texas. It was tasked to identify innovative and superior concepts to plan and employ information warfare in disciplines such as deception, psyops, physical destruction, security measures, information attack, and electronic warfare.

An organizational change was made at the air force level and a senior officer was designated as the functional manager with full responsibility for all intelligence resourcing and management. The new position carried the impressive designation of deputy chief of staff for warfare integration.

Force Transformation instituted the concept of network-centric warfare, a strategy linking all weapon systems in local and wide-area networks. A completely new defense intranet was developed linking the army, air force, navy, and marines to exchange information and control actions. INTELINK enabled significantly increased access to intelligence data, reports, analysis, and details by all military intelligence agents worldwide.

Simultaneously, a huge network consisting of deployable workstations hosting situational awareness, decision aids, and battle management software applications was created. Powerful computers incorporating powerful software with an ability to predict enemy courses of action, analyze situations, compute solutions, determine the most favorable one and recommend it to the commander. It provided a seamless, machine-to-machine interface by linking sensors, communications systems, and weapons systems in an interconnected grid called the Network Centric Warfare Solution. It not only gave commanders the ability to make superior decisions, but it also went the extra step and actually provided them with the most favorable option. It consisted of complex modules that had impressive names and equally impressive acronyms. Modules such as the DTIG, or Deployable Theater Information Grid; the TCTF, or Time Critical Targeting Functionality module; and the NCCT, a Network Centric Collaborative Targeting system. All modules linked together by MIJI, the Meaconing, Interference, Jamming, and Intrusion resistant machine-to-machine datalink.

Military Intelligence now started coordinating matters with its civilian counterparts. . It gained access to computers that had been developed by collaboration between the Department of Energy's National Nuclear Security Administration and the Sandia, Lawrence Livermore, and Los Alamos National Laboratories.

The civilians called it either the Accelerated Strategic Computing Initiative or the Advanced Simulation and Computing Initiative. To the military it mattered little; hardly ever did the armed forces ever use full names. Acronyms sufficed and ASCI was a neat acronym, indeed it had a ring to it. No one knew what ASCI meant; no one cared. Acronyms always took on a meaning of their own; they were new words that became part of a vocabulary so loved by the military. Just as the doctors confused their patients and occasionally themselves by complicated biological and biochemical terminologies, just as lawyers took refuge behind unintelligible Latin phrases, so did the military delight in using acronyms.

ASCI soon became Asskeek, and it did not take long for Asskeek to become Asskicker.

Asskicker was housed in the strategic computing complex within the Los Alamos National Laboratories. The hall that housed the machine was almost as large as a football field and required over ten megawatts of power to run it. The massive computer was capable of 7.73 trillion calculations per second. It used over 12,000 processors, in excess of 15,000 disk arrays containing dual controller accessible drives, 400 file server nodes, 12 terabytes of memory, and 600 terabytes of disk storage, all connected together with 2 miles of cable trays carrying over 200 miles of cable under the floor in a dual rail switch interconnect, fat tree configuration. To back up this monster, an identical machine was housed within the same building and, for off-site backup, a third was deployed in the Lawrence Livermore National Laboratory.

Asskicker was about two and one-half times as powerful as its predecessor, ASCI White. ASCI White was a development of ASCI Red and the two other terraops machines codenamed Blue Mountain and Blue Pacific. Each one was, in its own right, a massive machine, with impressive computing power even when working in an isolated manner. Tied together in a computing grid, these machines became truly amazing. Once assigned to the emerging grid computing infrastructure, they easily became the backbone of national defense and security, supporting a seamless, immediate flow of information among and within various government agencies.

Yet another network was also available. Another massive, distributed computing supercomputer network built around the supercomputers at the University of Illinois, University of California in San Diego, the Argonne National Laboratory in Chicago, and the California Institute of Technology in Pasadena. Together, these systems were programmed to distribute any assigned task among them, each one taking a portion of the calculations. It was called the Terragrid and had cost over $50 million to put together. Terragrid was gigantic. It could carry out over 13.6 trillion calculations per second.

There was more. Another supercomputer, able to perform 12 trillion calculations per second, was available at the Pacific Northwest National Laboratory. Flaunted as the nation's fastest nonmilitary machine, it was, in reality, an integral part of the military network, to be used whenever required. During one of his rare public interactions, the director of the laboratory had been asked by a persistent reporter the justification for such a powerful computer at a civilian facility acquired at a staggering cost of over $25 million. An inveterate scientist thrilled at his acquisition, he had responded breezily, "We have problems of national interest that require this computational horsepower." The reporter had persisted, "But surely 7,000 gigabytes of memory, 2,000 Madisons, the new Intel Itanium-2 processors, a 3,000-square-foot facility obviously generating immense heat that requires almost one hundred times the air conditioning normally required for such space was not what could be needed. Sir, could you give us an example of the problem that may need such power."

"Let's see now. One task could be to model the ground under the Hanford nuclear reservation to show what's happening and what could happen to nuclear and chemical contamination there. Another could be the study of the ground beneath Yucca Mountain in Nevada, which is being considered as a permanent underground storage site to safely store the nation's spent nuclear fuel for the next 10,000 years. These are monstrous models that cannot be studied in any other manner."

The reporter had been satisfied. She had no way of knowing that these two problems could be modeled by simply networking the fifty-odd desktop computers in her downtown office. Similarly, the director had no way of knowing that his supercomputer would not be used for such terrain

185

modeling only. He had no way of knowing that the computer in his facility "talked" regularly to pilotless drones flying in the remote wildernesses of Afghanistan!

The University of California was the key player in the supercomputing world. The campuses of Berkeley, Davis, Irvine, Los Angeles, Riverside, San Diego, San Francisco, Santa Barbara, and Santa Cruz managed three laboratories; The Lawrence Berkeley National Laboratory, the Lawrence Livermore National Laboratory, and the Los Alamos National Laboratory. Ever since their inception well over half a century ago, these labs and the university had been tied together in a close relationship. The three employed 18,000 people and received federal financing of almost $4 billion annually. It was the university that had prompted the U.S. government to institute a "work for others" program in which supercomputers of one facility could be used by others, thus furthering the distributed computing concept. A whole host of supercomputers employed in diverse tasks such as weapon design, energy research and development projects and other such assignments were tied into a grid.

Supercomputers needed superstorage. Spread across the supercomputer grids were multiple data storage systems, each able to store approximately 600 terabytes of data, roughly equivalent to 146-million full-length novels. This was made possible by the brilliant work done at the Carnegie-Mellon University, where an individual had developed software that greatly simplified parallel storage. He had come up with a set of secure commands that enabled devices to store and manage a variable quantity of data in a simpler and more secure manner. It was called object-based storage.

Powerful computers were good and so was massive, object based storage, but all this was useless if the data could not flow in real time. For that to happen, bandwidth was needed. Huge electronic pipes were needed to move the mountains of data created by the supercomputers across physical space. The solution had been provided by the Lawrence Berkeley National Laboratory. It was here that engineers had conducted extensive research in data flow to empower the supercomputing grid. To prove their abilities, the laboratory had run a real-world scientific application across the Ethernet at speeds in excess of 10 gigabits. It had put together a demonstration that made the visiting generals from the Pentagon sit up in their seats. The demonstration consisted of two powerful Linux clusters, each at the two ends of a pair of Force Ten Networks switches connected by two pairs of 10-gigabit Ethernet interfaces.

One cluster of dual-CPU Linux PCs ran the "Cactus" simulation code and fed data to another cluster of PCs that ran "Visapult," a remote visualization application that rendered the received data for real-time visual display and analysis. The experiment was designed to produce data on one cluster of computers and then

187

transfer it across the 10-gigabit Ethernet connection to another cluster, where it was to be displayed in real time. Using "Cactus," the application that had been developed at the Albert Einstein Institute in Potsdam, Germany, one supercomputer cluster, working in a distributed computing profile, modeled the collision of two black holes. It then created the visualizations of the gravity waves that would result from such a collision. This data was then transferred to another supercomputer cluster, where "Visapult" decoded it, reformatted it, rendered it and displayed the gravity waves on a large screen display. All in real time.

Every single person viewing the experiment was dumbstruck. Each one was impressed beyond belief. One individual was particularly interested in knowing the names of the companies that had put together this marvel of technology. Next trading day, a broker, acting upon the instructions of a Washington madam bought sizeable chunks of stock in obscure companies with cryptic names; Ixia, Finetec, Syskonnect, Force10 Networks, Quartet Network Storage, and others. While the broker was placing the orders, the D.C. madam's favorite client was busy writing his report. "Now that we've done 10 gigabits, it's time to start looking at 100. We need to provide additional governmental grants to the following companies that are working on the cutting edge of technology. A list of company names followed. It was surprisingly similar to the one with the broker. The report continued. "Failure to do so would mean that the Europeans, particularly the French, would overtake us in this race." This last statement would overcome any reservations the tight-fisted guys at the Hill may have had.

The secretary never stopped boasting. "Do we have a very robust machine-to-machine interface of command and control, intelligence, surveillance, and reconnaissance systems? Yes, we do. Do we have horizontal integration of manned, unmanned, air, surface, information and space systems? Yes we do. Can we provide executable, decision-quality knowledge to the commander in real-time from anywhere? Yes, we can."

SIPRNET, the standard Department of Defense secure Internet system for classified data was beefed up and expanded. SIPRNET terminals were installed on every ship, in each subordinate command center all the way down to the field level. The United States Navy developed FORCENET which further integrated all force elements throughout the battlespace.

The Marine Corps joined in. Its Shared Data Environment incorporated the standards, models, and data warehousing technologies required to establish the "common language" and enabled it to achieve total systems integration and interoperability.

The concept was further expanded by integrating allies into the battleforce network with the Coalition Wide Area Network, called COWAN.

Information superiority, however, could not be achieved without protecting friendly information, information systems, and information processes. In fact, as the services transformed into the world's most information-dependent fighting force, the U.S. military had to implement major reforms and upgrades to the existing capabilities of computer network defense, information assurance, operations security, counterdeception, counterintelligence, and counterpropaganda, all aimed at negating the ability of adversaries to exploit this reliance on information. A complete new backbone was developed to provide long-range, jam-resistant, secure communications for integrated operations and to support the concept of machine-to-machine interface. Using a network of space and airborne sensors and directed by highly responsive command and control systems, the backbone linked all computers into one seamless data network. It took the experts fifteen attempts to finally come up with a satisfactory design. The sixteenth attempt worked. LINK 16 was commissioned and made operational.

One final piece of hardware was essential to complete the Force Transformation Computing Network. This was the replacement for REACT, the Rapid Execution and Combat Targeting equipment. REACT was the hardware installed in all sensitive locations such as Minuteman launch control centers, B52 bombers, and nuclear submarines. Its purpose was to integrate the nuclear weapons launch platforms with the higher control authority, the president of the United States. It was through REACT that the president would issue the executive order to fire a land-based nuclear-tipped ballistic missile, or order an aircraft carrier battle group into action, or instruct a nuclear submarine to launch its deadly payload. REACT was the medium, the messenger.

The messenger was aging. REACT platforms employed technology that was outdated, technology that used the low frequencies of the electromagnetic spectrum. These frequencies were susceptible to jamming and interference and were capable of being compromised by a determined hacker. A completely new piece of hardware, extremely robust, not jam resistant but fully jam proof, able to hop frequencies across the entire range from the extremely high frequency to the very low frequency band was designed, manufactured, and integrated with the Higher Authority Communications Rapid Message Processing Element Processor.

REACT platforms were replaced with 'Messages, Instructions, Command and Order Consoles'. Amazingly complex stand-alone systems, using the newly built 64-bit processors, these machines were not only installed in every launch control center of the nuclear forces, but were also provided to each and every end user worldwide. Messages, Instructions, Command and Order Consoles were installed in operations centers, aboard ships, on land, underwater, in the air, on the ground, in space, in foreign countries, in each embassy, in each organization that was required to be connected to the U.S. Government. All instructions that were to be passed to any subordinate formation or organization would be displayed on the screens of these devices and printed out on the high speed, high resolution printers integrated into the system. The presidential order authorizing launch of nuclear weapons that had historically been conveyed via REACT would now be transmitted via these consoles.

The machines came with their own emergency power supply systems, their own integrated backup communication hardware. They were built of space age materials that could withstand a drop from 500 feet onto hard concrete. They were unaffected by the electromagnetic impulse generated by a nuclear explosion. They could operate in subzero temperatures and at heat levels where the operator would melt before the machine did. Messages, Instructions, Command and Order Consoles were the very cutting edge of technology.

The ultimate mark of distinction of these consoles could best be judged by the fact that they were equated with the supreme command authority. Instructions appearing on these terminals superseded any instructions given by any commander. A superior officer, issuing a direct verbal command, was to be disregarded if the instructions were in conflict with those appearing on the console. In fact, the superior officer was to be informed of this anomaly, and, if the individual persisted, he or she was to be removed from command and put under close arrest, confined to quarters until the matter was resolved.

Any message appearing on these screens was superior to all telephonic or teleconferenced instructions issued by anyone. Orders received on the consoles could only be superseded by new orders received on the same machines. There was only one exception. Only the president of the United States of America had the authority to issue an order that would take precedence over the electronic message. However, for this to happen, the order had to be given verbally, directly, face to face. The president had to be physically present and it had to be ascertained that it was really the president, not a double. Only then could the instructions of the console be overruled. These devices were the ultimate authority; they were the flawless superior commanders of the transformed force. They were perfect, immaculate, unemotional, and absolutely unambiguous.

If one was to seek some flaw in these wondrous devices, it could perhaps be their unfortunate acronym.

MICOC.

Even before the machines had arrived, the acronym had made its impact. "Are you expecting MICOC tonight?" "Wait till you see MICOC." "Do you have someplace I can put MICOC?" "Once MICOC is up and running, it can't be put down, even by a nuke!"

Many a pretty young uniformed thing had been approached with obvious come ons. "Care to see MICOC? "Like to touch MICOC?"

MICOC liberated the military in more ways than intended. It was surprising how many agreed to the various innuendos. Many were willing to see MICOC, feel MICOC, sit on MICOC, spend an evening familiarizing themselves with MICOC. There was even the somewhat excited comment by one officer, "MICOC, my ass." They never figured out whether the individual was resistant to change or simply ambitious.

Women's rights campaigners within the establishment took serious exception to the acronym and demanded that the name be changed. An irate female presidential adviser had stormed into the office of the secretary, demanding that action be taken. The secretary had been his usual questioning self. "Is MICOC bad? I don't think so. Can we change MICOC?" He assumed a thoughtful look, stroking his forehead with his forefinger, "Hmmm. What's in a name? That you call MICOC by any other name, it would still be MICOC. What shall we do with MICOC? I know, why don't you sit on it for a while. It should subside on its own."

The adviser was furious. "I don't think this is funny. Wait till the president hears about it."

"Don't bother. He's heard it. He's seen it, he's even played with it for a while. He loves MICOC."

The lady retreated in a huff.

MICOC was there to stay.

21

Most Americans, including many in uniform, believed that the command center for all combat operations was located deep within the Pentagon. They reasoned that it had to be a room similar to the one they saw each time a space mission went up; Mission Control at Cape Canaveral. It would be a huge workspace with banks of workstations, immense wall-to-wall displays, busy-looking personnel scurrying about, messages being flashed across the globe, orders being passed, instructions being given, results being recorded. Not many could have known that there were a total of eleven such identical control centers spread throughout the United States. In addition there were forty-three smaller centers at different locations worldwide. Somewhat austere, with lesser displays, fewer consoles, and limited seating, these smaller centers were, in terms of capability, the exact duplicates of their bigger, better-endowed counterparts. They enjoyed the same hierarchy, and from each of these centers, authorized personnel could control and access every aspect of the American war machine. Some, like the one in the innards of the White House, were stationary; others, like the one aboard Air Force One, aboard fleet command ships, inside forty-foot container trucks, in modified railroad carriages, aboard Chinook helicopters, on board a luxury ocean liner, were mobile. They used to be forty-four in number. One had been destroyed when the twin towers came crashing down on 9/11.

The hierarchy of control centers, the massive computing networks, the voluminous data banks and their associated control electronics needed a highly secure, indestructible control and backup system that would exercise oversight of the entire system — an apex location from where the entire affair was to be managed. This was housed in a facility that had been built in 1966 but still remained a viable, impregnable fortress. It was a perfect site, located deep inside a mountain outside Colorado Springs at the Cheyenne Mountain Air Force Base. It was an intricate complex, the erstwhile Combat Operations Center of NORAD, set inside tunnels that had been carved deep into the heart of the mountain itself. The exterior was constantly patrolled and protected by elite security guards, each armed to the teeth with automatic sidearms and semiautomatic machine guns. Scores of German Shepherd attack dogs provided added security to the forbidden structure above the entrance of which still hung the ominous sign, "Use of Deadly Force Authorized by All Personnel."

The natural protection provided by the mountain was further bolstered using layers of lead and reinforced concrete to prevent any radiation from entering the completely self-contained complex. The headquarters was redesigned to survive a direct hit from a 10-megaton nuclear weapon, and to ensure that the shockwaves of the detonation did not disturb the men and equipment inside, the entire structure was mounted atop huge springs that were over three feet in diameter. It contained food and water supplies for three months for all conceivable personnel who might be located in the facility. Uninterrupted power for lighting as well as for the computer systems was ensured through huge battery banks and multiple generators designed to come on line automatically in case of a power failure. Huge blast doors were the only entrances and exits to the base. Once closed, everything inside was completely isolated from the rest of the world. The isolation was only physical; the complex retained full ability to communicate with the outside world using state-of-the-art communications systems, with triple-redundant links to all command sites, all headquarters, and to each and every unit worldwide through MICOC. It was also linked into all major news and civil defense agencies to accept and release up-to-the-minute information on global military affairs.

One tunnel, slightly separate from the rest, was barred by another set of steel doors, another set of guards, another array of biometric identification devices. Behind these was installed the apex support system of the entire networked structure, the final recourse of the Distributed Computing Network. Two more Asskickers, back to back, the 'computers of last resort' in the hierarchy of the entire netcentric warfare concept.

Force Transformation ensured that commanders were provided with clear, coherent, real-time information of the global battle space. This information flowed through absolutely reliable, highly secure, large bandwidth channels and incorporated global data link integration of all ground, air and space platforms. This was no mean achievement. However, this crowning triumph of technology had a very dark side to it. Force Transformation had achieved something remarkably malicious. It removed the human element from all aspects of command and control and forced individuals at every level to put their absolute faith in machines. Computers now gathered data, computers carried out data analysis, microprocessors carried out electronic decision making, communications were based on digital messaging and security was based on computer generated encryption. All information flowed through computer-controlled information transfer systems. Force transformation went as far as to direct commanders that, when in doubt, they were to follow the instructions being displayed on their terminals instead of what they heard on the voice communication channels. Voices could be faked; the sound spectrum could be compromised. Video could be created in studios, uniformed commanders could be consummate actors. SIPRNET and the Data

Exchange Backbone were immune to attack.
Computer terminals were absolutely reliable. They
were to be trusted implicitly.

The professional warriors, the brave men and women
who bore arms and went in harm's way shared
Robert's view. They believed that they now had the
ultimate command and control structure in place.
Robert believed that his paper had been instrumental
in putting in place a structure that would be
controlled by the military and that Brawn would now
be firmly in charge.

The politicians however had a different perspective.
They viewed the process of Force Transformation as a
means to screw the professional soldiers in a truly
remarkable manner. They now had a tool that would
enable them to replace brilliance in soldiering with
machine-based logic. Machines would now handle all
aspects of warfare; there would no longer be any need
for military geniuses. No longer would there be a
need for any heroes; the machines would provide
logic based decisions. All situations would have
logical outcomes. The brains delighted in the fact that
the United States of America had created an all-
powerful, next generation, distributed computing
network with multiple redundant backups and
storage systems that would be controlled by them.
Brains could now conduct netcentric warfare. Force
Transformation could be used to do away with the
need for brawn.

Databases and programs from the central computers dispersed throughout the government departments were migrated to the new machines. With the old databases came the historic data and, with the old, proven programs came their secure code. Within one such data migration, unchecked by anyone, came a tiny piece of extra code.

Puck.

22

To test and refine the new system and the department's control over it, a recurring war game, Global Engagement, was instituted. It explored air and space contributions to joint war fighting ten to fifteen years in the future. Global Engagement created a level playing field and then examined the totality of modern warfare. In a structured forum, military and policy experts highlighted, discussed, explored, and defined war-fighting concepts and issues that would shape the future force. Another war game, designed to push the thought processes beyond fifteen years, was also devised. The "Futures Game" looked approximately a decade beyond Global Engagement to determine capabilities that would move the force toward its vision. Futuristic concepts, capabilities, and emerging doctrine were included in these war games to evaluate their future potential and generate the required interest. Computer-based war gaming became a major part of the syllabi of the staff and war colleges, because now computer-based wars were an integral part of the philosophy of the Pentagon.

It could have been a movie theater. It could have been a movie. The four people sitting comfortably in front of the large screens that covered the walls could have been ordinary people enjoying a movie in a home cinema basement. They were not. The screens were not showing any Hollywood production. This was no home theater; these were no ordinary people; these were no ordinary images. These images were being transmitted in real time, and they showed a pair of F-14s being catapulted off the deck of the USS John F. Kennedy somewhere off the coast of Baluchistan, a hostile and forbidding coastal province of Pakistan. The launch video was soon replaced by multiple video streams from a variety of sensors and cameras spread across the globe. And, through exceptionally high-quality speakers, there poured forth selectable, stereophonic sound to accompany the video screen of choice.

Airborne, the aircraft turned north, climbing to a comfortable altitude and leveling off. Flying together, yet spaced apart, they entered Pakistani airspace. The Pakistani radar controller could see the formation on his scope but did not respond. He had strict instructions to let the Americans fly in and out as they liked, at the altitudes they chose, at the times they chose, at speeds they elected to fly. The task of the Pakistani controllers was restricted to ensuring that any air traffic that could conflict with the flight path of the American aircraft was diverted elsewhere.

One screen was now showing an eerie picture of a
pickup truck racing across the Afghan countryside.
Actually, what the viewers saw was a thermal image
of the truck, not the truck itself. An unnatural black
and white image of a hot engine, the fuzzy images of
the four occupants in the truck, all a ghostly white,
white headlights, white taillights. A white spot at the
rear end, close to one of the taillights indicating that
one wheel was running hotter than the other three.
The screen showed readouts and computer-based
analysis of the raw data. It was a jeep with four
occupants, traveling at a speed of 57.34 miles per
hour, and it had a brake pad that needed fixing.
The unsuspecting occupants of the jeep were oblivious
of the fact that they were being tracked by an
unmanned aircraft flying above them, its sensors
locating and transmitting their ground position
continuously to satellites overhead that bounced the
data across the skies and downlinked it to multiple
destinations. The staff of the operations room of the
USS John F. Kennedy could see the image. So could
commanders of differing levels based in Qatar, Saudi
Arabia, Muscat, Bahrain, Kuwait, Germany, Brussels
and England . So could the staff at the Pentagon, and
so could the many intermediate decision makers in
between. So also could the president of the United
States, the secretary of defense, the special adviser to
the president, and the CIA chief—the four persons
watching the drama as it unfolded across the screens
in the command center within the White House.

The whole activity was being orchestrated by Asskicker. It had, within seconds, matched the infrared picture of the jeep with that of the personal vehicle of Mullah Omar, the leader of the Taliban. The IR signature matched perfectly. The acoustics of the machine were identical to those stored in the memory banks. Despite twenty-three days, nineteen hours, and forty-six seconds having elapsed since the left rear brake of the vehicle started catching, the mullah had yet to have the problem fixed. This was a positive ID with zero margin of error. The jeep was definitely that of the evil mullah. The occupants were yet to be identified. They needed checking.

Asskicker planned its next move and formulated a very specific order for the Predator. The message was routed through the twenty-year-old corporal who sat on the terminal in Jacobabad, Pakistan, a god-forsaken place in the middle of nowhere but now a major U.S. air base from where the pilotless drones operated over Afghanistan. As she read the message, the young airwoman had no way of knowing that she was being ordered by a computer. She didn't really care. Her boss, whoever he or she was, always communicated to her directly through the computer screen in front of her, the display panel of a gleaming MICOC. The boss wanted her to bring the Predator down to one hundred feet above ground level and position it three thousand feet behind the vehicle that was racing on the ground. Simultaneously, she was to activate the "sniffer." She twiddled with the controls, and seconds later, five hundred miles away, the Predator arrived at the desired position. Another instruction, another twiddling of knobs, another throwing of switches and the powerful sniffer on board the Predator was turned on. The female returned to her boring task of monitoring of the flight instruments of the Predator. She knew that the machine was executing the instructions because all lights were green and the data flow indicator showed that the sniffer was sending out a steady stream of information. Up to the same satellite, across the same skies, bounced off more satellites and then down to the ground receiving station, back to Asskicker.

A highly specialized field agent in Afghanistan began feeding data to an electronic analyst in the United States. Activated, the 320-sensor array device that had been created by NASA and endearingly termed E-nose commenced its routine. This marvel of modern engineering had been funded and developed by DARPA and used techniques developed after studying the electrical signals that flowed within the brains of dogs and sharks, the two animals that had the most powerful odor detection ability endowed by nature. It used biosensors, which actually were living organisms that could take a few molecules and, by cascading their outputs, amplify the smell many times over and then convert it into binary format to be handed over to the resident computers within the device.

Naturally, the sniffer data was voluminous. It covered the entire spectrum of olfactory emissions. Had it wanted, the receiving Asskicker could have matched the smell of the fuel being burnt by the vehicle to the particular refinery where it had been processed. It could also have determined the state of the vehicle's engine by the exhaust emissions. The computer was, however, interested in just one specific bit of information, one specific odor.

It initiated a reverse search. Instead of trying to match the sniffer data to the information stored within its database, it did the opposite. From its database it selected one specific data string and ran a match against the data arriving from the Predator. It was child's play for a machine that could handle 30 trillion computations in one second. Within nanoseconds, it had found the perfect match. Two identical values, two perfectly matched sets of zeros and ones. One stored within itself and one brought in from outside via the sniffer. Two identical odors, one from within the mullah's personal file and another from the Predator. MASINT was working perfectly.

The olfactory sensors of E-nose had no problem detecting the personal body odor of Mullah Omar. Asskicker had no problem matching it with its database. The evil mullah was on board the vehicle and, as always, he desperately needed a bath.

A value had been found, a condition had been met, the program could now branch into a new direction. Additional searches were completed, fresh instructions compiled, new messages transmitted.

This time the messages were relayed via satellite directly to the F-14s, now orbiting in the vicinity of the vehicle carrying Mullah Omar across the stark Afghan landscape. The satellite downlinked to the flight control computers; Asskicker and the F-14s were connected electronically, across over 12,000 miles, across continents, across oceans. Computers talked, one located in California, the others on board fighter aircraft patrolling the skies over Afghanistan.

Connect, Handshake, establish protocol, identify, verify, open ports, kill crosstalk, talk.

Machines talked. Asskicker, the superior being, asked the two aircraft to identify themselves. Who they were, what was their flight condition, where they were, what they were doing, and what could they do. The aircraft told the computer all it wanted to know, their serial numbers, engine data, position, endurance, range, payload, and a host of other details. The Asskicker already had this information, it was simply double checking. It even had the names of the crew, their rank, and personal numbers, which it had been fed by a computer aboard the launch aircraft carrier. It knew who the pilots were, where they lived, who they were married to, what their sexual preferences were, who needed to be notified in case they died.

Right now, Asskicker needed to do something else. As the feeble, slow, almost infantile computers on board the two aircraft chattered on, the supercomputer interrupted their litany. It instructed the aircraft what to do, how to do it, and when to do it. Asskicker fed the complete positional data of the truck into the navigation systems of the two aircraft. It then triggered various systems on, transmitters and receivers were activated, frequencies tuned automatically. Asskicker then proceeded to establish a conference call with the drone. Asskicker, the F-14s, and the Predator were now in a huddle. The Predator gave the F-14 the latest coordinates of the truck. The F-14 relayed the same data through its multiplexer bus to the JDAMs, the sleek and deadly bombs carried underslung on the aircraft. This established; Asskicker brought another party on line, the satellite orbiting over that region. The satellite in space now started conversing directly with the bombs on the F-14s.

Multiple computers were now carrying out repeated calculations to accurately predict where the JDAMs would land if released under the present conditions, from this altitude, at this speed. Asskicker, the Predator, the satellite, the aircraft navigation systems, the fire control computers, and the JDAMs conversed continuously, updating the ground position of the truck, the aircraft position in space, the conditions of flight, and the atmospheric conditions, while simultaneously updating a host of other, relevant information.

Asskicker had already given its approval, and, when the intercept geometry was found to be perfect, the fire control computers on board the lead F 14 sent a pulse of electricity surging down the wires to the bomb racks. The pulse triggered miniscule explosive charges built into the bolts that were holding the bombs captive on the belly of the aircraft.

The bolts exploded. Freed, the bombs fell earthward. They arced gracefully across the dark sky. Elegant artifacts of human engineering; sleek, beautiful, intelligent creatures, they headed for their target and, indeed, toward self-destruction. The date code stamped across their identification plates indicated that these bombs were barely two years old and that they had a shelf life of forty years. These bombs were not destined to sit on a crowded shelf for long. Barely out of the factories, their life would soon be ended. They would blow themselves up in a strange, foreign land.

Their brains activated, the graceful JDAMs started their own intricate routine. Each established a direct dialog with multiple satellites in the sky from which they were fed a constant stream of information. These inputs were summed, averaged, and refined. Each bomb calculated its latitude, longitude, its height, its position in space accurate to within a few inches. Simultaneously, each bomb talked to the Predator, which fed it another set of values—the position of the truck. The bombs worked out the desired flight path they needed to reach the truck. Tiny motors using compressed gases moved small fins to drive the bombs toward their target, which was the geometric center of Mullah Omar's truck.

The occupants of the truck had no idea at all that this hectic activity was happening around and above them. They were lost in their own thoughts. The driver was busy trying to figure out when he would have time to get the brake problem fixed. The young Afghan beside him was thinking that soon he too would be allowed to drive the vehicle instead of just being the driver's assistant. The two females behind were busy planning the day that lay ahead of them. One would gather the sticks to make the fire for breakfast while the other would make her way down to the fast-flowing stream along with the pile of laundry. She winced; the pile stank. If only the smelly mullah would use some soap and change his clothes more often.

The first bomb impacted thirteen inches off target. The second bomb's point of impact was obscured by the ball of fire that was, a few microseconds earlier, the target vehicle. The truck and its occupants were already history. The second bomb was a needless expense, an intelligent weapon wasted unnecessarily. These were costly, highly precise, explosive-delivery mechanisms designed to blow themselves up and destroy everything within their radius of effectiveness to bits, converting flesh and bones into obscene, quivering pieces of jelly, metal to jagged pieces, glass to shards. These were sleek, attractive, young devices, carefully engineered and specially designed to explode brutally in strange lands, among strange people, killing without distinction, with absolute disregard for the sanctity of human life. These were the creation of evil brains; these were artifacts that could be used without any remorse or guilt. These were expendable weapons that could be used safely and surely while those that launched them remained safe and protected in their luxurious surroundings, well out of harm's way.

As Asskicker updated its inventory of JDAMs, it also recorded the fact that there had been an overkill. One weapon had been wasted. It mattered not. There were thousands more in the arsenal.

The audience in every operation center watching the encounter broke into spontaneous applause. They cheered, shook hands, embraced one another, and congratulated themselves. Mullah Omer was dead. They had just witnessed the first real-life engagement of a target by Asskicker. A completely automated process, from start to finish, the only human interaction being restricted to operating a few switches, pressing a few buttons, activating a few processes. The complete process of target search, identification, selection, target to weapon matching, weapon selection, weapon launch, and control and guidance to the target—every single decision was made by the supercomputer.

These were the powerful decision makers of the new military order, and they were fully supported by sophisticated, technologically advanced weapons. By dovetailing automated decision making with overwhelming force and endowing it with precision strike ability, America had created the ultimate fighting machine. Capable, powerful, omnipotent, omnipresent. Impossible to neutralize. Sadly, no one had visualized that this massive might would end up being controlled by unprincipled minds. No one would have believed that the world's most powerful military machine would fall into the hands of insecure commanders; that its power would be wielded by unscrupulous leaders, and that ultimate force would become the ultimate evil. No one could have visualized that the immense power of the U.S. military would be used by corrupt and immoral individuals to destroy the world.

No one could have predicted Iraq.

It was Iraq through which the immorality that had permeated the global political process revealed itself. The world had watched as the United Nations inspectors tried to keep the inspections going; everyone had seen the world body trying to convince the United States and Britain that no weapons of mass destruction had been uncovered in Iraq. Those voices had gone unheeded. The warmongers, safe in their undisclosed locations, immune to harm, had already planned their move. They had already decided to invade Iraq. Despite the world crying for a peaceful solution, despite the United Nations and its inspectors saying that there was no imminent threat to any Western country, despite there being no linkage of Iraq with Afghanistan, despite every indicator saying that Iraq did not pose any immediate problem, the evil brains had tasked brawn to decimate the Iraqi people. A coalition of the willing had been formed by countries that needed the American largesse and were not averse to having their young men and women die needlessly in a strange and foreign land.

Iraq was attacked in an obscene manner. It was a murderous attack designed for shock and awe on a population already hurting desperately from decades of living under a tyrant. And, as if a despotic ruler was not enough, the poor Iraqis had further been forced to suffer sanctions at the hands of Britain and America for over ten years. Iraq was a nation that had been turned into a pauper by the "Oil for Food" program managed by the United Nations, a program that had sucked up billions of dollars in administrative costs from an already impoverished country. Iraq the undefended, Iraq the weak, Iraq the crippled was attacked by the might of the American armed forces, assisted feebly but willingly by the British, the Italians, and the Australians.

And now, a mission accomplished had turned into a mission frustrated. The coalition was coming apart. While its partners were gradually pulling out, America remained stuck in Iraq with absolutely no clue on how to extricate itself from the mess it had created. If the Americans cut and run, the country would rapidly sink into civil war and breakup. If they stayed, they would continue to suffer casualties. If they used additional force, that would only worsen things, and anyway, not much additional help was forthcoming. From the fifty thousand soldiers Britain had contributed to the coalition, the number had dropped to just a few thousand, and those too were kept in the south, close to the escape route, the sea port of Basra. The Brits were no fools. They had learned from history. More than once they had been trapped deep inside landlocked countries and had been unable to flee when the natives became "restless." It had become unwritten policy that the British would never be boxed in, never again would they be trapped deep inside strange territories in distant lands. It was not coincidence that they were quite content to stay in Basra. The jubilant and relatively inexperienced Americans were not so shrewd. In their enthusiasm to gain global approbation, they had rushed headlong into Baghdad, into the Sunni triangle, only to find that the welcome they expected was not forthcoming. The liberated were shooting at the liberators. There was murdering in Mosul, burning in Baquba, firing in Fallujah, torturing in Tikrit. There was kneeling in Karbala.

Lt. Col. Chris Hughes, commander of the 2nd Battalion, 327th Infantry Regiment, yelled to his troops: "Smile, relax." Hughes was leading a foot patrol in the Iraqi town aiming to befriend the locals when the crowd turned hostile and started hurling obscenities at its liberators. The situation turned ugly and it rapidly became apparent to the colonel that his soldiers would be overwhelmed and lynched. He commanded his soldiers to take a knee and point their weapons to the ground. The angry locals saw armed

215

to the teeth Americans kneel in the dust and signal surrender. The tribal Arabs understood. The crowd acknowledged the offer of subservience by armed intruders and the hostility dissipated. The crowd dispersed. Hughes drew praise from President Bush for his "skill and honor."

Bewildered soldiers from the land of the free, from the land of the liberated were stunned at the reception they were getting. Bright eyed, young fighting men and women were shocked at the manner in which those that they had liberated were treating them. Soldiers who had been brainwashed by the most blatant of propaganda to keep them scared and hyped up were now wandering across a land that was truly foreign in every sense of the word. Regulars and reservists had been motivated into believing that a raghead Saudi millionaire playing "follow the leader" in the barren wastes of Afghanistan could hurt the mightiest nation in the world. Normal, fun loving Americans had been convinced that a dimwitted Saddam Hussein, stupid enough not to know how to fight or indeed, how to run, could be a threat to the world's most powerful nation thousands of miles away. Gullible Americans were made to believe that the Arabs, having tasted the pleasures that oil could buy, would give up their luxuries just to spite the developed world. Unnerved Americans had been misled by the self-serving religious lobbies that propagated the myth that the existence of the Jews was threatened by the Arabs and that a threat to Israel was a threat to the United States. Americans had been suckered in by the intelligence agencies of foreign countries who were interested in keeping the American nation scared. Phobic America was now averse to reaching out and touching someone or, indeed, be touched by others. Americans, once easily the best of nations was systematically being transformed into the worst.

The Americans would remain mired in Iraq. The Arab-Israeli conflict would continue to fester. The conflict between the Palestinians and Israelis, both cousins, both natives of the historic lands of Sumeria and Judea, both Semites, had now been masterfully expanded to include the Americans.

American military might would now engage rock throwing, insult hurling teenagers.

Thermobaric bombs would now be used to indiscriminately dispatch men, women and children to kingdom come.

23

She was sleek. She was beautiful, she was intelligent. She was young. She was a teenage Palestinian girl. She had blown herself up with seven others in an Israeli café. She was Muslim.

"What is it with you guys? What twisted thinking goes on in your brains? Did you see her picture? Jesus Christ. So young, so pretty. And she looked bright too. Eighteen. Just fucking eighteen. And the Israelis. A complete family wiped out. Kids and all. What would make a girl do that? You are sickos. All of you. First, you guys breed like flies. Then you choose some real screwed up people as your leaders. Then you start pissing around with those who have a better quality of life than yours. You flock to the West and if the West does not accept you, you turn against it and start blowing yourselves up. What the fuck is it with you guys anyway? Why can't you enjoy the world and let others live in peace"?

P. K. responded. "It wasn't like that, was it? Hell, not too long ago, just twenty, thirty years ago, where were we guys? Where were the Muslims and their problems? Have you forgotten that back then the ones we worried about was the yellow peril? The Chinese. Everyone had us believing that the Chinese were out to get us. Then there were the Russians. The West said that the Russians were the problem. Where were the Muslims? Where was this Muslim problem? I'll tell you where it was. I'll tell you what happened. The Muslims helped you guys to bring about the demise of the USSR. With the fracture of the Soviet empire, the Warsaw Pact countries disintegrated. So did the Warsaw Pact. And what did you guys do with the organization whose sole purpose in life was to combat the Warsaw Pact countries? What did you do to NATO? Did you disband it? No way. No bloody way. It was too good a gravy train to put to an end. The armament industries of the West would have come to a grinding halt if NATO were to shut shop. If that happened, most Western economies would collapse.

"So what do you do? You screwballs take on board those very same countries that were until recently the avowed enemy. You expanded NATO. You strengthened a military alliance. And this you did without there being any enemy. Unbelievable. Absofuckinglutely unbelievable. Even though there was no longer any major threat to the West, it created a much larger, much more powerful military alliance. And then, one fine morning, suddenly, someone, somewhere, realized 'Oh shit, we don't have anyone to fight. Hell, we need an enemy to justify all this crap. Someone we can focus on. We need a threat that can keep the weapon factories churning out hardware for the killing fields that are yet to be defined. New battlefields were needed where taxpayers dollars could be spent.

"But there was a problem, wasn't there? There was no damn enemy. No one was big enough or strong enough or crazy enough to stand up to the sole superpower and a superfluous but powerful North Atlantic Alliance. Plus there wasn't any battlefield large enough or developed enough to fight. The traditional battlefield of Europe could not be duplicated in Africa or South America or Asia. It had to be a completely new enemy and it had to be a completely new battleground.

"I don't know who thought of it, but it had to be a true brain. It was, after all, a truly brilliant idea. Some genius came up with it. How about an enemy that is everywhere? How about a virtual enemy? How about an all pervasive, all embracing enemy? How about the freaky Muslims?

"So they found themselves an enemy. Ragheads, freaks, Jihadis, warlords, and warriors willing to fight just for the heck of it. Not for money, not for wealth, not for fame, not for worldly possessions, but for a belief. For a cause. We told them the Russians were infidels, we told them to fight the infidels. They fought and kicked the Russians out of Afghanistan.

We created the Taliban, the Mujahedeen, the Osamas, the Mullah Omars. And when we had defeated the Russians, when we had screwed the Soviet empire, we decided that these Mujahedeen could now be termed terrorists and projected as an enemy of the whole world.

"Boy, did they get it wrong. They really picked the wrong lot this time. They picked an enemy, a bunch of weirdoes who believe that dying is the best thing that can happen to them.

"Let me explain something to you. Something that the West has great difficulty in understanding. Suicide is not allowed in Islam. It simply isn't. Get this through your thick skull, R.F. Let it sink into your brain, N.B. A Muslim who commits suicide will never go to heaven. Muslims are prohibited from taking their lives for the simple reason that the promise of the hereafter is too damned attractive. Sure, there is the promise of Houris, virgins, rivers of milk and honey, eternal peace, eternal happiness. All this is there in Heaven. And this is exactly why suicide is prohibited. One would willingly die for these goodies, and He does not want people to take the easy way out to the next world. He wants us to face the music here. And you know what? This is also promised to the Muslims, He has said that there would be plenty of music to be faced. The Muslims would suffer; they would face conflict. They would constantly have to battle evil, fight wrong, face unbelievers. And then, in complete contrast to His earlier instructions to the Jews and

Christians, God told the Muslims to fight, to struggle, to wage 'Jihad.' Don't turn the other cheek, don't take shit lying down. Not for yourself, not for your clan, not for another Muslim. If you see another Muslim in pain, you must feel for him, care for him, fight for him. When your sisters are being burned at the stake, don't turn your face the other way, pretending that all is well. When your brothers and sisters are sent to gas chambers clutching bars of soap, don't pretend that they are headed for a shower. That nothing is happening. When Sabra and Shatilla happen, don't think that the dead were someone you did not know, and therefore you need not care. You have to care. So when the West decided to label the Muslims as an enemy, it took on something that it hadn't a clue about. It took on 1.3 billion Jihadis. And this number is growing much faster than you can imagine."

He waited for that to sink in before continuing. "And let me tell you something else. Don't go around believing what some Muslims tell you. That we are moderate, that the true evil is in the fundamentalists. Trust me, believe me when I tell you that there is no such thing as a moderate Muslim. Likewise, there in no fundamentalist Muslim. There is no enlightened Muslim, progressive Muslim, free-thinking Muslim. There are just Muslims. You are either a Muslim or a nonbeliever. There is no half measure here. If you are a Muslim, you have to subscribe to the fundamentals of Islam. In doing so, you are simply following the dictates of your God. You are therefore a fundamentalist; you have to be. Just as a practicing

Jew or a Christian has to be a fundamentalist Jew or Christian. The pope is a fundamentalist Christian, I sincerely hope that he is, just as the rabbi at the downtown synagogue has to be a fundamentalist Jew. All of us have to believe in the fundamentals of our religion, which, incidentally, are identical. Trust me when I tell you that your safest bet is with the fundamentalists. Because peace and love are fundamental to Islam, just as they are to Christianity and Judaism. You need to recognize and understand that, for a Muslim, the Christians and the Jews are fellow believers. You have absolutely nothing to fear from the true Muslims. We are all one."

"Piss off, P. K. You know that what you are saying is bullshit. Just who exactly do you think you are kidding? The next thing you shall be telling us is that those who kill and maim, those who blow up innocent bystanders and themselves, are peace-loving pacifists!"

"Fair enough. Let's see who these guys are. Who exactly are those who do such things? These are the weirdoes who have taken our religion and hijacked it for their personal aims. It again boils down to what I have always told you guys. It's the evil brains screwing the rest of the world. In this case, some smart sonsofbitches have hijacked Islam for their own evil ends. Getting the poor, the uneducated, the deprived, the needy to follow their evil ways by giving them the hope that this is the route to salvation. You really think a mother, any mother, wants her child to blow himself or herself up? You think that there are people out there who breed for this purpose. You couldn't be more wrong. It is the feebleminded being brainwashed into doing things that suit others. And you know damn well what I mean. This is something you do extremely well in the West. Getting the ignorant, the stupid, the illiterate to behave in a certain manner is an art form taught in all universities across the world and practiced to perfection by the media.

"Osama bin Laden. He is nobody. A lone, insignificant individual. A person who decided to forego his life of luxury and instead fight the Americans. Big bloody deal. True, he hated the Americans. But then, who doesn't? If hating Americans qualifies you to be a member of al-Qaida, then someone somewhere should be really worried. The whole damn world is al-Qaida! "And then what do you do? You guys come up and glorify these nuts. Terrorists, terrorists you chant. You bring crappy personalities on television, portraying them as experts; experts, my ass. Pathetic assholes who pose as experts and go around trying to glorify demented sickos such as Osama and his lot. Terror, guys, is like beauty. It lies in the eye of the beholder or, should I say, in the mind of the viewer. It is you and your media that terrorize the public. Not Osama, Not Saddam, it is you, your freaking actions that terrorize the nation.

"And this is the problem. I really need you to understand this. Because if you don't, you will continue making the same damn mistake over and over again. You will continue believing that Muslims are terrorists; that they are the root cause of all evil in this world.

"You are afraid to admit the real reason for your scare. You will never admit that the real reason that Muslims scare you is because the things that scare you mean nothing to them. They do not get scared when bombs rain on them; they do not scare when tanks are sent in against their rock-throwing children. They do not scare when Jenin and Rafah happen. They are not terrorized in Bosnia. Nor in Iran, nor in Pakistan. They do not wilt under sanctions; they do not compromise as their loved ones are butchered. Irrespective of what Man can do to them, they remain steadfast in their belief. That is what terrorizes the West."

"Bravo, Bravo, you brave lot," said Robert, mockingly, clapping his hands.

"No, no, hang on, R. F., hear me out. You are the ones who have glorified Al-Qaida. You talk of a complex, loosely knit organization; a widespread network; a bunch of sleeper cells; intricate financial arrangements; a hierarchy of leaders, deputies, commanders, cell captains, soldiers. You talk about involved messaging systems, about slush funds, about madressahs, about complex command and control. And on top of it all, the evil leader, a renegade Saudi millionaire pissed off at America and someone who has elected to fight your 'evil empire,' using all his resources. An amazing genius who has set up a most elaborate network of operatives, sleepers, and active agents, a multitiered, multifaceted organization that has chapters, offices, distributors, agents, regional bases; the whole corporate structure of a multinational operating on a global scale with an intricate network of banks, financial institutions, trading houses, communication centers, travel agencies, safe houses, the whole works. It is the Mafia, the Cosa Nostra, the Bretton Woods sisters, the Big Seven, Microsoft, the church, the drug lords all rolled in one huge, amorphous, evil mass. From the caves of Afghanistan to the bars of Boston, from the forests of Indonesia to the desert wastes of the Middle East, from the rain forest of the Amazon to the Chechen countryside, al-Qaida has spread itself and is actively trying to destroy civilization, demolish the world as we know it. It is evil, it is criminal, it is Muslim. And therefore, because it is Muslim, terrorism and violence must be part of the Muslim faith.

"What you have actually done is glorified a pathetic, impotent group of disenchanted, dysfunctional individuals who, if left alone, would have faded unsung into the wilderness of the Afghan countryside. Instead, a terrified West has now propelled them to prominence. And, by equating al-Qaida with Islam, the world has done itself a huge disfavor. Indeed, it has done something truly disastrous. By raising the bogey of Islam, the West has really screwed itself. It has created a terrorist organization that has over one point three billion members.

"Just think of what the West has achieved. Recognize the irony of it all. What was it that Osama wanted? The removal of Americans from Saudi Arabia. What he could not do in a lifetime of struggle and toil, George W. Bush accomplished in less than three years! The Americans are out of Saudi Arabia. Where Osama failed, George succeeded. By this twisted logic, George Bush must therefore be a true Muslim, a patriotic Saudi, a member of al-Qaida.

"Who cooked Saddam's goose? Not the Iraqis, not the Sunnis, not the Shias, not the Kurds, not the Arabs, not the Iranians. For over two decades the unfortunate Iraqis struggled under the oppressive yoke of Saddam. Nothing could shake off the iron grip this evil man had over the citizens of that historic land. Numerous coup attempts, innumerable plots, all fell by the wayside and ended with the plotters being executed in the most horrific manner. The majority of Iraqis, the Shias, were kept isolated, oppressed, confined and unable to join up with their spiritual centre, Iran. George W. Bush changed all that. He liberated the Iraqis, he freed the Shias. He enabled the Iranians to extend their influence across Iraq, well into Jordan and Lebanon. The king of kings, the shah of Iran could not do it, nor could Ayatollah Khomeini; George did, and did it almost effortlessly. So what is it now? Isn't George a true Muslim, a devout Shia?

"George is not only a Shia, he is also a Kurd. These poor buggers have forever wanted a separate homeland. This has not happened because the Turks would not allow it to happen, Saddam would not allow it to happen, the Iranians would not allow a Kurdistan to emerge. Saddam slaughtered and gassed to death those who dared even think about it. Turkey would never tolerate such a territorial aberration. Iran banished those who even contemplated such an eventuality. Kurdistan is a very distinct possibility now. George Bush has made this possible. George W. Bush, the Kurd nationalist, Bush the Muslim, George of al-Qaida.

"The Israel-Palestine conflict has raged for ages. No one has been able to solve this festering problem, not one person, not one organization, not any international body. George W. Bush is going to solve this issue, make no mistake about it. His road map may not be working right now, but trust me, it is going to happen. He shall prevail. He has set in motion the series of events that shall ensure the Palestinians get their homeland and this oppressed race can thus begin its journey toward normalcy. George W. Bush must be a Palestinian, a Yasser Arafat in a 10-gallon hat instead of a rag. George is going to liberate Palestine, just as he did Afghanistan.

"Who could have beaten back the relentless evil of the Taliban? Everyone seemed powerless and unable to stop them; complete nations were being held hostage to this distorted version of one of the fastest growing religion of the world. The Americans stepped up to the plate and assumed this responsibility. They took up this challenge. George saved Islam from the unbridled spread of this maniacal version of a truly noble religion.

"And Pakistan. Who reformed the madressahs in Pakistan? Who stopped the millions of dollars being pumped into distorting of our religion? The frigging Brits could not liberate our North-West Frontier Province. They tried for two hundred years to tame it. We have been trying since 1947. Who actually does it? Good old U.S. of A. Americans are true Muslims, active Jihadis, loyal Pakistanis, fighting for the cause of Islam. Goddamn amazing."

24

"Maybe you have something there, P.K. with your weird theory of brawn and brain. Here is a guy that was both brawn and brain. You cannot get any better than this icon. He graduated magna cum laude from Harvard University and he was also a fearless fighter; a true hero in every sense of the word. He fought in the Spanish American War. He was the one who formed the Rough Rider regiment; he is the one who commanded it as a colonel".

Robert was eulogizing his favorite personality, the twenty-sixth president of the United States, Theodore Roosevelt. "I bet you guys don't know that he is the only American president ever to be awarded the Medal of Honor."
"I didn't know that but I do know that he was awarded the Nobel Peace Prize for ending the war between the Japs and the Russians," said Niles.

"I knew that. I know that he is the first American to get both the Nobel Prize and the Medal of Honor. Of course he had to wait for the medal until he was very dead and until Bill Clinton was in office but he did get it," said P.K.

Robert continued, "His face is carved into Mount Rushmore. He is the youngest of the four guys there. He was an amazing person. Do you know what he once said? He said that 'to sit home, read one's favorite paper, and scoff at the misdeeds of the men who do things is easy, but it is markedly ineffective. It is what evil men count upon the good men's doing.'"

Robert then crystallized his thoughts into words. "We can't just sit around while our world is coming unstuck around us. We have to do something. Those who stand by watching idly as rape takes place are as much to blame as the one who rapes. Perhaps more. We have to act. We must. We have to stop this madness. We have to restore sanity before we destroy ourselves."

"Yes, absolutely. We need to take over the world. Boy, you do have a fertile imagination. But then, I guess, having your head up your arse automatically means that it is well fertilized. What you need to do is pull your head out of your arse, Robert!" Niles said, taunting.

"Hey, let's declare martial law," P. K. chimed in. "We are good at that in Pakistan."

"I'm damn serious. We have to do something. And martial law might not be a bad idea."

"You've got to be nuts. Do you realize what you are saying?" an incredulous Pervez asked.

"You cannot be bloody serious, Robert," said Niles, echoing P. K. "We've played together, fought together, screwed together. We have been through thick and thin together, but this is crazy. What's with you R.F.? You are asking us to commit suicide. No, not that, you are asking us to destroy the very institutions that we so passionately believe in. You have to be crazy."

"Don't you 'crazy' me, Niles. You both know exactly what I am asking. I am not asking you to give up what you stand for but to fight for exactly that. I am asking you to stand up for what we have always believed in. To fight evil. To serve our nations, to serve humanity. We have fought, we have killed, we maimed, we have destroyed for the sake of peace, for the betterment of our masses, for the progress of mankind. But now, just look around you. What are we doing? Now we don't seem to give a rat's ass for mankind. We are no longer worried about morality. We are killing for the sake of killing. And, you, P. K., you and your freaking mullahs. Your Jihadis; they are no different from our neocons, our screwed up brains, who think that they have the solution for the whole damn world. For the love of God, look around you. Can't you see the cancer that is within ourselves? Can't you feel it tearing us apart. Nations, races, tribes, religions, the complete globe is threatened. Mankind is destroying itself."

They knew. They understood. Each had felt the same anguish; they had seen the malaise develop. Indeed, they had been part of the entire process.

Niles decided to carry the conversation further. "OK, OK. Let's just suppose for a moment that we do decide to fix things. That we do go ahead. Any idea how you are planning to do it? How exactly do you plan to take over the world? Run into the nearest telephone booth, put on your costume, and zoom off into space, saving the world. You've been watching too many movies, my friend. You of all the people, you know damn well the strength of the U.S. armed forces. How in hell do you think you are going to take on the world's most powerful military machine? How exactly do you plan to take on the most powerful establishments of the free world?"

"I have no fucking idea, but don't worry, I will think of something. We will think of something. Something will come along, and when it does, we shall know," said Robert.

It was P.K.'s turn to express concern. "I hope you realize that this is the whole frigging world we are talking about, not just our three countries. What about Europe? What about Russia, China, India? There are a whole bunch of nations out there. You simply cannot forget about them, R.F."

"I really don't think that this is our major worry presently. We shall deal with it when and if we come up with something. And, anyway, if we do it right, we should have everyone on our side."

"Look, if you are really going to go somewhere with this, we shall need all the help we can get. Maybe we need to bring in some of our old friends. Rahul is a big wheel in the Indian establishment. I can't do it but you can. You could talk to him, Niles. And the Russians; they are still a major player in this game. Maybe I should sound out Aleksandr," said P.K.

"Look, we know all about you and your Russian 'friend' but this is not the time", his voice heavy with sarcasm as he enunciated the word friend forcefully. "We don't have to do anything at this time, especially with the frigging Russians. Let's just keep this to ourselves," replied Niles.

"Not a problem. Let's keep it quiet but I do wish you would change your perception of Alex. He is one of us. He is a fighter pilot, just like us. I have told you more than once that he is really a very nice person," responded P.K. "Remember, I met him first in combat. You get to know the true nature of a person when he is fighting for his life. I have found him to be a genuine human being."

"Time will tell, buddy, time will tell," said Robert.

25

An eagle was fucking a bear. This unholy union was taking place in a barren wasteland known as Afghanistan. As it engaged in this perverted act, the eagle, prudent as ever, was using protection. To safeguard itself, it was using a condom, a prophylactic with the brand name "Mujahedeen." At the time the majestic bird had no idea that while this measure would prevent it from catching any disease from the powerful bear, the prophylactic itself would infect its user with a devastating sickness. A horrible, lingering disease that would mutate friendly, welcoming arms into gnarled, ugly, finger-pointing stubs. An affliction that would destroy the eagle's historic ability to smile and welcome strangers, an illness that would shrivel open minds into closed organs incapable of objective thought. The evil disease would generate phobias of an unimaginable kind, triggering irrational knee-jerk responses upon seeing beards, burqas, hijabs. It would render immobile loquacious tongues that had always delighted in free speech. It would atrophy emotions, numb the senses, create fevered brows. An entire nation would be infected, losing its freedom, its frank and open society, its love for all things beautiful, all creatures great and small. The disease would cause a horrible reversal to take place. America, a nation that had once sought tired, huddled masses from across the world would itself be transformed into one. A war weary, withdrawn mass, longing to be liberated from the fear that now consumed it.

The Mujahedeen would inflict a crippling blow to the beauty that once was America. A lamp beside a golden door would soon, sadly and irrevocably, be extinguished.

The United States of America had decided to confront the Union of the Soviet Socialist Republics in Afghanistan. It was using proxy fighters, now called Mujahedeen but later to be reclassified as religious zealots, militant Islamists, Jihadists. Muslims had been cunningly motivated to fight a holy war and the "Muj" had flocked to Afghanistan from the world over. Bearded youths, clean shaven adults, teenagers, octogenarians, able bodied, crippled, male, female, black, brown, white, yellow, they had all gravitated toward the killing field of Afghanistan, responding to a call for Jihad, a religious war against the heathens who had occupied the Stan of the Afghans. Staying in the background, Americans staffed, planned, scouted, provided the best of intelligence, the finest of satellite reconnaissance, the sharpest of highest resolution pictures to assist the holy warriors in their endeavor. They supplied them with the latest weaponry in massive quantities. They gave them cutting-edge technology—Guns, rockets, bombs, surface-to-air missiles, attack helicopters—and to make sure that the Russians understood absolutely clearly that America meant business, it gave the Pakistani nation the finest combat aircraft ever built, the General Dynamics Fighting Falcon, the F-16.

The Pakistanis were thrilled beyond belief. They did not realize that the aircraft were given to simply send a message to the Russians and that the Americans cared little whether the Pakistanis flew the F-16s or parked them somewhere in the desert. The aim was to tell the Soviet leadership to lay off Afghanistan. The aircraft were given to send a message that the Americans were willing to provide the latest in technology to a dicey military dictatorship just so that the USSR understood that Afghanistan and all points south of Afghanistan were off limits for the Soviets. By entering Afghanistan, the Russians had gone a step too far. They would have to go back. The Soviets would be made to leave Afghanistan, whatever it took. America was willing to put in the money and the hardware; the stupid Muslims were willing to lay down their lives in the name of Allah, and the naïve Pakistanis would fly the F-16s in every conceivable role. The highly professional and combat ready air force of Pakistan would use the world's finest day superiority fighter in all roles imaginable. Even as an early-warning platform and a night interceptor.

The pilot was simply doing his duty. Perched high above the rocky, inhospitable terrain of the North-West Frontier Province in Pakistan, laid back in the steeply reclined seat of his aircraft, he was busy twiddling knobs, pressing buttons, listening to the ALR-69 Radar Warning Receiver, selecting threat libraries, identifying blips, monitoring radios, working the APG-66 radar, selecting tilt angles and scan modes, zooming in to targets, locking, unlocking, trying to identify, sort and prioritize the threat posed by each one of the aircraft he could see on his radar screen.

It was, however, a duty that the pilot loved immensely. Whenever he eased out of bed at an unearthly hour, he couldn't help thinking that what he was doing was not unlike a cheating husband sneaking out of a conjugal bed for a seamy rendezvous with a secret mistress! Deep within his heart he knew that, as he kissed his sleeping wife good-bye and she replied with a dreamy murmur, that he was actually going to his other, undying love. This the sleepy wife also knew. Had he been doing this for earthy, carnal pleasures, time would have diminished both the desire and intensity of this nightly tryst. This was different. This was eternal love. Years of fighter flying had not lessened the thrill and the emotional rush he felt each time he headed for the cockpit.

Tonight was a particularly busy one. A major ground action was under way, fully supported by air power.

Out there, in the inky black distance, lay Afghanistan, a primitive land populated by a primitive people, primitive in concepts, primitive in action, primitive in beliefs, primitive in lifestyle, now transformed into the most modern battlefield on the globe. Afghanistan was no stranger to war. It was located at the crossroads of civilizations. It straddled the path that great warriors had crisscrossed. It was a melting pot of races, origins, colors and creeds. There were the tall, fair-skinned, blue-eyed, blond-haired Afghans who could have traced their ancestry to the Aryans of Central Asia. There were slant-eyed, stubby-nosed, flat-featured Afghans whose ancestors had ridden with the Mongol hordes that had descended on this inhospitable land from the North. Then there were the dark-skinned, greasy-haired, short statured people who had their roots in the vast Indo-Gangetic plains of the East. Afghanistan was a land that consisted of a number of smaller, distinct fiefdoms, each ruled by a tribal warlord, each warlord shepherding his flock in the manner and style of his choosing. Rivalries were common; so was fighting.

Spanning these divisions were the Powindahs, strange people, nomadic gypsies who spent their entire lives on the move. In summers they moved to the mountains and in winters to the plains. Those who could not keep pace with them were left behind to die. This was a land of survival, this was the domain of the fittest. This was virgin land unspoiled by civilization, populated by a people who had simple thoughts and led simple lives. It was a land of pristine splendor and pristine values. Afghanistan was a land governed by the immutable laws of Islam. These hardy people lived their lives according to the Koran. Five times a day, the Afghans would stop whatever they were doing, and, facing the house of Abraham, facing Mecca, they would pray to Allah, The One. Five times a day the Afghans joined the one point three billion Muslims spread over the globe in "Salaat," the Muslim prayer. At the appointed times, all activity stopped and every able-bodied Muslim man, woman, and child alike faced Mecca and prayed to the Divine Giver, the Forgiving and the Merciful, the Rehman, the Raheem. Prayers over, they would resume whatever they were doing. Mostly this meant a return to fighting.

Perched at his vantage point, looking deep into Afghanistan, the pilot did not know that down below was also located that particular rock on which the representative of the U.S. government, Paul Wolfowitz, had stood, elevating himself above the tall, swarthy Afghans gathered around. He had come half way around the world to address the "Mujahedeen" and had raised his hand, pointed his finger upward to the heavens, and exhorted the simple folk that it was their duty assigned by their God to fight the invaders, to wage a holy war against the Russian infidels. Wolfowitz had urged the Mujahedeen to commence Jihad.

He had succeeded. A non-Muslim had succeeded in motivating the simpleminded Muslims to take up arms against an infidel enemy in the name of Islam. The religious warriors had fought with a ferocity and careless abandon that was stunningly remarkable. Without fear of dying, without regard for life, without caring for home, hearth or family, able-bodied men, feeble octogenarians, children of indeterminate age, and even women had pitched in to take on a fully equipped Soviet juggernaut. The peasants of Afghanistan had engaged in combat with an armed-to-the-teeth superpower.

And surprisingly, the peasants were winning.

The complex military maneuvers the pilot could see being orchestrated in the far distance as he patrolled the skies at Cap Station Alpha was but another gory episode in that Jihad. Down below, in the craggy, barren mountains, a group of lightly armed Muslim fighters were absorbing a devastating joint air-land assault by the Soviet armed forces. The small, square airborne radar screen was aglow with multiple targets at various ranges, different altitudes, and differing speeds. Those four blips down below, close to the ground, were night attack helicopters, orbiting the combat zone, probably attacking some "enemy" ground concentrations, whereas the six faster, higher targets had been conclusively identified as specialized ground attack aircraft in a surface attack pattern, dropping flares, lighting up the area for both the helicopters and themselves as they pounded the earth below. The four blips further back, patrolling at fifteen thousand feet, were obviously fighters, judging by their speed and other parameters that the pilot had analyzed. And the lone blip, well in the distance, lumbering ponderously across the sky in a defined orbit was almost certainly the command center, an airborne post from where this major ground assault, fully supported by air power, was being orchestrated. The other blips dotted across the screen were aircraft transiting back to base having done their bit, and soon another set of blips would be visible, indicating that fresh replacements were arriving. This was something quite unusual. Something big was happening down there.

The rules of engagement for the Pakistani pilots were amply clear. The nation had absolutely no intention of getting involved with the Soviet forces. Its leaders had not forgotten the U2 spy plane that had been shot down over the Soviet Union and the capture of its American pilot, Francis Gary Powers. That flight had originated from a Pakistani base in Peshawar, and the USSR had threatened to wipe Pakistan off the face of the earth. Pakistanis could not risk a repeat of that scary event. They knew that the Americans were being generous and friendly because it suited them. This had happened before, and, when the American's need had been met, when the job had been done, the shortsighted Pakistanis had been left to fend for themselves. Deluded, naïve, immature Pakistanis, acting suave and polished in international forums without any understanding of power politics, thinking that nice begat nice, that one good turn deserved another. Simpletons with no idea of what hardballing it with the big guys meant, had finally awakened to the harsh reality of life. They were learning to stand up, to think for themselves. They did not want the eagle to migrate to sunnier climes, leaving behind a wounded bear in their backyard. A pissed off bear who would then chew the Pakistani ass. It was the Afghans who were to fight the proxy war for the United States. Pakistan would be restricted to being the conduit, the staging post, the training ground, the interface.

Despite the American desire that the Pakistan Air Force use the F-16 more aggressively, despite a general desire by all concerned to prove the world's most agile fighter in battle, the Pakistanis had elected to remain cautious and had planned that the F-16s would only be operated within Pakistan and only for self-defense. Any fighting that took place could only happen in Pakistani airspace. Any aircraft to be shot down had to be engaged in such a manner that the wreckage would fall in Pakistan, thus ensuring that that the country could substantiate its claim of self-defense.

The pilot tensed. Afghan aircraft were now crossing the border. They were now violating Pakistani airspace. The hostile aircraft would head in, fly approximately ten miles into Pakistan, and then turn back for what appeared to be a bombing run. In fact, it now looked as if their bombing target was also inside Pakistan. This was something new because although the border was ill defined and it was impossible to tell where one country ended and the other started, both sides had very clearly demarcated lines that they did not cross. Both parties stayed well inside their own territory.

The F-16 was primed, fully ready for any eventuality. Its deadly gun, capable of firing six thousand rounds a minute, was armed. Under its wings it carried two standard Sidewinder missiles, the older version that was capable of homing on to the exhaust of an aircraft but only from the rear. If the enemy was facing the aircraft head on, these missiles were useless. To cater to this shortcoming, this particular F-16 also carried two Sidewinder Lima missiles, the latest addition to the Pakistani weapon inventory, flown into the country under utmost secrecy just a few days ago. These were deadly weapons, designed to engage aircraft with unerring accuracy from any angle, even head on. These new missiles were also primed and ready, their seekers cooled to optimum temperature, ready to start growling at the first sign of any hot metal in their field of view. The specialized seeker heads on the new missiles were able to detect the smallest of temperature changes, miles out in front. And they were growling now. The missile-seeker heads were seeing the aircraft attacking the Mujahedeen, inside Pakistani territory.

The pilot was delighted at the air situation that presented itself. He could finally engage violators of the Pakistani airspace in full conformity with the rules of engagement. He turned his aircraft around, planning his maneuver, going deeper into Pakistan before turning to face the threat once again. He then descended to a level lower than that of the target aircraft so that it was framed in stark contrast against the cold night sky. He thumbed his radar controls and locked the target on his radar. Shifting his vision to the heads-up display, he located the green square that indicated the target was somewhere in that box and uncaged the missile seeker. As the released detector swung instantly to the source of the heat it was seeing, it drove a digital diamond into the green box which started flashing urgently. At the same time, the unmistakable chirping sound of a missile locked on to a target rang clear over his headset. A quick recheck of all systems indicated "GO."

He fired the missile. The left wing of the aircraft lit up in an orange glow as the missile took off on its deadly mission. A flash of flame and then, as the rocket motor burnt out, everything was enveloped in inky blackness once again. The pilot waited expectantly and soon it came, the brilliant flash, a sign of the explosion of a missile finding its target. It was followed by the streaking shower of burning metal as the debris of the stricken plane plummeted earthward.

The F-16 turned and headed back to the CAP station. Once there, he checked the situation on his radar scope once again. The blips on the screen were now moving uniformly back into Afghanistan. There was however, one difference. There was one less blip.

He radioed Control. In predefined code he told the duty officer what the outcome was. Control decided that the F-16 was to be replaced by another, fully fueled machine to continue the vigil. The secure speech radio crackled and ground control sent out its instructions.

"Night Owl, this is Control. Pancake, Pancake, Pancake. Vector 080. Angels 50. Voice on Tango. Eyeballs Three. Exit using Departure Gate Romeo Zulu, Squawk two three on three." And then, a friendly and heartwarming "Congratulations, Sir. Have a nice flight back home."

The pilot ramped the throttle all the way to the forward stop, tilting the lever outward, and pushing it to the limit. The afterburner lit, its five stages cutting in sequentially, and as each stage lit up, the pilot was pushed further backward into the seat with an accompanying dull thud. Simultaneously, he rolled the aircraft over onto its back and pulled back on the rigid control column. The aircraft hurtled toward the ground at a rate that would have thrilled Sir Issac Newton. Nothing drops faster to the ground than an aircraft pointed downward with its engine in full afterburner. The engine screamed, the afterburner roared, the machine outpaced its own noise, it over took its own acoustic waves. Within seconds, the F-16 was racing ahead of its own sound.

Two muffled explosions, barely distinguishable apart, reverberated across the terrain below, thunderclaps of sound trapped and sound released. Had there been anyone down below in the impassable terrain, they would have heard the blasts as they ricocheted across the sides of the naked granite mountains before being lost in the desolate wilderness, echoing into oblivion. At the right moment, honed to perfection after countless such dizzying descents, an instant determined more by instinct than by referring to instruments or gauges, the pilot pulled back on the control column and the throttle lever, arriving at an amazingly accurate level-off altitude of 5,000 feet above the terrain on a heading of 080 degrees with the airspeed indicator settling down at cruising speed.

A Fighting Falcon was pointed home base at the assigned altitude at the desired speed.

Cap Station Alpha had been vacated. The pilot was going home, a kill under his belt!

26

The United States Air Force has its Red Flag, the United States Navy its Top Gun program. The British have their Central Trials and Tactics Unit. The Pakistan air force has its Combat Commanders School. Even the erstwhile Iraqi air force had the "Madressah Al Qital Al Javvi," a school for aerial combat. Air forces the world over have an institution where they carry out advanced training for air combat leaders. Not unnaturally, the Union of Soviet Socialist Republics had one too. The Yevgeni Pepelyaev Institute for Aerial Strategy and Aircraft Employment was named after the top-scoring Soviet ace from the 64th Fighter Aviation Corps, a group that had been sent secretly to assist the North during the Korean War. Soviet pilots flying stubby MiG-15s had shot down over 1300 aircraft of the United Nations during that war, while losing 345 of their own. The prestigious institute was staffed by the finest combat pilots of the Soviet Union and was dedicated to the development of aerial combat tactics.

Colonel Aleksandr Vladimirovich Rustovesky was rightly proud of his position as commanding officer of the institute. His name was the latest addition to a long list of outstanding combat commanders that was headed by none other than the legendary Ivan Kozhedub, the highly decorated hero with sixty-two German kills to his credit during the Second World War. Alex was also proud of the fact that command of the institute automatically accorded him the privilege of direct contact with the Kremlin, a fact amply depicted by the top secret letter that now lay on his desk. The Kremlin was concerned about the lack of results being shown by close air support squadrons in Afghanistan. This was because the Americans had introduced Stinger missiles into the theater, which had forced the Soviets to switch to attacking at night to negate the deadly missile. While they had managed to stop losing aircraft, they had also stopped being effective and, as a result, the ground offensive was bogged down. The colonel and his staff were to examine the problem and find a suitable solution. The institute was not found wanting. It came up with a complex pattern of night ground attack maneuvers based on multiple aircraft flying in a coordinated manner, using flares, target markers, and other navigation aids to ensure successful delivery of precision-guided munitions. As Colonel Aleksandr put the final touches to the plan, the professional fighter pilot in him suddenly surfaced. He realized that he could use this situation to his advantage; he could get back in the cockpit and fly operationally in the Afghan theater. He therefore closed his remarks by stating that he would personally fly into Afghanistan and train the first set of crews in this new attack tactic himself. His recommendations were accepted in full.

The reception at the Bagram Air Base was as deferential as expected. The reasons were plenty. Eager students were receiving an instructor, the field staff was being honored by a visit from headquarters, a party member was arriving amid the proletariat, an aristocrat was mingling with the plebeians. But above all, a highly respected air warrior was arriving among those eager to emulate him. He ordered the base commander to arrange a briefing at twenty hundred hours and have all aircraft readied for a night mission. He was going to sleep and was to be awakened at six o'clock sharp.

The briefing took place as planned. The aircraft were ready as ordered. The formation taxied out into the pitch-dark Afghan night, took off, and headed east, where the ground battle was raging. After all the aircraft were airborne, the colonel deployed them in accordance with the briefed pattern. With a confidence born out of knowledge and experience, Colonel Aleksandr talked freely on the radio, ordering, instructing, briefing, guiding, adjusting; a chess master was setting up his board for an intricate game. Arriving in the combat zone, he established the bombing pattern and, as the leader, he was the first aircraft to roll into the attack pattern. The sky lit up as the huge flares wafted down on their parachutes, illuminating the area, transforming night into day, enabling him to see the targets and refine his aim. The bombs impacted the Mujahedeen positions with tremendous accuracy.

Airborne Command and Control was ecstatic. The operations officer congratulated the pilot, showering praise both because it was due and also because they were fully aware of the colonel's status, ass-kissing being a universal article of faith. The second aircraft followed, the third, the fourth, the first again.

Everything was going according to plan; the bombs were slaughtering the enemy. The colonel decided to take on a second, slightly more distant, enemy position, and the entire formation positioned accordingly. Once again, the colonel led the formation into the new attack. As he saw the bombs impact the targets with enviable precision, he smiled.

The radar warning receiver on Aleksandr's aircraft chirped. It was signaling that somewhere out there, in the black sky ahead, a hostile radar was tracking his aircraft. He examined the indicator and, sure enough, just as he had expected, there it was, the definite signature of the APG-66 radar, carried on board the F-16. His smile broadened as he recognized the agony that must be going through the mind of the pilot flying the F-16. There was nothing that he could do. His aircraft carried the impotent Sidewinder missiles that could only engage receding targets. The Pakistanis were flying potent platforms with impotent weapons. The Americans were not stupid; superpowers never were. Just as the Soviets had distributed toothless weaponry throughout the world, so too had the Americans. They had given this third world country their latest fighter platform but without any decent weapons. Yet, it did not hurt to be cautious. Alex flipped the transmit button and instructed all members in the formation to pump flares on their way out to neutralize any missile the Paki aircraft may be planning to launch.

He had no way of knowing that the F-16 had already launched a missile and that the all aspect weapon was well on its way. He had barely completed his transmission when a blinding flash engulfed his aircraft and a fierce explosion blew his aircraft apart. Alex's cockpit erupted, lights began flashing, a strident alarm bell started clanging loudly, and the aircraft tumbled out of control, pitching and yawing wildly. In less than a second, the Soviet fighter pilot not only assessed, analyzed, and understood the situation but also came up with the remedial course of action. Alex reached up and tugged firmly at the handles located above his head. After what seemed an eternity he was explosively ejected out of the plummeting remains of what was, moments ago, a highly capable ground-attack aircraft. An individual who had, two seconds earlier, been sitting comfortably in a cockpit of a modern fighter bomber aircraft found himself tumbling uncontrollably in a cold, black, empty sky.

His mind worked frantically. He had no way of knowing what lay below him, whether he was going to land in a valley or on a mountain peak. Not knowing this, he pulled the ripcord immediately, because he realized that if he were headed for a peak, he would hit the mountain before the automatic parachute opening mechanism would work. As the parachute blossomed, jerking him with a violence that shook him to the very core, he assumed the landing posture, knees together, slightly bent, ankles together, feet angled correctly, forearms crossed across his face protecting it, hands gripping the parachute risers firmly, ready to hit the quick release mechanism. He did so because he had no idea whether his landing would take place in the next minute or ten. Alex would wait, crouched in the landing position, for an interminably long time, because he was falling into a valley, a remote, desolate valley in the foothills of the Himalayas, in the lawless, undefined territory that was the North-West Frontier Province of Pakistan.

Although he had been anticipating it all along, when it eventually came, the landing was surprisingly hard and sudden. There was no warning for him to go through the shock-absorbing maneuver he had rehearsed repeatedly during training. He hit the ground squarely, the shock traveling up his body, jarring his every bone, taking his breath away. The parachute collapsed around him, engulfing him. Even as he winced in pain, his trained mind recognized that he was very lucky, because there was no wind to drag him across the ground. He was also not sliding down any steep slope. He appeared to have landed on flat ground, and as he lay there, absolutely still, recovering his breath, he went over the facts in his mind, meticulously repeating each perception. No wind. Good. No slope; most likely level ground. Good. Deathly silence. That was good too. It meant that he was most probably away from any habitation and that, in turn, meant that his arrival would have gone unnoticed. He wiggled his fingers and toes and then moved his arms and legs and finally swiveled his head from side to side. No pain, no fractures. Excellent. Yet he lay still and unmoving on the cold earth. He remembered what had been drummed into his head during training. If one was unable to see where one was headed, one was not supposed to move. He knew that he had to stay put until he could be sure that it was safe to move.

He pulled at the parachute canopy, sliding it over himself, aiming to reach its edge so that he could emerge from the shroud. This done, he gathered the cloth canopy and bundled it into a ball. Even when freed from the parachute, he could see nothing, it was a pitch dark, moonless night. Lying prone on the ground, he started pulling the cord that was attached to his harness aiming to reel in the survival pack that was attached to the other end. He placed the pack and parachute close to his body, knowing that he would need both for the coming run to safety.

He could not, would not, move. He remained supine on the cold ground. He knew that inside the pack there were matches; he also carried a flashlight in one of the many pockets of his flight suit. But he could not risk using either one of them. He glanced at his watch, big luminous hands pointing to big luminous digits. Sunrise was still a long way away. Staying spread-eagled on the ground, he started feeling the space around him. He was lying in what appeared to be soft dirt. Off on to his right side, close to his right leg, there appeared to be a boulder. On his left, dirt. Ahead, more dirt. He pivoted his body, now facing the boulder he could not see, and ran his hands along the stone. It appeared to be large. He tried to feel around it, above it, checking its dimensions. He rolled over on his back and looked up at the starry sky. He located the Big Dipper, the Belt of Orion, the North Star. Alex spent the next hour listening, crawling, examining, evaluating, calculating times, distances, searching through his memory, remembering topography, geography, astronomy.

Aleksandr determined that he was between five and fifteen kilometers from the border between Pakistan and Afghanistan. The long descent indicated that he had landed in a valley. He hoped that he was not on the wrong side of the eleven thousand-foot high ridge that he knew ran parallel to the border. Dawn would tell. He now knew where north was. Knowing that, he knew the direction to head for safety. He raked the soft earth with his bare hands, drawing a crude compass. The position indicated by the stars would be crosschecked with the sun when it rose.

Aleksandr also determined that the area extending in a rough circle of about four meters around him was relatively flat. The northern side had a large rock that he could not reach the top of, even if he stood up. Adjacent to the large rock was another, smaller rock that had some prickly shrubs on the far side. The spikes of the shrub were very sharp and of a stinging variety. Between the two rocks there was enough space for him to crawl into. Aleksandr squeezed himself between the two rocks and burrowed back as far as he could. He took a mental inventory of the survival aids he carried in his pocket and the kit that came with the parachute. He had already decided not to use the matches, the emergency radio, or any of the other items until he could see where he was and what the surroundings were. He pulled the parachute around him to keep himself warm and began the long wait for dawn.

All actions taken, his body relaxed, and his mind gave up its focus. He now had time for his first emotion. As his body broke out into an involuntary shiver, Alex realized that it was not the cold that caused that response; it was fear. He was in hostile territory. Fear was good. It would ensure survival. Squatting in the crevice, bent double, his knees gathered together in his tired arms, he rested his forehead on them and started rocking gently. A, bruised, battered and tired body relaxed. A drained mind soon drifted off into sleep.

Alex awoke to the pitter patter of falling rain. The soothing, whispering sound of nature as it poured forth its fluid onto a parched earth. His mind struggled into wakefulness as he looked up and saw the sky, the stars now gone, the bright glow of day having replaced the inky darkness. Wedged between the rocks, he could see the bright sky and the twin moons that hung suspended above him against the velvety blue background, so close that he could almost touch them if he stretched out his hand fully.

The hissing sound of falling rain, twin suspended moons, warm fluid trickling down his face—a perplexed mind reluctantly awaken from sound slumber desperately sought solution to the puzzling inputs.

The twin moons rapidly resolved themselves into a large, milky white, fleshy bottom; the rain, into a golden stream pouring forth from a shaven, hairless vagina. His brain was still trying to assimilate this information when the eyes sent in another urgent message. The eyes were telling the brain of a round, distended orifice located in the immediate vicinity of the source of the golden stream. Emerging from this orifice was a sizeable projectile, brown in size, smooth in texture, offensive in smell. It was headed directly for his face. Aleksandr's brain promptly deciphered the information it had received.

A woman was crapping on his face.

Instinct overcame intellect.

Aleksandr screamed.

For the rest of his life, Aleksandr would rue this scream. He would recall how very fortunate he had been to have landed in a really isolated spot. The female's choice of location to relieve herself was adequate proof of the remoteness and the privacy of his hiding place. He would chastise himself, curse his luck. If only he had kept quiet. If only he had stayed put, if only he had moved his head to one side, if only he had let the Pathan female complete her toilette in the barren countryside. If only he could have been awake when it happened. He would have been prepared. She would have departed, and then he would have emerged from his hiding place. He would have found that he was just one kilometer from the border. A brisk walk would have had him back among friends in less than an hour. If only his mind had not been numbed by sleep; if only he had some warning. If only he had been a bit more patient, Alex could have turned this adversity into a privilege. A truly memorable incident. Not everyone gets a chance to be inside a toilet bowl, looking up.

But he hadn't. He had screamed and scampered out of the way, out into open ground.

As screams go, it was a whopper. And it had the desired effect. The golden rain stopped immediately. The projectile retracted, the distended orifice puckered up. Unfortunately, there were some other undesirable effects. His scream triggered another, far louder, higher pitched shriek. The naked backside tumbled off its precarious perch, landing on top of Aleksandr as he darted out of his hiding place. They tumbled together, rolling off the small plateau, down the sloping ground. A Pathan peasant girl, her torso and face covered by a burqa, absolutely naked from the waist downward and a Soviet colonel, still enveloped in the parachute he had drawn around himself. As they rolled downhill, the cords of the parachute entangled the two writhing bodies into one inextricable package, one screaming, the other swearing.

The tangled mess, man, woman, burqa, parachute, survival pack, risers, and cords finally came to rest at the bottom of the slope, inseparably wedded, unable to move. By this time, Aleksandr's face was firmly wedged between the gloriously naked thighs of the demented female who continued shrieking her head off. The colonel's face was buried in a warm, wet Afghan vagina and, as he struggled to breathe, the Afghan female finally stopped screaming. She started breathing unevenly and the more the colonel tried to dislodge his face, the more labored her breathing became.

Yusufene Khan jerked his head up at the first cry. He saw her sister tumbling down from the hillock she had climbed to answer the call of nature. He immediately recognized the danger and guessed that she had been attacked by some animal or stung by a scorpion or bitten by a snake. He picked up his AK-47 and ran toward the unfortunate sister. Others too had seen and heard. They too followed. A mother, a father, children, dogs; the entire caravan headed for the girl. No one was quite prepared for what they saw. Bare flesh of a virgin female. A semi naked girl entwined with a man. A foreigner. A complete stranger with his face buried in an Afghan woman's crotch.

Yusufene Khan had never seen a naked woman in broad daylight before. That the naked woman was his sister was beyond belief. It was the ultimate humiliation, a shame, a family disgrace. What was worse and utterly disgusting was that she had a man between her legs. He reached for his knife and cut the ropes that entangled them. The girl scampered free, her burqa dropping down, finally covering her exposed body, restoring her modesty. Completely hidden to the world once again, she cowered to one side. The man, freed from his parachute, tried to stand. Yusufene kicked the man viciously in the stomach and as the man crumpled to the ground, he followed it with another kick in the groin that had Alex writhing on the ground, bent double, an agonized whimper escaping his gritted teeth. Yusufene grabbed the foreigner's shock of hair, pulled his head back and positioned the knife to slit the exposed throat. By now the father had reached the scene along with the other elders. He grabbed hold of his son's forearm and told him to back off.

Yusufene Khan flared up. The man was a stranger, a foreigner, a "farangee." He had brought shame and dishonor to the family. He would have to die. So to his sister who had also exposed herself publicly. She would be next to be killed. The father was annoyed. "Don't be an idiot," he chided the son. "Don't rush it. Let us find out who this vile man is. What is he doing here?" The girl was dispatched to the tent in the distance with the other females. Aleksandr was stripped completely. Yusufene Khan gathered together the belongings of the naked person. He folded the parachute canopy into a manageable size and placed the collection within it, everything except the watch, which he slid into his pocket. He secured the bundle tightly with the parachute cords. The same cords were used to secure Aleksandr's legs and hands. Bound hand and foot, stark naked, he lay on the dirt and the Pathans squatted around him. They talked.

Aleksandr could not understand a word of what they were saying, but he could easily interpret the tones. Angry, placating, objecting, arguing, soothing, pleading, grieved, vicious. At one stage, one big, burly Pathan stood up, seized him roughly, turned him around, spread his buttocks, inspected his posterior and then displayed him thus to the seated audience. Guffaws and lecherous laughter followed. Even Yusufene joined in. For over an hour they debated, discussed, and argued. Finally the old man stood up. He approached Aleksandr as he lay helpless on the cold ground. He stood over him, forced his legs apart and with the barrel of his AK-47, he prodded his manhood, poking his genitals with the cold metal while lecturing to the crowd. They closed in, looked at the limp appendage, nodding their heads, muttering to themselves. "This is it," Aleksandr thought. "This is where they chop my manhood off and stuff it in my mouth, sew it up, and let me die." He had heard that the Arabs did that to their captives. Maybe the Pathans did the same.

Someone produced the Pathan dress, the baggy trouser, "shalwar" and the long, flowing shirt, the "kameez." He was untied, dressed up, and then bound again. They put him atop a camel, slung across the hump like a sack of flour. Aleksandr was going on a trip.

Little did he know that he had just been saved by something his mother did forty odd years ago. Much against the wishes of a father who did not believe in any god, the Jewish mother had prevailed. She had insisted that the son born to her be circumcised. Aleksandr was saved by his foreskin. Rather, by the lack of one.

The tribal custom of the Pathans dictated that a fellow Muslim had to be tried by the Jirga, the council of elders. The old man had pointed out to the rest of the crowd that the captive was circumcised. He was obviously a Muslim, and being a Muslim, he could not be executed here in the wilderness. They would have to take him back to the village where he would be tried and sentenced. He had also cautioned the burly man who had inspected Aleksandr's posterior that he would have to wait until that time before he could sodomize the captive. The expectant Pathan was annoyed. So too was Yusufene Khan. He would now have to wait to redeem his sister's honor. The father too was annoyed. He was upset that the caravan would now have to go back to Pakistan. They had just been a few hours away from their destination, a secret meeting place where the foreigners, the "Roussies" were waiting to sell them vodka, guns, knives, pornography, and other stuff they would smuggle back to be sold in the thriving black market bazaars of Peshawar. They had almost reached their meeting place with the Russians and now, because of this Muslim, they would have to go back. Reluctantly, the caravan turned around.

As it turned out, they did not have to go back all the way to the village. Soon, the big metal birds came. They circled low over the group, scanning the small caravan from above. The men sitting inside the metal birds waved to the tribesmen down below. All waved back except one, because he was strung across a camel, bound hand and foot. The helicopters landed, and the men who had been waving disembarked from the machines. They talked to the leader, took over the prisoner from the Pathans, and flew off. The old man was relieved, because they could now resume their journey toward Afghanistan as originally intended. Life could go back to normal. Everyone could be happy again. All except the big burly Pathan. He had been looking forward to enjoying the virgin sphincter of the foreigner. Instead, he would have to make do with his usual consort. Reluctantly, he turned his lecherous gaze toward Yusufene Khan. Their eyes exchanged unspoken messages.

"Tonight." Big burly Pathan.

"Not tonight." Yusufene.

27

Aleksandr strained his ears and could just barely make out one side of the dialog between the pilot and his controlling agency. The pilot was informing Control that they had recovered the downed Afghan pilot and needed instructions on how to proceed. Despite his discomfort, he could not help being amused by the fact that the Pakistanis did not know that they had a Soviet Colonel in their hands and thought that they had captured an Afghan air force officer. As the pilot read back the instructions received, Alex learned that he would be taken to a forward-operating airfield, where a C-130 cargo aircraft would be positioned to receive him. He was relieved to be in the hands of the Pakistan army. He knew that they would treat him properly; they had to. The barbaric tribesmen were not bound by any obligations, any law or any treaty; Pakistan was.

The aircraft was there as briefed, ready for takeoff, ramp open, engines running. The helicopter landed, the captive was bundled rapidly from the helicopter into the C-130, and even before the occupants had time to settle down, the aircraft was racing down the runway, its ramp closing after the aircraft had become airborne. Staying low, following combat-evasion tactics, the C-130 headed toward Islamabad at maximum permissible speed. Overhead, patrolling fighters provided air cover in case the Afghans decided to kill their pilot before the Pakistanis forced him to talk and divulge military secrets while inside the aircraft, Inter Services Intelligence personnel gagged and hooded Alex and conducted a thorough body search on the bound individual.

Blindfolded, deprived of sight, Aleksandr's other senses were working frantically to analyze the situation. Landing, stopping. No, taxiing. Obviously staying on the runway. The whine of a powerful motor, a rush of fresh air. An aircraft ramp opening. Rough hands dragged him out, forcing him into a vehicle. Head forced down. Doors slammed shut. Approximately eighteen minutes driving time to somewhere. Screeching brakes. Barked commands. Electrical solenoids popping metallic bolts. Doors opening. Metal hinges rasping. Solid steel doors slamming shut. And now, all sounds echoing hollowly. Metal studded boots striking bare stone. Cold, long corridors. One hundred and two paces and then a turn to the right. Another thirty paces, a turn to the left. Stop. Whining motors. More, excited voices joining the group. Electrical doors closing. Descent. Forty-three seconds. Exit. Eighty-four steps. Cold. Stale air. A door opening reluctantly, raspingly.

Hands uncuffed. Door slamming shut. Receding footsteps. Silence. Utter silence. Very cold.

Aleksandr rubbed his hands together, massaging the wrists where the handcuffs had dug into his flesh. It took him a while to realize that he could remove his blindfold. He did. It did not help much. Everything stayed pitch dark.

The bundled parachute, tied in complex tribal knots, lay on the table of the major from the ISI. The dreaded Inter Services Intelligence, referred by many as the government within the government of Pakistan. Intended originally to provide strategic intelligence for military purposes, the organization had taken on a role and task well beyond that of intelligence gathering. It created intelligence. It manipulated events. It decided on how the State of Pakistan was to be ruled, by whom, and for how long. It decided on all affairs, internal and external, how the citizens were to be managed and how Pakistan's neighbors were to be handled. It was the organization that was the intermediary for the American war of proxy against the Soviet Union. The Americans interfaced with the ISI, the ISI organized and controlled the Mujahedeen, the Mujahedeen fought the Russians. The Americans channeled huge amounts of weapons and money through the ISI for the Mujahedeen effort, the ISI kept a portion, the Pakistan army kept another and the remainder went to the fighters. The Americans were fully aware of this siphoning but were not perturbed as they already had plans to remedy this. At a later stage they would take care of the illegal stockpile that the Pakistanis had built up in a place called Ojheri Camp. The cache would go up in a deadly display of fireworks. One fine morning the residents of the twin cities of Islamabad and Rawalpindi would be sent scurrying for cover. As missiles and bombs exploded across the landscape, the entire airspace would be shut down, all surface traffic would come to a halt. The earth would glow red hot for almost one week after the massive warehouses that housed the illegal stockpile were torched.

As the major unraveled the package and its contents came into view, his eyes lit up. As he examined each article more carefully, his heartbeat picked up pace. When he opened the wallet and saw the identity card inside, he jumped up and dashed for the door. Identity card in hand, he barged into the brigadier's office and excitedly informed the brigadier of the contents of the bundle. The brigadier did what the major had done. His dash took him to the general's office, where he told the portly figure seated behind the massive desk of what he had found. As the boss of the most powerful organization of the country, the general had no need to jump or run. He picked up the handset of the hotline and the president came on the line instantly. The general informed the president that he would come to meet him and therefore the president should remain available. He then turned to the brigadier and let forth a volley of abuse. He told the brigadier that he had been very foolish to handle the situation the way he had done and then issued instructions on how he wanted things done henceforth.

The brigadier scurried back to his office, where the major was waiting patiently, and unleashed a tirade at the major. How could the major have been so thoughtless to have the Russian in such a location? Did the major not know the significance of this? Did he want to put Pakistan squarely in the crosshairs of the Soviet war machine? The brigadier then informed his subordinate that he had briefed the general on how he was going to handle the situation and the general had agreed to his plan. He then proceeded to pass on the instructions he had received from his boss.

Aleksandr had by now determined that he was in a stone room. Stone walls, stone floor, a stony ceiling. Standing erect, he could touch the ceiling easily. There was nothing on the floor except a hole in the corner — somewhere he could squat and relieve himself. The door was cold metal. There was a two-inch gap both above and below the sheet metal. Surprisingly, the place appeared clean. It had a powerful smell of disinfectant.

Hurried footsteps echoed down the corridor. A key turned and the metal door was kicked open viciously with a force that would have crippled the occupant inside had he been within its swinging arc. Aleksandr was grabbed by the two muscular, mustached men, handcuffed, blindfolded, and dragged out. Flanked on both sides, each arm firmly gripped, he was hauled across the stone corridor once again. Eighty-four steps. The whine of the lift. Aleksandr remembered, counted, and waited. Sure enough, it took forty-three seconds for the lift to stop. Right turn. Thirty paces. Turn to the left. He was going back the way he had come. He anticipated the sounds of solenoids popping, a steel door opening, the metal hinges rasping, the door closing, the barked commands. He anticipated the clean fresh air, the smell of freshly mown grass assailing his nostrils even as he was forced into a car and flanked by his two escorts. This time the vehicle stopped after approximately one hour and thirty minutes of fast driving. They disembarked, Aleksandr's hands were uncuffed and the blindfold removed.

Aleksandr found himself standing in the driveway of a beautiful colonial mansion built of solid stone, complete with a massive porch covering the circular drive that enclosed a perfectly manicured garden with rose bushes in full bloom. He could also see the many individuals who dotted the landscape, standing at a distance, some with automatic weapons, others with sidearms, watching stonily. He saw a short-statured, smartly dressed man coming down the stairs, hand extended, who addressed Aleksandr in impeccable Russian, "Welcome, welcome, welcome. Colonel Aleksandr Vladimirovich Rustovesky. Welcome to Pakistan."

They went inside, into the beautiful villa with the checkered, tiled corridors, the ornate chandeliers, the gleaming, paneled walls adorned with hunting trophies, guns, and portraits of distinguished-looking military men. They walked past an imposing lounge within which Alex could see a well-stocked bar running the length of the far wall. They turned the corner and entered an elegantly furnished suite. They walked across the large sitting room, which lead to an even larger bedroom with a magnificent double bed on which were laid out a set of fresh clothes, a crisp, laundered local dress, the " shalwar-kameez." The Russian-speaking Pakistani, who was scurrying along, talking incessantly, was obviously very keen to please the visitor. He told Aleksandr that he was assigned to the respected colonel as his escorting officer and interpreter. The colonel was a guest of the Pakistan government and if there was anything he needed, he just had to ask. He was to stay in this guest house until the authorities were able to figure out how to return him to the Soviet Union. "If the colonel could have a bath, freshen up, change, and then join us for dinner. That would be nice. And, oh dear, oh yes. You can call me 'M. C.' All my friends do." The colonel nodded vaguely. In the short time he had known his interpreter, he had come to the conclusion that this was one individual he did not like.

The Russian had been through an unbelievable twenty-four hours. He had ejected over hostile territory. He had been pissed on, crapped on. He had been stripped, gagged, bound, prodded, probed and violated in almost the worst manner possible. He had been dragged, kicked, punched, and beaten. He had been strapped on the back of a camel, pushed into aircraft, shoved into vehicles, thrown into a cold, black stone prison cell, deprived of his dignity, his honor. He had been kept hungry and thirsty. Despite this, despite all these harrowing experiences, Aleksandr had not lost his ability to judge men. In just a few minutes he had assessed the detestable personality of M. C. He could not have however known that, while his friends did call him M.C., so did his enemies. So indeed, did everybody. Everyone delighted in calling him M. C., because the letters stood for "Madar Chhoud," Urdu for Motherfucker. Only two people called him M. C. because they were the initials for his name, Mian Choudhry. His wife and son also called him M. C. They were not the two.

Aleksandr ran the bath and, as the water gurgled into the tub, he showered briskly, lathered himself generously, aiming to wash out the Afghan female from his body and remove the deposit left by the soiled hands of his Afghan captors. He wanted to sanitize his body, erase the smell of the foul camel, and purify himself once again. Cleansed by the shower, he stepped into the warm bath, slid into the welcoming water, and closed his eyes. He would have loved to drift off into sleep, but this was no time for relaxing. His tired body would have to wait. His mind would have to remain fully active. He had to think, assess, evaluate, and plan. He went over the events of the last few hours.

He had already figured out that the C-130 had landed in Islamabad, and he had been incarcerated in a prison somewhere in that city. After being removed from the stone cell, he had been driven for about one hour and thirty minutes. His new location therefore had to be within a radius of about one hundred kilometers around Islamabad. When he had arrived at this new location, he had seen the tall mountains quite clearly, up close. This meant that he had traveled north of Islamabad. He climbed out of the bath, drying himself with the soft fluffy towels as he walked up to the window from where he had a clear view of the huge, unbelievably wide river that meandered in the distance. There was nothing between him and the river. No walls, no barriers, no locked gates, no barbed wire. Had he wanted to, he could climb out of the window and take off for the distant river and then on to freedom.

Aleksandr did not follow this course of action for two reasons. First, because he was a colonel in the Soviet air force and he knew that the Pakistanis would not harm him. More important, however, Aleksandr did not run because he knew his geography. He realized that the hilltop villa provided him an unobstructed view of the mighty Indus River, the mighty sparkling, blue waterway that snaked across Pakistan, bringing crystal-clear water from the icy glaciers of the Himalayas to the thirsty plains. As he strained his eyes, he could make out the other torrent merging into the huge blue-water stream. Alex had spotted the Kabul River, a fast-flowing muddy river, rising in the

273

Sanglakh range west of Kabul city, flowing through Afghanistan, into Pakistan, past Peshawar eventually to fall into the Indus. This was the waterway his namesake, Alexander the Great, had used to invade India in the fourth century B.C., and now, many hundred years later, another Aleksandr was standing at this majestic confluence of two historic rivers. Alex could now put a name to his location. He knew that the meeting point of the two grand rivers was named Attock. And if he was viewing Attock, then his vantage point, the hillock overlooking the confluence could only be the Attock Fort.

A cold chill ran through Alex's body. He sank into the nearby chair. He was in the dreaded Attock Fort. No bars were needed, because no one dared escape from this place. No barbed wire fences were needed because the fort was ringed beyond visual range by an insurmountable stone wall, thirty-five feet high and eighteen feet across. Originally a massive mud and stone wall but now reinforced with steel and concrete, it had a moat on the inside; a deep man-made swamp flooded with stagnant water and infested with alligators. There was another ringed area between the wall and the moat and this was enclosed in a steel fence in which roamed the dogs. Pit bulls, Dobermanns, Alsatians and some other cross breeds defying definition that had been created in the imaginative kennels of the Army School of Veterinary Medicine. The animals were fed distantly from high above. From the crest of the wall were tossed down chunks of raw meat of indeterminate origins. The

274

animals made crematoriums and graveyards unnecessary. They were cheap and reliable; they were even preferred over the minefields that dotted the area.

There was only one way out of the fort, and that was through the front door. One could walk out of the front door, but that was a privilege almost exclusively reserved for the hosts. The guests at Attock Fort normally exited to the next world. Indeed, they sought exit to the next world impatiently as it was vastly preferable to staying alive inside.

Despite what Aleksandr had been through since his ejection, never once had he felt really scared. Now, in the luxurious suite, shaven, bathed, clothed in crispy clean garments, he was petrified. He was in Attock Fort. The model facility that the staff at the yellow-bricked Lubyanka Prison was constantly motivated to emulate. He was in the dreaded fort that was respected worldwide for its efficiency, its results.

Aleksandr had not eaten for over twenty-four hours when M. C. came to escort him to dinner. They walked to the dining room together, their footsteps tapping across the polished wooden floor, the escort once again trying desperately to ingratiate himself with the visitor. Two other men were already seated at the table when they entered. Both stood up in unison and greeted him. "Salam alaikum." He nodded, preferring not to make the customary "Walaikum Salam" response, which he knew well.

"Obviously ISI personnel; obviously there on business," said Alex to himself. There was no point in any introductions as they sat down at the elegantly laid table. Pure china, sterling silver. Liveried servants served the soup, which was deliciously tangy, full of spicy aroma. M. C. enthusiastically explained the ingredients of the soup. It was originally a South Indian dish called "Mooloo Ka Tunni," which meant "Water of the Tamarind," but this had been corrupted by the English rulers of the subcontinent to its present form of "Mulligatawny." It was an intricate concoction based on the sour fruit of the tamarind tree and included hot peppers, spices, lentils, and boiled rice. Aleksandr savored the tangy flavor, the spicy taste. One of the ISI goons said something in Urdu. Everyone laughed. Seeing the quizzical look on Alex's face, M. C. explained.

"If you are ever in India, don't eat the soup." As Aleksandr raised his eyebrows, M. C. continued, "They put other things in it."

"What other things?"

"You don't want to know," M. C. said with a giggle. Aleksandr shrugged his shoulders and continued. It was wonderfully rich in taste. Hot to the tongue, it made him feel warm and flushed. He desperately wanted to take his mind off the problem he was facing; his being at the Attock Fort, dining with the ISI. This was a deadly situation, something was terribly amiss. If he could drown his thoughts in the spicy food and the flowing wine, he would be considerably relieved.

The spicy meatballs served on a saffron-colored bed of aromatic rice that followed had an even richer taste. And the grilled liver of lamb, wrapped in strips of animal fat, served on a skewer. He was now enjoying the amazing flavors, his mouth was aflame with taste; the food was wonderfully delicious. This was his first authentic oriental meal and he decided to enjoy it fully and take his mind off his uncomfortable situation. The powerful aroma, the exotic spices, the hot pepper sauces had him flushed, but this heat was easily washed away with the vintage wines the waiters served. Despite being located in a nation that had strict prohibition, the fort seemed to be doing all right for itself as far as its wine list was concerned.

As they ate, they talked. Aleksandr knew the routine, he knew what to expect and had already decided to answer most questions as truthfully as possible without giving away any critical information. The guys doing the talking were not idiots. He knew that. And he knew that they knew that he wasn't one either. The questions had been routine, even boring. When did he come to Afghanistan? How long had he been doing this? Was it difficult? What were the targets they were attacking? Why was such a senior person flying? And the small talk. How did he like the dress? Had he known any Pakistanis earlier? What did he think of the place? How did it feel to be stuck between the thighs of a Pathan woman? How was the camel ride? Aleksandr found himself enjoying the meal, the excellent wine, the hot, spicy food, the easygoing conversation. Not a bad way to end what had been a disastrous day, he thought to himself as the alcohol relaxed his mind and body.

Meal over, the hosts asked if he was ready to retire. Aleksandr nodded, and M. C. escorted him back to his suite. He hung around asking if there was anything the colonel wanted, anything at all. Aleksandr declined, and a reluctant M. C. departed. Aleksandr headed for the bedroom, pulled back the covers and slid into the cool, luxurious bed. He could not find comfort because of the shalwar-kameez; the dress hampered his movement; it bothered him. He wondered why the Afghans, the Pakistanis, the Pathans all seemed to love it. They wore it for all occasions, formal events, informal ones, for going to town, for staying home. Males and females, both wore the same basic style. For them it was the only dress, good when awake and good for sleeping. Not for him, he decided. The long dress was too restrictive, he removed it and drifted off to sleep.

28

It had to be a nightmare, a horrible dream that would go away as soon as he opened his eyes. He forced his eyes open, but it did not go away. This was no nightmare, the pain was real. Aleksandr's brain reeled into wakefulness as an indescribable pain flooded his senses. A pain, the likes of which he had never experienced before. It was an unbelievable agony; it was mind numbing and he was unable to focus his thoughts or his eyes. He had a vague recollection of being grabbed roughly by his arms and then being dragged down a long corridor. He remembered being forced into the hard chair. Through watery eyes he tried to focus on the surroundings. The bare stone floor, the stark, solitary, incandescent lamp hanging overhead, swinging lazily, bathing him and his surroundings in a cold, harsh glow. He was completely naked, seated in the only chair in the room. Against the wall, he could make out the two shadows. He squinted, trying to make out their faces, trying to confirm if they were the same two who had been seated at the table, the ones with whom he had shared a meal. The third person he recognized instantly. M. C. was standing right next to him, pushing his head back, questioning him; asking him.

"Talk, Colonel. Talk to me? Tell me. Tell me. Colonel, can you hear me? Colonel, Colonel Aleksandr, tell me, tell me, what is it?" M. C., his voice urgent, anxious, insistent.

One of the two shadows said something to M. C.

M. C. grabbed Aleksandr's face in both hands, pushed it up, staring him in the eyes. "Colonel Aleksandr. I know that you can hear me, Alex. Talk to me. You have to talk to me. Answer me."

Aleksandr tried to focus, he tried to force his mouth open to speak but no words came forth. His tortured body was aflame with pain. He had difficulty keeping his eyes open. All he could feel was the penetrating pain that invaded deep into his body. His nakedness was now covered in sweat, his face was flushed, his heart was pounding wildly. He could not believe that there could ever be so much pain. He gritted his teeth and clenched his hands, grabbing his bare thighs, sharp nails digging into soft flesh, tearing it. Blood oozed from the torn skin.

He willed his mind to restrain him, to discipline him. He forced his mind to focus. Slowly, very slowly, the pain ebbed. Aleksandr lifted his head, saw the two shadows watching him stonily. Yes, they were the same two he had had dinner with. He tried to straighten his back and sit up. Through clenched teeth, he began. "I am Colonel Aleksandr Vladimirovich Rustovesky of the Soviet air force. I demand . . ."The sentence trailed off unfinished as once again the crashing pain ripped through his body, tearing into his very guts. A pain so devastating that his torso slumped forward, his head was thrown against his knees, his tortured body sagged, sweat now flowing profusely from his brow. His jaw dropped open, a trickle of saliva dripping forth.

He did not know how long he remained thus. He seemed to be drifting in and out of consciousness. As he came to, he thought he saw the man nod once again. And once again, he felt as if someone had stabbed him with a red hot poker right through his body. Once again the pain flooded back. Sharp, indescribably sharp pain radiating into every corner of his body, ripping his innards, his mind, his brain. A long, drawn-out moan escaped his lips. He was now jerking uncontrollably; sweat was pouring out of his body. Alex was naked, bent double, blood oozing from where his nails had ripped through the skin. He slid forward off his cold perch and slumped to the floor.

They hauled him up. One of the shadows spoke. "Come on, Colonel Aleksandr. Get a grip on yourself. Don't tell me that the Russians can't take a bit of pain." The other laughed. They picked him up from the floor and forced him back into the seat. Another burst. Another searing burst of gut-rending pain shot through his body. Alex now had difficulty controlling his facial muscles. There was an evil, bitter taste in his mouth, a nauseating smell assailing his nostrils. There was nothing else he could feel, nothing he could see, hear, or smell. Just a huge sea of pain in which his helpless body was floating, being buffeted and racked by powerful waves. If only he could die, if only he could be put out of his misery. If only they would shoot him. He tried closing his mouth, gritting his teeth. He bit his tongue. He tasted blood.

Another devastating shock of pain surged through his now-limp body. His eyes lost their focus completely. The room darkened. Mercifully, Aleksandr fainted. When he came to, M. C. was slapping him and sprinkling cold water on his face. He was still in the cold seat, still naked, bent double, the two shadows still hovering in the background. There was now a third person, a white-coated, bespectacled man. He was holding something sleek and shiny in his hand. Aleksandr fought to gain control of his body. His mind was working erratically as he tried to focus his eyes. "Please help me. Please. No more pain. Just stop the pain, please stop the pain," Aleksandr whimpered. The interpreter strained his ears to pick up the whispers of the Russian colonel. He tried to understand the language the colonel was speaking in failed. M. C. had qualified as an expert in Russian. Not gibberish.

M. C. cradled the man's head in his palms, consoling him, soothing him, telling him to give in, not to fight his body. "Relax, don't panic. This is for your own good. This is not going to hurt you." The white coat approached Aleksandr. He primed the hypodermic syringe, found a vein in Aleksandr's unresisting arm, and injected the contents into the devastated body. Aleksandr passed out once again.

The two shadows, the white-coated man and M. C. now worked rapidly but with measured concern. They pulled Aleksandr's limp body off the seat and lay him on the floor. They washed his body thoroughly. They then dried him and wrapped him tightly in a blanket, enveloping him in a woolen cocoon. Someone yelled a command and a stretcher materialized. Aleksandr was placed on the stretcher, carried outside into the night, into the waiting ambulance. Lights flashing, siren blowing, two motorcycle outriders in front, a military jeep behind, the convoy emerged from Attock Fort, headed toward Islamabad at breakneck speed.

When Aleksandr finally awoke, he found himself in a hospital bed wired into an array of machines. The cannula on his forearm was connected to an intravenous solution dispenser that dripped its contents steadily into his bloodstream. The pain was gone, and although he felt weak, he realized that all was well. He wiggled his toes, his fingers, his hands, his tongue, his lips, and was relieved to find that his body appeared intact. As his eyes swept across the room he saw a person sitting on the chair across the room, rocking himself gently. The individual, seeing Alex awaken, came over and spoke to him in his native language. Alex heaved a sigh of relief. He was back amongst his own.

"It's good to have you back, colonel. We're lucky to have saved you. For some time it was touch and go." Alex had never envisaged that he would be so delighted to hear someone speaking Russian. The man proceeded to introduce himself. He was the first consul at the Russian embassy in Islamabad and was there to monitor his progress. Aleksandr was still a captive, still in Pakistani hands, but he was being well looked after. "You have been through a very rough time, Colonel. But this is to be expected. The first time can be very, very tough. Indeed, the first time is always terrible; the pain can be amazing." Aleksandr smiled weakly, indicating assent. He realized that it was his fault; he should have been a bit more cautious. First timers never jumped off the deep end. He should have taken it one step at a time. Pakistani spices were an acquired taste. It was a taste that the mouth adapted to much faster than the stomach, the intestines, or indeed, the rectum. Aleksandr had been introduced to the fiery Pakistani food the hard way. He had thrown caution to the wind and had eaten the hot, spicy food with recklessness. His body had protested and he had been violently sick. The gut-wrenching pain was now gone, but his rectum was still tender. It was a pain that the muscle would never forget. For the rest of his life, whenever he passed an

Asian restaurant, his sphincter would twitch involuntarily.

Sadly, the reflex would go unrecorded, unsung. The Rustovesky twitch was not destined for fame. Ivan Pavlov had beaten him to it one hundred years ago.

Alex would, however, have grudging admiration for the wily Asians. They always wanted to get the maximum from anything, to get the biggest bang for their buck. The ingenious Pakis had optimized everything, even their food. The masochistic, pepper eating, spice-devouring race enjoyed each meal twice.

A recovered Aleksandr was moved from the hospital to a suite in the visiting officer's quarters of an army mess. As the two governments finalized the diplomatic formalities of having the downed pilot repatriated, Alex was made as comfortable as possible. He had also acquired a regular visitor who had been introduced as a fellow professional; a fighter pilot. The two conversed haltingly through the interpreter, but then Aleksandr decided to make M. C. superfluous and dispense with his presence. One fine morning he startled everyone in the room by conversing in impeccable English. M. C. was no longer required, and everyone was glad to see him depart. The two professional pilots could now discuss airplanes and fighter flying openly and excitedly. Aleksandr looked forward to the visits of his newfound friend, who had, at their first introduction, asked that he simply be called "P. K."

The chief of the ISI looked at the officer across the table pensively. His debriefing was quite encouraging. The officer had made friends with the captured pilot and the two had hit it off very well. He had also managed to get quite a lot of information regarding the airborne equipment that the Soviets were using in Afghanistan. It was nowhere close to the sophisticated equipment that the Americans claimed was carried aboard Russian aircraft. The Soviets were actually operating with ancient technology and outdated equipment. The Americans had, as always, blown the opposition completely out of proportion. The boss of ISI understood the brilliance of the American strategy. To convince the gullible American masses that their tax dollars were being well spent, the enemy was always portrayed as superhuman. Whether it was the Hondurans, the Nicaraguans, the Cubans, the Columbians, or the Afghans, the American public was always told that American forces had to fight against powerful enemies of mighty nations whose massive armies were equipped with sophisticated space age weaponry. America always fought against fearful odds—against the mighty Dominican Republic, the armed-to-the-teeth nation of Haiti, powerful Guatemala, the vast modern military machine of Panama, the legendary Presidential Guards of Saddam Hussein. The opposing forces were always superbly equipped, heavily armed, brilliantly trained, and exceptionally well-commanded. The chaotic, ragtag columns of ill-dressed fighters, the flocks of impoverished children, the cringing, frightened women, old men, cripples that the media showed on the TV were simply clever disguises used by the enemy, but they weren't clever enough to fool the Pentagon. The actual enemy was composed of powerful, evil forces that had to be killed before they destroyed the free world.

"Mercifully, we do not have to prove anything to the public; we do not have to fight for budgets or face appropriations committees. This is one of the good things about military rule," thought the ISI chief as he forced his mind to concentrate on the issues facing him. He was pleased that the two pilots had got along well. The Soviet colonel would remember his stay favorably and would report this fact to his superiors and this would auger well for relations between Moscow and Islamabad. He picked up the green phone and dialed M. C., who had been rendered surplus so precipitously. As they spoke, the chief winced, cursing himself on his choice of the man. Such a pain in the ass, a lousy subordinate, his only redeeming feature being a pretty, vivacious wife, a devoted female willing to go to any length to see her husband prosper and be promoted. He stroked his mustache as he gave instructions to the eager subordinate.

"I have a plan that would do wonders for our relations with Moscow. We shall have the Russian be the guest of a regular Pakistani family for a couple of days. I shall tell Pervez to play host to the Russian, as they seem to be getting on quite well. As for you, I want you to monitor the entire affair from a distance.

Keep a watchful eye for as long as the Russian is with Pervez. I want you to be in your office round the clock. Eat there, sleep there; just make sure that you don't crap in the corners. Just don't screw up. I don't need to remind you that your case is coming up for promotion shortly. Make absolutely sure that nothing goes wrong." He then briefed P. K. on how to handle his houseguest and dismissed him. This done, he rang up M. C.'s wife and gave her the same news—that her husband's case was coming up for promotion. He was on an important assignment and would not be home for a while. Could they meet? They sure could, said the socialite; wincing at the thought. Lately, the chief had become a real pain in the ass. Literally.

When P. K. suggested that Aleksandr move into his home while they waited for the formalities to be worked out between the two governments, Alex agreed readily. It would get him out of the sterile atmosphere of his present quarters, and it would also give him a chance to see how the Pakistanis lived. He moved into P. K.'s guest bedroom with only one condition; that no spicy meals were to be served.

P. K. took him on a tour of the town, and Alex walked the crowded bazaars, mingling unobtrusively with the natives. Dressed in the shalwar-kameez, the blue eyed, fair-skinned Aleksandr easily passed for a Pathan from the northern areas. Lounging at home after a hearty meal served by P. K.'s wife, the two fighter pilots spoke their minds frankly as they discussed flying, life, religion, politics. The two professionals understood each other amazingly well, and they debated issues in a lively, yet friendly manner.

"You really believe that the Americans are out to help you. Think again, my friend. The Americans have never helped anyone. The only people they help are themselves. We know. We have been there. We fought with them, side by side. You forget what happened. You forget the race for Berlin? You forget the cold war? You forget the shit they fed you about us, the evil Communists? Enjoy it while it lasts, my friend, because if we are ever pushed out of Afghanistan, you will be next. It will then be your turn to be buggered. So, get ready to bend over.

"You Pakistanis are really simple people. No, no, I'm sorry, I take that back. You are not simple, my friend, you are stupid. You believe that America is a leader of the free, that it aspires to make the whole world a free world. That it looks after the downtrodden. Hah! You think the Americans care about the poor, the hungry, the sick, the dying. Think again.

"Which nation is it that dumps millions of tons of food into the sea? Which nation is it that wastes the most natural resources? Who is it that prevents medicines from being sold cheaply in the disease-stricken countries of the world? Who encourages the sweatshops of the East? Who props up the drug dealers, the poppy fields, the coca plantations, the synthetic drug labs? America. Capitalist America. You think they care? Think again." He paused, took a deep breath and continued. "Tell me something. How many people go to bed hungry each night in this wonderful world of ours?"

"I don't know, Alex," said a surprised P. K., not understanding the change of topic but sensing that the guest needed an answer. "I really don't know. Maybe fifty million, a hundred million, I have no idea."

"I'll tell you. It's over two hundred million people. Each day, across the globe, across this wonderful world of ours, two hundred million human beings do not get to eat a decent meal. They eat roots, leaves, insects. They starve, they die. And, Pervez, understand this. They starve while America, your America, spends over $30 billion each year feeding their pets—thirty fucking billion."

"That's $2.5 billion each month. Almost a $100 million a day! Think about it. They spend this huge fortune on animals while their fellow beings starve all over the globe. Their pets eat better than half the human population of the globe. That's $30 billion. It's enough to feed the poor of the entire bloody world. But no. they would rather spend it on the cats, dogs, fish, birds, reptiles. On animals. That's $30 billion pampering, cuddling, nursing, celebrating their birthdays, giving them gifts. For what, you may well ask? What do they get in return? Love. Love, they say. Balls. The pets bite and scratch their owners; they crap on the carpets, urinate in their beds, hump their legs, eat their food, force them to take them out on cold wintry mornings and evenings; they actually get them to be their slaves. Shit, they even have some of their masters believing that they are divine. Do you know that there are Americans who believe that dog is God spelled backward." He paused, amazed at his own intensity. Alex could really get worked up whenever the discussion was about America or Americans.

"Alex, at least that part makes sense, a god spelt wrongly for a people thinking wrongly. But please don't forget the problem of the dog or the tomcat. There is an associated pain of being loved. You get pampered, nursed, cared, for but you also get your balls chopped off. You get neutered. Castrated or spayed."

"Damn the dogs; they are not the issue. It is the damn injustice of it all. There are millions and millions of human beings out there who are worse off and would willingly give them the love they want. The people could trade places with them! They too could fetch slippers, bring in the newspaper; they too could chase the mice, keep guard over kids. Think about it. Aren't there people doing that already in your beautiful, free America? The millions of illegals who do all the hard work, the dirty work for them. Where do they live? What do they eat? What do they have? Not one tiny fraction of the fun the dogs and cats have. Given the right incentive, they too would willingly ride in the front seat of the car, head stuck out, gawking at the passersby. They too would willingly hump the legs of their keepers whenever they felt like it. Or stick their faces in their crotches. Hell, they'd even lie in front of the fire licking their balls. If only they too could be given the same deal as the dogs get. They too would do it all."

Pervez let it pass. He was relieved that the conversation had taken a casual and humorous turn. He was, however, sobered by Alex's revelation. He had no idea that America spent $30 billion a year on pet food. He did, however, know the figure well, because it was the total national debt of Pakistan—$30 billion. It would take his poor nation many, many generations to pay it off.

The piercing call of the muezzin calling for the morning prayer made them realize that they had talked the night through. Dawn was breaking, Pervez went to say his prayers, Aleksandr to sleep.

As Pervez prayed, his mind kept repeating the remark Aleksandr had made at one stage of the discussion. "Russia is not a country, my friend; it is a vast empire. What's happening in Afghanistan is just a hiccup in our glorious history. Even if we are forced out, we shall be back. Trust me. We shall be back in Afghanistan. And then, my friend, we shall come to you. To Pakistan."

Soon, it was time for him to go home, Aleksandr was taken to the local television studios. In front of the cameras and in the presence of an international press, he read out a speech that had already been vetted by both governments. It talked of a faulty navigational computer, a lost aircraft straying into Pakistani airspace, an intercepted aircraft, a recovered pilot. A Soviet colonel had been a guest of the Pakistani government and was now being repatriated.

Colonel Aleksandr Ivanovich Rustovesky of the Soviet air force went home.

29

The cash register had broken down, and P. K. stood patiently in line at the checkout counter, waiting for it to be fixed. He glanced at the pretty female behind him. Immaculately attired, perfectly made-up, strikingly pretty, head erect, she held herself like a queen. She, in turn, could not help staring at the attractive foreigner in front of her. God, he was a handsome one, he was. The athletic body, that skin, the color of that skin. Nature was very unfair. Here she was, spending all the free time she could afford, out in the sun, rubbing all kinds of lotions all over herself, desperately trying to add some color to her body, while here was this foreigner, with the perfect natural color, so beautifully tanned. Their eyes met. "Those eyes, Oh my God, those eyes," she said to herself. He nodded, smiling pleasantly, displaying a row of even, white teeth.

"Hi. Good Morning." She realized that the voice wasn't brown and a smile of delight crept across her face. She was pleased that he had provided an opening; excited that they could converse. The words came tumbling out of her mouth, rushing forth before better sense could prevail, before her normal reserved self could stop her. Before the weary mind could prevent the heart from releasing the bubbling, effusive girl that had long been buried under marriage, responsibility, childbirth, parenting, mortgages and dreary wives clubs.

"Oh my God, what a beautiful tan you have. It is amazing, I keep trying and trying and this is what I get and look at you, just look at you." So saying, she held up her bare arm against his exposed forearm, a pasty white limb against another the color of chocolate milk. "My God, what I wouldn't give to have a skin like yours!" Frankness, truth, openness; expressions of the heart straight from the heart, without the sobering, controlling influence of the matronly brain.

P. K. was equally delighted at the outburst. It was so natural, so warm; she was such a charming person. It was now his turn to surprise the attractive female. "You can have it, you know. It's really very simple, quite easy, actually." As her eyes widened, he continued mischievously, "You see, my color is not permanent, it rubs off. All we've got to do is to rub our bodies together, preferably with a lot of sweat thrown in. And then my color will transfer on to you!"

She frowned; a foreigner speaking her language in an immaculate manner confused her as much as what he seemed to be implying. Then, having understood the foreigner's bold but unfeigned humor, she broke out into spontaneous laughter. She nudged him, a firm elbow prodding a firmer, younger body, "Get away, You, you . . . you naughty, naughty . . ." she trailed off into silence, unable to complete her sentence.

Two strangers, never met before, would never meet again, had, for one precious moment, come close together in a frank and carefree manner. Two humans had shared emotions without guilt or fear, two souls had come together even as the two bodies remained widely separated. Each would have gone their different ways without any exchange of words but they had been lucky. Fate had provided them a few extra minutes of waiting in line. She wished that the cash register would never be fixed; she hoped that time would stand still. Sadly, it was not to be. Though the machine could not be fixed, the girl behind it decided to accept cash directly from the customers. The tanned foreigner went his way; the pretty matron, hers.

That night, a tired husband would climb the stairs of his home cautiously and disrobing quietly, slip into bed gingerly, trying not to disturb a sleeping wife. He would fail. She would awaken, a groggy female, disturbed yet delighted at the intrusion. In the darkened bedroom with the faintest of lights filtering through the curtained windows, she would turn toward the intruder. Half asleep, eyes closed, she would pull the dark-skinned, black-haired, dreamy-eyed foreigner toward herself and make violent passionate love to him. As the heat became unbearable, she would throw the covers off. She would moan, scream, bite, and scratch; she would rake her nails over his bare chest. She would ride the dark foreigner to a long forgotten destination. Drenched in sweat, she would arrive. A delirious body would be racked by orgasm after orgasm, each one more intense than the preceding one. Sweating, shattered, completely depleted, she would finally let go of the chocolate-skinned stranger and drift off to sleep reminding herself to check her tanned body the next morning.

Elsewhere, far away from the satiated female an ecstatic P. K. would pace his apartment, unable to sleep. Standing in the queue ahead of the pretty female, exchanging small talk as the cashier calculated his bill, he had found the solution.

"Guys, guys, I have it. I know how we can take over the world. I have the answer. I found it at Wal-Mart.

"Piss off, P. K. Why don't you grow up?"

"No, no, seriously. Listen. I was in the express checkout lane of Walmart when I realized how it can be done. I just had six items. Razor blades, gum, shit like that. As the girl rang up the stuff, the cash register failed. So what does she do? She rings a bell. The supervisor comes over. She too could not fix it. They told me to go to the next lane. I requested them to take cash, 'please, just take the cash.' The lady behind me said that they should fix the machine. She could wait. She was quite nice, really, the woman behind me. Anyway, the supervisor tried to fix the machine, but couldn't, so she decided to take cash directly. I gave the girl a twenty-dollar bill. My bill was $11.56. I had worked it out in my mind in about two seconds. It took the two females five frigging minutes to work out the cost of goods, deduct it from twenty bucks, and figure out how much to return to me. And they got it wrong! Would you believe it? They got a simple piece of math wrong! They gave me an extra dollar.

"That's when it hit me. Nobody uses the brain anymore. It's all left to the computers. They just believe the computers. Whatever they see on the screen, they believe."

"And this is good news? This is going to help us win?"

"Don't you see? We don't have to take over anything. We let the computers take over. We only control the computers. How's that for an idea?"

"Oh shit. You are right. Damn. You may have something there."

"I know that you can do great things with computers, P. K. I've seen you do them. It cost me five hundred bucks. But remember, that was something very different, something quite basic. This is big, very big. Times have changed. You could never do it again. Do you really think you can get into the computers of the Pentagon once again? Can you control them now as you did.then? No way. You cannot get into the massive, highly sophisticated machines being used now"

It was Niles who replied. "I said it then, I'll say it again now. If it can be done, P. K. can do it. I know that he can do it. But so fucking what? It doesn't mean anything at all. Where do you plan to go from there? What does it mean even if we take over the whole damn system? Have you any idea what this leads to? Can you handle it? Can we handle it? Can anyone handle it? No, sir, this is just too damn big for comfort. I hope you understand this. It is not a joke or a silly bet."

"Yes. Yes I do. And, yes, we can handle it. And, yes. Yes, I can do it."

"Pardon me if I piss on your roaring fire. You guys need to get your heads examined. This is not like hot-wiring a car or trying to charm the pants of a reluctant virgin. This is deadly serious. This is messing with the world's only superpower. This is, as you would say, Robert, hardballing it with the big guys, in fact the biggest guys."

"Listen, we are not going to do anything in a hurry. Let's just take it one step at a time. Let's first find out exactly what P. K. can control. Let's first see what he can do. Once he can come up with something workable, we can then decide the next step."

P. K. knew that it could be done. He knew that Puck was alive and well. That it was lying in wait, hibernating in servers all across the Internet. P. K. checked on Puck periodically, analyzed its state, and then ordered it back into hibernation. It had become a habit with him, but to be able to do what was now being expected of it, it needed to evolve, to adapt, to incorporate the latest distributed computing and emerging netcentric technologies. P. K. realized that this meant more work. It also meant that an innocent hobby had now become a deadly serious matter. His computing skills, developed casually but passionately over the years, were now to be used as instruments of war.

Puck would, however, need to be tested. P. K. had to test the system, but it would have to be a benign test. He could not take the chance of alerting the Pentagon. It would be an act of supreme folly to invade the military computers at this early stage. The capabilities of Puck would have to be tested on some other, less sensitive, but equally complicated network. A target had to be found. It had to be something very similar, something important and global in scope. The choice was quite obvious.

Puck would target SCADA, the Supervisory Control and Data Acquisition system that used computers and communication components to enable access between the vast, prolific network of computer systems, Programmable Logic Controllers, Remote Terminal Units, subnetworks, and vendor maintenance support, all linked together via the Internet and also across older, analog modem lines. SCADA was a huge arrangement of thousands of computers linking systems and infrastructures connected to each other through the Internet. SCADA controlled the power generation and distribution networks of the West.

30

On August 14, 2003, the network server controlling the central Ohio electrical grid started running a small subroutine that was not a part of the program installed by the facility. It prompted the 375-megawatt Conesville Unit 5 generator to go off line. At exactly the same time, an identical subroutine in a server located in Detroit shut down the 785-megawatt Greenwood Unit 1 located north of the Detroit area. A third server in northern Ohio turned off the 597-megawatt Eastlake Unit 5 in northern Ohio. Another subroutine in a fourth SCADA computer tripped the massive circuit breakers of a transmission line in southwestern Ohio, disconnecting a total of four high-voltage lines from the national electrical grid. Electrical connections between eastern and northern Ohio were disrupted. Power stopped flowing into northern Ohio from the eastern part of the state. Having executed the illegal instruction set, the very same computers that had triggered the shutdowns and deactivated the lines started remedying the faults. Unaware that it was they that had themselves ordered these actions, their powerful programs started complex processes of error analysis and error correction. Power that had been flowing over those lines was shifted to other lines. Smaller, less-capable lines. These began to overload. Lines overheated, voltages dropped. Amperes increased. Unable to bear these variations in load distribution, the computers started dropping users from the service.

Industrial, commercial, and domestic customers consuming about 600 megawatts worth of power were disconnected automatically from the grid.

When this did not help in eliminating the problem, all the lines able to move power into northern Ohio and onward into eastern Michigan from eastern Ohio were disconnected. Seconds later, power lines bringing in electricity to the north from southern and western Ohio were also disconnected.

Another surge, another fault, another correction, another problem. Twenty more generators in Michigan tripped. As the generators tripped, the 345kV Perry-Ashtabula-Erie West transmission line started overloading and tripped off line.

Power flowing in from Pennsylvania along the southern shore of Lake Erie was shut off.

Power that had been flowing clockwise around Lake Erie reversed direction and began flowing from Pennsylvania to New York to Ontario and into

Michigan. This surge of energy flowing out of Pennsylvania caused the four lines carrying the power to disconnect. Within four seconds, Pennsylvania was separated from New York. Additional power plants failed, additional generators stopped generating.

Another computer stirred into action. Another dormant Puck awakened. The Branchburg-Ramapo 500kV line running through northern New Jersey, part of the grid stretching from the Rockies to the East Coast and south to Texas was disconnected from the main grid.

Northern New Jersey blacked out.

A cascading effect caused the transmission lines between New York and New England to be disconnected.

Up north, lines around Niagara Falls disconnected, separating New York from Ontario.

Ontario plunged into darkness. Eastern New York followed, as did southwestern Connecticut.

FirstEnergy Corporation and Detroit Edison computers, massive, complex, intricate, powerful and highly efficient machines had been attacked. Puck had rampaged across the electrical grid. Disrupting the electronic highway, it had induced massive surges in the Eastern seaboard Electrical grid. Thousands of megawatts of power had surged one way; thousands had bounced back.

Puck caused a massive blackout, the largest in North American history. It shut down everything from the bright lights of Broadway in New York to streetcars in Toronto. Within seconds, Canada and the United States lost a total of 62,000 megawatts. Some 50 million people spread over 24 thousand square kilometers were affected. Seven American states, two countries were plunged into darkness. More than 100 power-generating plants and over 22 nuclear reactors were disabled.

The energy secretary stated that it would take weeks before the reasons for the blackout were known. Across the Atlantic, Silvio Berlusconi, the Italian prime minister, made disparaging remarks about the power cuts in the North America, assuring his people that such an event could never happen in Italy.

Further east, twelve thousands miles away, P. K. was tracking the blackout. Well before the news channels started reporting the facts, well before camera crews started transmitting pictures, Puck had already sent in its report via the World Wide Web. The Web, used to trigger the event was also used to provide feedback.

For P. K. it was a failed experiment. Too much, too devastating, not enough control. Not a successful test. More work was needed. Lessons had to be learned, the process needed to be refined, systems had to be tweaked. Puck needed to be made more specific, more targeted. He worked almost continuously for two weeks.

Puck was retrained; mutated.

On Thursday, August 28, 2003, a computer controlling the British national grid started running a small subroutine buried deep within its millions of characters of code. A massive power failure struck the city during the evening rush hour. A quarter of million people were caught in the London Underground when the outage hit. Thousands others took to the streets. Another quarter of a million people were affected when parts of the mainline rail system came to a halt. While some stations had emergency lighting, most were plunged into darkness. Train stations were evacuated because of overcrowding. Life came to a virtual halt.

Electricity was restored to London within an hour of the outage, which was blamed on an improbable failure in the national grid. National Grid Transco called it a freak event caused by two faults happening in quick succession. It was, they said, the result of a problem with a 275 KV cable feed from the national grid in the Wimbledon area of South London, compounded by the fitting of a wrongly rated part in a backup system. The British spokesman who came on the air to explain the outage said that it was similar to what would happen in a house if someone fitted a 1 amp fuse instead of a 5 amp fuse. It was simply an "unusual occurrence not even vaguely on the scale of what happened in the United States."

Once again, Silvio Berlusconi cast aspersions, this time on the British grid, blaming it for its antiquated state. Italy could never have such a crisis, because Italy imported most of its electricity from the nuclear power plants of France. To deliver this imported power to Italian consumers, the country had the most advanced power transmission and monitoring system in the world.

P. K. realized that Puck had been somewhat ineffective this time. He had obviously made too much of a correction and hence there was too little a response. Another tweak, another modification, another mutation. This done, another exercise was needed. Why not check out Senor Berlusconi's claim?

At 3:31 on September the 23, 2003, the computer that controlled power lines feeding Italy with power from the nuclear reactors of France decided to execute a branch instruction. It commanded the main computer controlling the Italian grid to drop one power transmission circuit off the line. This, in turn, caused another line located in Switzerland to overload. A cascade similar to the one that took place earlier in North America and England followed. Overload, tripping, alternate routes, additional overload, more tripping, generators going off line, power stations being shut down. The result was a complete shutdown of the French power transmission to Italy.

Italy experienced the worst power outage since the Second World War. Most of the country's 58 million people were affected. Over 110 trains with more than 30,000 passengers on board came to a grinding halt. The air traffic system collapsed causing flight cancellations and innumerable delays. Rome had been holding an all-night festival with museums, bars, and shops open at the time of the blackout. Thousands of people who had been participating in the festival found themselves stranded at subway stations, unable to travel anywhere. As the outage wore on, and the public remained stuck in the open, the public toilets of Rome were overwhelmed the facilities were inundated. The Italians decided to relieve themselves in the corners of the buildings. There were plenty of dark corners everywhere, except of course in the Colosseum. It had no corners. The Roman Emperors of yore probably knew well the public propensity to use corners as toilets.

It took over three days to restore power to all parts of Italy. As in the North American and England experiments, there was confusion about the cause, and there was considerable finger pointing among everyone involved, this time on an international level.

Three countries blamed each other for the disaster. Swiss and French energy officials said the responsibility was Italy's, while the Italians insisted that the power cut originated in France. Later, experts would agree to place the blame on nature. They issued a press statement that said that a tree branch had hit a power line, causing the outage. On one point they all agreed—the Italians, Swiss, French, Brits and Americans. Each nation firmly believed that there was no possibility of any foul play. These were freak occurrences, rare events that would never be repeated again. The Italian prime minister was not available for comment.

While the experiment had finally been successful and, indeed, was quite impressive, the three friends were in agreement about one thing: SCADA was not the Pentagon. It was not the military. It was not DISA, it was not Asskicker, it was not cutting-edge encryption.

It was not enough for P. K. to breach SCADA. He had to prove that he could breach the Pentagon. He had to be able to control the distributed computing netcentric information grid.

Only then could they decide on the future course of action.

31

The general commanding the coalition forces in Iraq
was delighted with the instructions displayed on his
screen. MICOC had just displayed the presidential
order for the force commander to begin an immediate
withdrawal from Iraq. He was both thrilled and
relieved. Thrilled that he would now be able to spend
Christmas with his family and relieved because the
last eight months had had a debilitating effect on his
troops. Things had now reached a stage where it was
almost impossible to keep their morale up. It was now
becoming necessary to use the threat of punishment to
ensure that they continued doing their duty. He could
not blame them; there was no way the troops could
continue swallowing the bullshit that had been fed to
them from day one. "Liberators arriving to a
humongous welcome!" "A triumphant army being
welcomed by a population that loved them!" This was
nonsense. The truth was that they were getting shot
at, they were being abused, his soldiers were being
ridiculed. Children would follow them on the streets
making rude gestures; men would take off their

sandals and show the soles of their feet to the liberators; they would give them this Iraqi equivalent of the finger; women would lift their veils and spit in their direction. Wizened old men had taken out their shriveled members and urinated, facing them, openly, defiantly. Some young men had even mooned them. They must have been educated in the United States, the commander guessed. He was glad that all this was now going to end.

He summoned his second in command, another brave son of an immigrant father. The coincidence was amazing. The bulk of American troops in Iraq were nonwhite. The whites remained stuck in desk jobs back in Washington, and those with colored skins — black; brown; yellow; men and women with Mexican, Latin American, and even Middle Eastern names — ended up fighting in Iraq. Just as there was an old Europe and a new one, there were Old Americans and New Americans. It was the duty of the New Americans to fight; the Old Americans had to plan. "Let's do this very carefully, one step at a time. There is no need to inform everyone and end up with another disaster like that of Saigon. Assholes falling over each other trying to get on board helicopters, aircraft, ships, boats, anything, everything," he briefed his subordinate. "The instructions are here, but let's keep them to ourselves for the time being." The subordinate, thrilled at the prospect of going home, agreed readily. He asked the commander when and how the instructions had arrived, and the commander told him about the message on the MICOC terminal.

The subordinate couldn't resist the temptation. "Its great news, isn't it, Sir. You must be really happy. Don't you feel like kissing MICOC?"

The general knew that the evacuation had to be planned meticulously. It could not be like the exit from Vietnam. Vietnam had been a disaster that no one cared to talk about. It was better left dead and buried. No one wanted to be reminded of that ignominious exit from a lost war, the mad dash for safety with absolute disregard for discipline, rank, protocol, manifests, order, law. He would never forget the soldier who had pushed him aside as he dashed toward the overloaded helicopter. "Fuck you, lieutenant," from a man who had fought alongside him in the jungle, a man on whom he had been willing to let his life depend. It was something one never forgot.

Caution and secrecy were essential. MICOC instructions had been specific and had explained in detail why this secrecy was needed. The evacuation had its detractors, both in uniform and out of it. The move was to take place slowly, secretly, without fanfare, and without publicity. The message had warned that there might be definite, overt attempts to prevent the pullout, and the military commander had to be extremely careful. The only civilian to be taken into confidence was the person who led the Provisional Authority.

The leader of the Provisional Authority was furious. He could not believe what the general was telling him.

There was absolutely no way the troops could be pulled out at this time. There was no logical reason for this sudden departure. It would spell disaster both for America and Iraq. He picked up the phone and dialed the White House.

"What exactly is the plan, Mr. President?"

Initially annoyed, then incredulous, the president listened. "Let me get back to you." He hit the speed dial button.

"What the fuck is going on, Donald?"

Donald, first questioning, then incredulous, listened to the president. "Let me get back to you."

Impatient, unable to wait for a response, the president hit another button.

"What the frigging hell is going on, Condi?" And, as the president explained the situation to the equally astonished female, she too responded with an identical response.

"Let me get back to you." Another speed dial button was punched.

And so it went, no one knowing what exactly was going on, until someone suggested that they ask the commanding general in Baghdad. The secretary called Baghdad. The chairman of the Joint Chiefs of Staff

313

called Baghdad. The secretary of the army called Baghdad. Each one got the same answer. "I have my orders, Sir. Straight from the president."

And therefore, the president of the United States of America called the commanding general in Baghdad. "Just exactly what are you doing, General?"

"Sir, I'm doing exactly what you told me to. You sent the orders, and I am executing them."

"Are you out of your fucking mind? I gave no such orders."

"I'm sorry Sir, but I have them. I have them on MICOC."

The staff worked rapidly, looking into the logs. Sure enough, it was there. The presidential order to recall the troops from Iraq. Quietly, without fanfare, without publicity.

The president was stunned. He knew that he had not given any such order. And anyway, such an order could not be sent out without considerable debate and the due process of decision making. How could this have happened? Could he actually have sent out a message without anybody else knowing? Was he having a relapse? Was he losing his mind once again? These were questions that could be answered later. There was work to be done. The withdrawal had to be stopped.

They were assembled in the situation room, the key advisers and the members of his inner cabinet, trying to recover from the fiasco. The staff had already put through the videoconference call to Baghdad. The face of the general appeared clearly, centered on the large video display. "We can get to the bottom of this later; right now we need you to stop your evacuation plan. We have no intention of leaving Iraq. Let me make that very clear to you, General."

"Understood, Sir. Loud and clear. I shall take the necessary steps immediately. I would however need you to supersede the MICOC command, Sir."

"Not a problem." The president understood the requirement. A MICOC order could only be rescinded by another instruction on MICOC. The procedures were very clear. Faces could be created, voices copied, video conferences hijacked. There was only one secure and foolproof system within the U.S. communications system, and that system was MICOC. It was constantly checked, monitored, and fully protected by DISA. He turned to the defense secretary, who was already well ahead of the situation. He had almost finished hammering out the short message on the MICOC terminal. Thousands of miles away in Baghdad, the general could see the secretary as he typed out the message, knowing that it would appear on his MICOC screen immediately after the secretary hit the SEND button.

The SEND button was pressed and they watched the general in Iraq. He just kept sitting there. A deadly silence ensued, broken by the secretary.

"So, what's keeping you?"

"I thought you were sending me a message."

"I did. I just sent you the order."

"Not to me you didn't. I'm still waiting."
The secretary rechecked the routing, the address block, the green lights signifying all systems were running fine. Everything was correct. The message should have gone. It must have gone. He checked the status column. "Message Sent" And next to it; "Message Displayed on Addressee Terminal, Awaiting Acknowledgement." It had gone.

"Quit fucking around, General. We can see that you have the message. Acknowledge receipt" The secretary of defense was visibly annoyed now. "How can this sonofabitch piss around with me like this in front of the president," he thought to himself. He would need to sort him out later.

"Like I said, Mr. Secretary, I'm still waiting," the general responded, impassive, unmoved.

The secretary pulled up the message on the screen and sent it out once again. Once again, the general indicated that he was not getting any message on MICOC.

The maintenance crew was called for. This was the first time an unscheduled maintenance call had been asked for on the system that had logged over a million hours of cumulative terminal time worldwide. Indeed, this was the very first time the system had experienced a failure. Too bad it had to happen with the president watching.

They found nothing wrong. Baghdad was asked to send a test message to the presidential terminal. The system showed that it was delivered immediately. The terminals were talking to each other normally. There was no apparent problem. The order was relayed to Baghdad for a third time. Nothing appeared on the Baghdad terminal. They tried it over a dozen times without success.

In Baghdad, the general was keenly watching the video screen and the drama unfolding on it. By now he had fully understood the situation and was actually somewhat amused by the whole affair. "God, these buggers are good," he thought to himself. But they weren't all that good. They could not fool him. It was not easy to hoodwink a seasoned guy like him. Although everything appeared pat, he could detect the flaws. It was just a bit too smooth. The adviser was definitely an imposter. The real adviser's mouth was a lot wider than that. The president; perfect features but not the mannerisms. He was not shrugging his shoulders as often as the actual president did. The defense secretary had not once asked a question and answered it himself. The charade with the maintenance team coming in—now that was really a nice touch. These guys were professionals. They almost had him fooled. Clever sons of bitches; they had been able to hack into the telecommunication network. They had tapped into the video network; they had compromised the audio links. They had almost pulled it off, but they had forgotten one small detail. They had forgotten that they were dealing with the most powerful artificial intelligence system that existed in the world. They could not penetrate MICOC.

An irate president now assumed command. "Let's cut the crap, asshole. I want you to call off this withdrawal. Right Now. General, this is an executive order from the president of the United States of America. Understand it. Execute it. NOW."

"Yes Sir, I'm sorry Sir. I understand fully that you are the president of the United States, and I respect your decision." The general stood up, reached across the table to the switch that controlled the video conferencing system. He bent forward, bringing his face closer to the camera that was sending out the streaming video all the way to wherever this team of clowns was. He knew that at the far end his face would now be filling the screen. He spoke in a measured tone, carefully, emphasizing each word. "As for the executive order, try sending in over on

MICOC." He paused, smiled, and then continued "Asshole." He switched the system off. He had work to do.

A deathly silence fell over the situation room. The president was the first to recover. "The fucking greaseball. The motherfucking greaseball. I want that son of a bitch in my office first thing tomorrow morning. I'll have his ass for breakfast. The bastard, the fucking bastard" he fumed. "Just get him over here."

Silence reigned supreme. The defense secretary knew better than to answer, and so did everyone else. They knew from past experience that when he got like that, only a fool would try and reason with him. A fool or, her. All eyes, almost in unison, turned toward the adviser. She could do it. She could handle him. She could get away with it. He always listened to her. "Sir, we have a problem."

The president could hardly contain himself. Visibly agitated, his voice was now a few octaves higher when he spoke. "You're fucking wrong. We have no fucking problem. I have no problem. I tell you what. I tell you who has a problem. That sonofabitch has one. One helluva motherfucking problem. He has no idea what's coming at him."

"No, Sir, This is a really serious problem, and it is with us. You want him out? You want him here tomorrow morning? Fair enough." She paused. "But how do we get him out? How do we tell him to come here?"

It took almost two whole minutes for the message to sink in. His brow deeply furrowed, the president looked at the stony stares of all his subordinates as his mind tried to comprehend what the adviser had just said. As understanding came, the president slumped forward in his chair. He cupped his head in his hands, staring down on the carpeted floor. Rocking back and forth, he moaned softly, "Oh, Shit. Oh Jesus, oh Shit."

MICOC was down in Baghdad. The last instructions would be followed to the letter. The president had ordered a troop withdrawal, it would happen. There was only one way to stop the event from happening. A direct, face-to-face presidential command. The general would not come out of Baghdad to receive it. He could only be ordered out over MICOC, and that was not possible. There was only one remaining alternative.

The president of the United States would have to go to Baghdad to give the order, face to face, to the errant general.

32

Just give them the problem and they will find the good in it. Or the bad. Whatever you want done, they shall do it. It's their job. This is what spin doctors do. They specialize in twisting any situation to the required outcome. And quite naturally, the spin doctors who work for the GOP are the best. They are, as the president himself has acknowledged on more than one occasion, "simply marvelous."

The trip to Baghdad, dangerous and necessary as it was, would be used to good advantage. The spin doctors would do it, just as they had worked the recent State visit to Britain. The Land of the Two Queens, as it was commonly referred to by some: Elizabeth II and Tony Blair. One wedded to the House of Windsor and the other betrothed to the House of Bush. The trip to London had been made to meet face to face with Tony, but, as one British wag had put it, "It's extremely difficult to meet a person face to face when that person's face is buried up your ass."

The spin doctors set the stage. The president would fly in on Thanksgiving Day. He would eat with the troops, issue the face-to-face order to counter the MICOC command, and exit promptly. No one was to know, not even his bodyguards. The First lady was told only a couple of days in advance, the children, just hours before he left. His parents were not told until they sat down for the dinner. Having prayed to the Lord, thanking him for the bounty that He had bestowed upon the family, Bush senior raised his eyes and saw the disadvantaged bird. Intrigued, he asked the daughter-in-law if one-legged turkeys were now the fashion. That is when she told him. She had taken the other leg and packed a Thanksgiving meal for a husband who was on his way to Iraq.

Bush Senior understood. The visit was in keeping with tradition. Nixon had gone to Vietnam, Lyndon Johnson made two wartime trips to Vietnam, and Eisenhower had visited Korea. He was reminded of his own visit to the troops at a desert outpost in Saudi Arabia on Thanksgiving Day when the first Gulf War took place. That was a different war, a different time, but it was the same enemy, same Saddam. Now, his son, the president, was visiting troops in Baghdad. It was good for morale. It was the done thing. Presidents always visited the troops in the field. So did comedians. Sometimes it was difficult tell which was which.

The ride from the ranch to the airport was made in an unmarked vehicle. The occupants traveled slouched down and used baseball caps to cover their faces to get past the prying news reporters who were always hanging around the Bush residence. It took them over forty-five minutes to make the trip, because this time they could not drive merrily through red lights and traffic jams. There were no wailing sirens, no flashing lights, and they had to observe the traffic rules. For what was perhaps the very first time, a president of the United States of America encountered traffic.

The intelligence agents remained at their posts as George Bush was hustled into Air Force One at Texas State Technical College, which had once been a military base. Air traffic control was simply informed that the aircraft had to be flown back to Washington for some unscheduled maintenance; there was no mention of any occupants of the aircraft. The plan was to land at Andrews Air Force Base outside Washington and change to a different, smaller aircraft for the ultra-secret dash with just a few aides on board. The switch was supposed to take place in a huge hangar, hidden from view to avoid the possibility of any chance observer.

George Bush however refused to change aircraft. He was not going to sneak into Baghdad on "some crappy 757"—a reference to one of the four Boeing 757 aircraft that were used for other senior officials of the government. It was then decided that the 747 would be used but that the flight plan would show that the aircraft was a Gulfstream 5 business jet. In the hangar, the selected staff and the specially assembled press contingent that included five reporters, a television production unit consisting of three persons, and the five photographers who would take the still shots, climbed aboard. Everyone was asked to surrender their cell phones, pagers, and other electronic devices, which were stashed in yellow manila envelopes and retained by the security officials. They were ordered not to raise the window blinds at any stage of the flight and were further informed that the aircraft would be flying in absolute radio silence. It would also not be identified by its usual call sign, "Air Force One."

In the excitement of the visit, they almost forgot the "football," the briefcase that held the codes for nuclear deployment and without which the president never moved. An agitated army officer, responsible for the "football" while the president was on the ground, rushed up the stairs to hand it over to the air force officer whose duty it was to guard it while airborne.

The presidential aircraft was, to the casual observer, similar to all the commercial 747s flying the skies. A closer examination would however, reveal some substantial differences. The skilled observer would not take long to recognize that the aircraft was actually the most well-defended airborne platform that flew the skies. Special antennae, chaff and flare dispensers, electro-optical sensors and jammers dotted the beautiful structure. The observer would also recognize the in-flight refueling receptacles that were seen on military aircraft only. This capability enabled

Air Force One to stay up in the air almost indefinitely; an attribute that was crucial in an emergency situation.

While the exterior differences may only have been appreciated by a skilled observer, the differences within the aircraft were readily recognizable by even the most nonobservant of individuals. The only similarity between Air Force One and the commercial airliners was the triple-decker arrangement.

The upper deck was reserved for the cockpit and, behind it, for the communications equipment. This was the world's most advanced airborne voice and data communications center. The electronics aboard the aircraft were by far the most remarkable feature of Air Force One. The aircraft had over 238 miles of special wiring, heavily shielded and specially designed to withstand the electromagnetic pulses that would originate from a nuclear blast. The wiring network connected over a hundred onboard telephones, intercoms, fax machines, computers, and display panels. Using both normal and highly secure voice and data communications, the president and his staff could reach anybody in the world irrespective of whether the aircraft was on ground or aloft.

The middle deck was where most of the passengers sat. They entered through three doors, two of which were located on the lower deck. Journalists normally used the rear door of the lower deck from where they climbed the staircase to the rear section of the middle deck. Here they traveled in first-class luxury on comfortable, spaced out seats. The crew and staffers used the lower door at the front of the plane. From here, they could proceed directly to the cargo area or climb a staircase to the front section of the middle deck. Cockpit crew and communications staff climbed further up using the internal staircase near the middle deck entrance.

The third door was at the front of the plane on the middle deck. This was reserved for the president. This was the door that the president of the United States would use to enter the plane, and it was from here that he would normally turn around and wave to the crowd assembled to see him off. Once inside, he could make a left turn to the president's suite and office or go right, ending up in the galley and the dining room, which also doubled as a conference room whenever required.

As President Bush reached the top of the stairs, he turned reflexively and waved, only to realize that this was quite unnecessary as there was nobody to see him off. A few ground personnel down below were surprised at the presidential gesture and waved back hesitatingly. George entered the aircraft and turned left. He headed straight for the bedroom located all the way in the front of the aircraft. Slumping into the leather sofa, he told the attendant that he would eat dinner once the airplane was airborne. She was to serve him the meal out of the brown paper bag the First Lady had handed him as he left the ranch.

As the aircraft climbed through eleven thousand George closed his eyes and, head bent, hands folded, he said a prayer. He prayed to God and thanked Him for all that he had received. Except Saddam, goddamn Saddam. This done, he picked up the turkey leg and bit into the soft, juicy meat viciously. He missed being with the family on this special day.

Baghdad International Airport was blacked out when Air Force One landed. The plane itself had no lights, no emissions. Once on the ground, the aircraft, unseen, unreported, taxied to a remote corner of the airfield and shut down its engines. Humvees swarmed around the aircraft as the passengers disembarked. As always, the official photo and video crews were first to disembark so that cameras were already rolling when the president emerged. The motorcade traveled from the plane to the mess hall in pitch darkness. All vehicles kept their lights off; the drivers were wearing night-vision goggles.

The troops had been told that they were gathered in the mess hall at Baghdad International Airport for a Thanksgiving dinner with a VIP guest. Paul Bremer, the civilian administrator in Iraq, went through the little routine he had rehearsed over three dozen times with the coalition force commander, Lt. Gen. Ricardo Sanchez. In the mess hall, in front of the six hundred-odd soldiers assembled for the special thanksgiving meal, he inaugurated the event by telling the soldiers it was time to read the president's Thanksgiving proclamation. He then paused, looked around, and attempted to deliver the routine he had so meticulously planned, but, despite the multiple rehearsals, he almost screwed it up. He stumbled on the words. In an embarrassingly hesitant manner, he asked if there was "anybody back there more senior than we" to read the president's words. George Bush emerged from the wings. The room erupted; soldiers clambered atop chairs and tables to bark, hoot, yell and "hoo-ah" their approval. Bush had a hard time fighting back the tears. He told the troops he was "just looking for a warm meal somewhere. Thank you for inviting me to dinner."

A plastic turkey, elegantly laid out on a dummy Thanksgiving spread, was handed over to the president. He carried the tray across the entire room, mingling with the troops, and then took up position behind the counter to dish out the meal. He however did not sit down to eat the sweet potatoes and corn from the chow line. "We thank you for your service, we're proud of you, and America stands solidly behind you," he said. "You are defeating the terrorists here in Iraq so we don't have to face them in our own country. You're defeating Saddam's henchmen so that the people of Iraq can live in peace and freedom. We did not charge hundreds of miles into the heart of Iraq, pay a bitter cost of casualties, defeat a ruthless dictator, and liberate 25 million people only to retreat before a band of thugs and assassins," Bush told about 600 soldiers from the 1st Armored Division and the 82nd Airborne, "No, Sir, we are in it for the long haul. No getting out at this stage." Not too many people understood the significance of this message. In fact only 350 troops could have understood it. They had been detailed for the first evacuation flight. They were shocked. And awed.

This done, Bush then went into a meeting with national security adviser Condoleezza Rice, Bremer, Sanchez, and four members of the Iraqi Governing Council. The members of the Iraqi governing council were requesting more money, better facilities, and additional privileges from their masters. The president approved the release of extra funds and then headed back to the aircraft for the return journey. He asked the general to drive the Humvee and he climbed into the passenger seat. He also told his aides that he wanted to ride alone with the general. When the vehicle was moving, he turned to the driver. "I am really pissed at this. Have you any idea what a major screw up this has been? Its not that I am blaming you, but, boy, am I pissed off. The first fucking MICOC failure and it had to happen in Baghdad. Just my damn luck. I have to travel to this hell hole. Anyway, I am here, and I am formally superseding the MICOC order. You are to forget about coming home. We are in this for the long haul. We are going to make Iraq a free and stable nation, whatever it takes."

"I understand fully well, Sir. I also hope that you recognize my limitations. I was just following orders. Your orders, Sir," said the general, pulling up at the base of the stairs leading to the 747 entrance. "And Sir,

329

I apologize for the inconvenience that I may have caused you."

The president got out of the Humvee. He turned around, looked the general in the eye and said, "It's OK, General. It's done. As for the apology," George leaned forward, thrusting his face into the general's, and said, "Send it over on MICOC, Asshole." He then broke into his typical laugh, shoulders shrugging uncontrollably.

The president bounded up the stairs, his step sprightly. Reaching the top, he turned, waved to those down below, and winked exaggeratedly at the general as he continued smiling broadly. He turned and entered Air Force One, saying to no one in particular, "Let's get the fuck out of here!" As the aircraft took off, his staff informed him that there had been two more bombings in Baghdad that day. Two more American soldiers had died. The remnants of the Iraqi regime were still active and were creating problems for the coalition forces. He made a mental note to instruct the Joint Chiefs to ensure that when they went into their next adventure, be it Iran or Syria, they had to address this issue seriously. They would need to fix this unwanted problem in all earnest. The remnants. These assholes always caused a major problem for the United States. They were the ones who made victory elusive. There would have to be no more of this nonsense. In all future operations, the General Staff was to ensure that the dead-enders, the stragglers, the remnants; these were to be the first target.

The 747 slipped out of Baghdad as surreptitiously as it had slipped in. Twenty-seven hours later, a tired president, irritated at the failure of the machine, climbed into bed muttering to himself, "Fuck MICOC."

A dutiful wife rolled over.

The trip was timed to give George Bush maximum exposure; it was specifically planned for a day when most Americans were at home. They were watching football games when the announcement came that George Bush had been to Baghdad. Some networks interrupted programming with news of the trip. The president's popularity, which had been steadily declining, was given a tremendous boost and the visit was seen as a major publicity success. The spin doctors had been very successful. U.S. forces in Iraq had become the target of regular, deadly attacks, and George Bush has been heavily criticized for his policies, particularly by the Democrats, who spared no opportunity to turn every issue into a political vulnerability for him. And this had been a particularly bad month. Over five dozen U.S. soldiers had been killed by hostile fire, more than any other month since he had declared the end of major combat in Iraq. The Baghdad trip was a huge success in reversing the decline in popularity of the president. The American public was overjoyed. They thought the world of a president who was willing to take major risks. Only a few days ago, a cargo plane had been hit by a surface-to-air missile over Baghdad, and it had to make an emergency landing, its missile decoy pod on fire. They saw a president mingling with his troops, recognizing the soldiers and their sacrifices that were contributing to the safety of their nation. America recognized a commander in chief who was not afraid to be in the line of fire.

The Iraqi reaction to Bush's visit was somewhat different. "As far as I'm concerned, he's welcome to come and he's more than welcome to leave," said Abu Mohammed, a cigarette vendor. "He should have taken the troops with him."

Abu Ismail, a Baghdad cab driver, was more succinct. He muttered, "Fuck Saddam, Fuck Bush. Fuck them all."

33

The ability of Puck to compromise MICOC proved conclusively that it was possible — that the sophisticated Defense information network could be controlled and manipulated. When he, Robert, and Niles next met, it was with an air of confidence that it could be done, that the computers could be made to do their bidding. This final meeting took place at a distant bed and breakfast retreat up in the Welsh countryside, in a town called Portmeirion. It was a charming place that housed a collection of some of the major architectural follies of the world. The three friends were fascinated by the buildings that had been collected on the small Welsh peninsula. Particularly intriguing was the bronze statue of Hercules and his burden. What had caught their imagination, however, was not the statue but the plaque that was attached to the pedestal with the cryptic message, "To the summer of 1959, in honour of its splendour." They had debated the passion, the delirium, the ecstasy that must have been the origin of such an intense dedication. They agreed that this was truly a befitting tribute to time, a monument to one singular summer that must have been so overwhelming, so intensely personal and joyous that it motivated someone to pay homage in this unique manner. It was more than a simple tribute to love, it was more elegant than an emperor declaring his love for a departed companion in the form of the Taj Mahal, It was much more emotive than a king bestowing a gift of a palace at Versailles to a loved one. It was much more because Hercules at Portmeirion was an anonymous tribute. It conveyed only the emotions without assigning them a name. This was a genuine, timeless tribute to love, to life, to emotion. They wondered whether, following that splendid summer, had there been a dreary winter? Were there broken hearts, souls torn apart by the cruel whims of fate. Was there anguish, remorse, misery, death?

They wondered because they too would build their own Portmeirion. Here, in tranquil surroundings, away from the hustle and bustle of a city, the three friends would put together their tribute to Mankind. They would build their future and that of the generations to follow. Safe and secure from any eavesdroppers or snoops, the three would put together their plan that would promise a better future for all.

"Now is the time to back off if anyone of us thinks that this is not a good idea." Robert did not want either of the two to think that they were being forced into this.

"I just need to understand what and how the three of us are going to be working this issue. Who is in charge? Who reports to whom? What exactly is the command and control aspect of this venture?" asked Niles, wanting to ensure that there were no conflicts down the line. Always pragmatic, always a stickler for detail, Niles needed to be absolutely sure that they had covered all possibilities.

"This is not something you can figure out from a textbook; there are no set rules. This is a unique situation and, being unique, it cannot have a precedent. There are no standard procedures, no fixed policy. We can only work with the broad principles and concepts; we must play the situation pretty much by ear, as stuff happens," said Robert, knowing full well that the venture that they were embarking on could not, did not have a planning guide. They were fighter pilots; they knew the rules, the principles, the laws, the do's and the don'ts. But ultimately, when pitched into combat, they had to fight the fight according to their gut feelings, their instincts, depending on well-honed skills acquired over years of aerial combat.

P. K. clasped his hands, assumed an air of seriousness, and intoned, "As we know, there are known knowns; there are things we know we know. We also know there are known unknowns; that is to say we know there are some things we do not know. But there also unknown unknowns—the ones we don't know we don't know."

"I know one thing for sure. You don't have to act like an asshole. We are dead serious here."

"Sorry, just couldn't help it."

"So, it's decided. We shall go for it. Right. Now let's get down to the nuts and bolts. We need to sort out a lot of things."

They talked. They discussed, they debated. They identified strengths, weaknesses, friends, foes, neutrals. It took them three days to define the strategy for the coming encounter and plan the mission in as much detail as possible. Finally, two plans were finalized, each being assigned its own unimaginative name, Plan Alpha and Plan Bravo.

Robert was to be the overall leader of the mission. He was also assigned the onerous task of being the front guy, the one who would face the music, if ever it had to be faced. When required, he would have to be out there, in the cold. R. F. would be the one who would face the authorities and tell them that they had been trumped; that they did not stand a chance of defeating the plan. Niles would be required to handle the diplomatic end. He would have to bring the United Nations on board and convince them of the New Order. This was something he would be able to accomplish relatively easily because of his deep personal relationship with the secretary general and others who mattered at the Secretariat. P. K. was responsible for the operational aspect of both plans.

He would remain in the background. He was the one who would control Puck; he would be the one who would harness the computers. His role was crucial, because both plans required full control of the computing networks and it was absolutely essential that all automated systems be brought under complete control. Pervez had to ensure that the distributed computing network was taken over and that all data flows and communications were managed as required. As the three stood up, Robert addressed them both directly. "I think we may want to let your friend Alex know about this. We don't want the Soviets freaking out thinking that this is some capitalist plan against them."

It was decided that P. K. would travel to Moscow and brief Aleksandr about the plans.

34

P. K. headed home via London. Arriving at Terminal
Three of Heathrow Airport, he walked over to the far
end of the hall to the left luggage office, where he
deposited his bags and then took the lift up to the
departures hall, proceeding directly to the Aeroflot
counter. He bought a round-trip ticket on the next
flight to Moscow and, after a short wait, boarded the
flight for Domodedovo Airport. Clearing customs and
immigration at Moscow, he took a cab to the square
close to his destination. He disembarked, thrust a $20
bill into the outstretched hand of a grateful taxi driver,
and then proceeded to his friend's apartment. He rang
the bell repeatedly but there was no answer.
Resignedly, he went back outside to wait in the cold.
He had no idea how long he would have to hang
around, but then, he had no option. He had made the
trip to meet someone who had once been an enemy
but had become a friend. He had come to meet a
fellow fighter pilot from a different world who
nonetheless shared similar values and ideals.

The last message that P. K. had received from Alex had been after the fall of the Taliban regime in Afghanistan. The Americans had bombed and blasted the desolate country, aiming to achieve total submission of an errant population. They would fly in from neighboring countries, from aircraft carriers, from Spain, from Europe, even from the United States. Aircrew would carry out assigned tasks and go back. The Americans controlled the skies but were nowhere to be seen on the ground as they continued to labor under the deluded doctrine that air power could do it all; that the land below could be controlled from the air above. And as they stayed aloft, the first foreigners to enter Afghanistan, the first boots on ground, were the Russians. It was then that Aleksandr had sent the e-mail. "I told you we would come back. We're back! And guess who paved the path for us to return. Your friends, the Americans. They laid a carpet for us to travel on. The Americans carpet bombed all obstacles in our path."

P. K. had been impressed. The Russians were being escorted back into Afghanistan by the very forces that had pushed them out ten years previously! The Americans were actually busy clearing the path for the Russians to march into Kabul. The Russians understood strategy. They were after all, the grand masters.

He caught up with the man as he approached the apartment complex in the posh district of Moscow. It was a dumbfounded Aleksandr who greeted his friend and immediately asked why the Pakistani had turned up at his house without any forewarning. "Is everything OK, my friend?"

"Yes it is. There is no problem. I was in the neighborhood and thought that I would stop and say hello."

Together the two entered the dark apartment; as usual, the electricity wasn't working. They sat down in the flickering light of the fire Alex lit, and as they looked at each other in the dimly lit apartment, each realized that age was catching up with them. There was more white in their hair. The Russian still sported his salt-and-pepper mustache; the clean-shaven Pakistani had an even grayer stubble showing. Both faces had lines where earlier there had been none. Both appeared a bit weary; shoulders of both now seemed to sag a little.

They talked. It was actually P. K. who did most of the talking. He told the Russian of Niles, of Robert, of Puck, of Iraq, of Afghanistan, of the United Nations, of America. He then talked of the plan the three had conceived in broad terms, hoping that the Russian would understand, hoping that he would realize the need for this unusual and dangerous move. Visibly agitated, in a voice choked with emotion, an astounded Aleksandr finally interrupted Pervez. "What exactly do you think you are doing, P. K.? Are you out of your fucking mind? Are you are brain dead. Has your brain stopped working?"

Undeterred, P. K. persisted in his attempt to explain his actions to his friend.

He talked about the horrors of war, the pain and the suffering that the common man was undergoing. He talked of those who carried absolutely no risk, of those who did not care whether other sons and daughters died for their crazy ideas and beliefs. He argued how the smug politicians, safe in their bunkers, sent hundreds and thousands of innocents to their graves as they carried out their evil plans. He talked of young men and women dying in foreign lands, in strange environments, in unlikely situations, unwanted, unloved, unsung. He talked of corporate greed, the lust of wealth, the milking of the third world, the anger, the sorrow, the pain, the fear. As the night grew longer, P. K. continued with his emotive speech, and Alex continued listening.

And Aleksandr understood. He had witnessed the devastation of Iraq; he had seen the criminal bombardment of Baghdad from the comfort of his home. He had seen Afghanistan being repeated. It was a similar campaign to the one in which he had been a participant. He had once been party to similarly wanton killing and had watched casually as dead bodies were hauled off by the truckload or shoveled into hastily dug trenches. He had seen the blown limbs, splattered flesh, torn bodies, devastated families. And he could now see very clearly those very same individuals who had kissed the Russian ass were now busy kissing American posteriors.

Opportunists, carpetbaggers, greedy sonsofbitches. Money-making individuals who had no aversion to trafficking in drugs, guns, missiles, human beings, children, body parts, you name it, they were willing to buy and sell as long as there was a buck to be made in the process. He had seen it in Israel and Palestine; he had witnessed meaningless death and destruction in Chechnya. Man liberating Man in a novel manner. Man killing fellow Man.

Aleksandr had to understand, because he had also been a victim of opportunistic politicians; greedy, plotting individuals who had used him and the military for their own warped aims. It did not matter to them how many people died or how many homes and hearths were destroyed as long as they politicians remained safe and their positions remained protected. They did not care about the rest of the world; they most definitely did not care at all about the third world. What had really upset Alex was the realization that they did not care too much about their own citizens. The proletariat was expendable. The aristocrats had to rule. Russia had always been an aristocracy. It had once been czarist, an aristocracy by birth; it was now an aristocracy by appropriation, by dominion.

Aleksandr was able to understand because he had been party to the coup against Gorbachev only to realize that all he had ended up doing was replacing one wily brain by another, somewhat feebler one. Disillusioned, he and eventually ended up opposing

342

Yeltsin's reforms and had then led an armed uprising to oust his former friend from power. He had failed; he had been arrested and imprisoned. Although a new parliament had granted him amnesty a year later, Aleksandr had continued to oppose the government. He remained a firm advocate of Russian expansion to the boundaries of the former Soviet Union. He vocally advocated the reunification of Russia, Ukraine, and Belarus. The Derzhava, a loose coalition of ex-Communists and other hard-liners had even nominated him as its presidential candidate, but he had withdrawn the nomination. Aleksandr remained a thorn in the side of the Kremlin both because of his concepts of fair play and his desire to seek betterment for the masses. However, no one was willing to state the real reason why he was not liked by the establishment. No one wanted to admit that not many Russians liked Jews.

They stayed up even as the night grew long, discussing the startling plan that P. K. had revealed. Outside, it had started snowing and the KGB tail assigned to follow P. K. ever since he left the airport, cursed his luck. He was forced to remain out in the open, braving the cold.

It was Alex who wound up the discussion. "Listen, Pervez, I don't think that you have a chance in hell. I really don't believe that you can pull this off. I would once again advise you to reconsider this. Friendship or not, you need to be very, very clear in your mind that you cannot trust the Americans or the British.

Take it from a person who has the experience. Russia has been through this more than once. And we have been let down every time. There is no way that you can get the capitalist West to treat anyone else in the world as an equal. And there is absolutely no way that the American nation can treat anyone at par. Trust me, take it from me." And as P. K. started to protest, he raised his hand and said, "I know, I know, this Niles and Robert, they are your brothers, your childhood friends. You want to insist? OK, you do that. I just hope that you have got it right. Me personally, I don't believe it."

And then Alex continued. "But I shall also tell you this. If anything can work, this is possibly it. There is no way anyone can take on the American might conventionally. It has to be something totally different. And as far as being different goes, your plan is crazy enough to work."

"I don't want you to do anything Alex, I came simply to let you know. I want you to know. If we fail, just say a little prayer for me. If you can, that is. But if we succeed, I need you to be part of the new order. You will need to convince your people that we are a good lot. You will have to stand with us shoulder to shoulder to build a new world."

"I don't think I shall need to convince anybody. Your actions would speak for themselves. I am very sure that no one is going to interfere. From what I have understood, nobody can. If you control the American military arsenal, no one would be stupid enough to take you on. But, for the sake of this world, if you do succeed, don't screw up in the aftermath. Don't make it like Iraq. Don't end up with a conquest without any plan for the future."

P. K. left the building next afternoon and headed straight to the airport, a relieved KGB shadow tailing him. The immigration officer looked at his passport and noted the date of arrival. He asked P. K. why he was leaving so soon. Did he not like the country? Why had this visit been so short? P. K. knew better than to lie. He told the officer about Alex and how, when he was in London, he had decided to say hello to an old friend who, it was rumored, was dying. Thank God that this was not true. P. K. was asked to step into the adjacent room. Here, another, obviously more senior person went through the questioning again. Once again, P. K. repeated his story. The official hammered out something on his computer while he told P. K. very politely that he had to check with his boss. P. K. resigned himself to missing his flight but the reply came through in less than fifteen minutes. His story checked out. The records at Kremlin showed that the two had been friends since the Afghan war. P. K. was OK.

The officer was now all over Pervez. No, he could not go back through the normal departure channel. He was a respected visitor and had to be treated in a privileged manner. The officer would personally escort the visitor to the aircraft. Would he like a private waiting room until the aircraft was ready to depart? Would he care for some refreshments while he waited? A bottle of special Russian vodka appeared mysteriously from somewhere. Would he care to taste it? Had he tasted Russian meat, he said winking at P. K.. He could arrange some immediately. A gourmet quickie could be arranged in a private "dining" room, wink, wink. PK refused all offers politely but could not avoid being escorted to the aircraft door.

At the aircraft entrance, P. K. said good-bye to his newfound admirer. The officer then pressed a piece of paper into his hand. If only the friend could talk to his contacts at the Kremlin. Could he please arrange for a government flat to be allotted to him and please, please could he get a pay raise. He was desperate to put a roof on his family's head and provide them three square meals a day.

"Soon, soon, my friend, it shall happen soon. This I promise you."

Poor bastard, thought P. K. as he entered the cabin. These were the masses the leaders loved. It was simple people like these who elected them as leaders and it was these innocents that could then be screwed by the leaders. Because that is what you did to those that loved you; you fucked them wholeheartedly.

P. K. returned home and readied himself to launch Plan Alpha, the first of the two plans they had so meticulously conducted. Alpha was a peaceful and benign plan, aimed at achieving the desired results without any overt action or violence. It was designed to create awareness among the masses that they were being led by devious, incompetent, uncaring individuals. It aimed to expose the evil machinations of the incompetent leaders so that the public would revoke the misplaced trust they had placed in these devious individuals. Puck would work behind the scenes, seeking out incriminating evidence against world leaders and push it into the open, into the public domain. This, the three friends hoped, would force a velvet revolution that would in turn trigger accountability of the leaders and thus ensure that necessary changes were made.

If Plan Alpha failed and if the situation did not improve, the final recourse would be Plan Bravo, an overt, aggressive, military plan. Hopefully it would never be exercised and would remain a paper option. P. K. put his coffee mug on the table, pulled out the keyboard drawer and typed the simple command, "Alpha Go."

He hit Enter.

Puck responded. It was more than ready for this task. It had reached the very depths of the computing world. It had made its nest in the most unlikely of places. Puck was no longer a virus. It was an amorphous entity that spanned the globe.

347

Plan Alpha was launched. The world was set on a new course.

There was no turning back now.

Epilogue

At first she thought that it was a disgruntled reader sending the newspaper a pornographic message. The sender was not identifiable, the message was dubious, and she almost trashed the e-mail. But she was intrigued by the body text. It had a peculiar urgency to it. "Please help us. Please save us. We want electricity in our homes, not in our arses! Please do something." The newspaper reporter hesitated and then made up her mind. She decided to take a look at the high-resolution JPEG images attached to the message.

The shocking scandal of Abu Ghraib hit the international media the following day.

They were obviously genuine; the documents had all the markings of the administration. The media magnate was amazed at the contents. This was no routine leak; the anonymous sender had to be someone high up in the government. This was hot stuff—collusion between two heads of state deciding to invade another sovereign country. He launched an internal investigation and when the facts tallied, he published the story.

The U.S. government auditing officer peered closely at the e-mail through thick-rimmed glasses. He could not believe his eyes. The figures were amazing. If it were true, the U.S. government had been overcharged by millions of dollars for the fuel supplied to the forces fighting in Iraq. All transactions that were showing up on his screen were actual copies of actual records of classified correspondence. He was a bit distracted by the sender of the e-mail; Robin Goodfellow. There was no return address, no identification of any sort. He elected to pursue the interesting case. A major financial racket was unearthed. The politicians tried their best to brush aside the major financial racket as "accounting errors."

The documents on the computer had come from an untraceable source but were positively genuine. The content was stunning. The National Security Agency of the United States was asking the British Government Communications Headquarters to bug the United Nations offices of the six countries that were the "swing" voters in the resolution to invade Iraq. The newspaper decided to go ahead and publish the story. The British public was furious. The individual who leaked the story was fired from her job and charged with an offence under the Official Secrets Act but the case was dismissed within half an hour because the prosecution declined to offer any evidence.

Eerie messages containing highly credible and factual documentation of failings of political leaders started cropping up on computers worldwide. These messages were addressed to individuals who cared about what was happening in the world and were in a position to use the information to advantage. Wily politicians and political aides started being exposed.

The American public was treated to mind-blowing disclosures involving White House officials and other key personnel. Heads started rolling. Presidential aides were sacked. Fund-raisers and donors were discredited.

The majority of Spain's population, which had all along been against the war in Iraq, finally triumphed. Jose Maria Aznar, the vocal prime minister was forced out of office.
In April 2006, the Italian government introduced electronic voting and vote counting procedures. The computers that calculated the results showed that Silvio Berlusconi, an aggressive advocate of the U.S. attack on Iraq polled a losing number of votes and was removed from office.

A secretary of defense was removed. A CIA boss was retired. An American ambassador to the United Nations was rejected by the world body. An unqualified individual nominated to lead the World Bank was forced to resign.

Anthony Charles Lynton Blair became the first-ever prime minister of the United Kingdom to be questioned by the Metropolitan Police while in office. Tony Blair, the most willing member of the coalition to attack Iraq, resigned from office after his popularity dropped to 26 percent.

The world watched the world's only superpower anguish over its failures in Iraq and Afghanistan. People the world over followed the media, listening to news and watching live feeds on TV. Some were saddened, most took a perverse delight in the predicament of the superpower. Everyone reveled in the stunning disclosures that were made periodically. No one could have known that someone out there was working for them. Someone who would ensure that Justice was served; that Right would triumph.

Greedy Bankers and avaricious brokerage houses would be forced into bankruptcy. Evil politicians would be forced out of office. Leadership would be wrested from the undeserving, the incompetent.

Puck would deliver.

www.ingramcontent.com/pod-product-compliance
Lightning Source LLC
Chambersburg PA
CBHW020353260626
47156CB00007B/2087